K W

The Shot

To Pauline

Thanks for all your support!

Love

Content note

Content note: Just so you're aware, this book contains mentions of cancer in a secondary character, and discussions of unhealthy/difficult familial relationships.

K W THOMAS

The Shot

The Shot
First edition published 2023
by Pear & Bear Publishing
ISBN: 978-1-8382264-5-9 (ebook)
978-1-8382264-6-6 (print)

Copyedited by Judith Leask
Cover design by Elizabeth Grey
Typeset by Eleanor Abraham

1

MICHAEL Hedley liked order, neatness, clarity. He preferred the objects in his life to be functional, or beautiful, or preferably both. So it was a measure of how much he bloody loved Cleo Carrigan that he was currently sitting on the floor of his living room, surrounded by a pile of what he could only describe as utter shite.

"Why the hell has this bollocks been in the back of my cupboard all these years, Cleo?" he asked his ex-wife, best friend, and apparently long-term abuser of the Michael Hedley storage facility. "It was marked 'Important Stuff', so I never threw it out. But there's half a menu from a Chinese takeaway in Bedlington here. I don't think they deliver to either London or California."

From LA, Cleo gave him a mildly embarrassed grimace over the phone screen. "I'm sure it was important at some point."

"And this bundle of ribbon?"

"Erm, pass."

Michael shook his head. "It's not surprising that we couldn't live together for long, is it?"

She grinned. "Not in the slightest. You're itching to throw it all away, aren't you?"

"So badly. But I'll keep it, on the off chance there's actually something important lurking among these random pieces of paper and bits of twig."

"There are twigs in there?" Cleo hid her face with her free hand.

"No, I'm taking the piss."

"Dickhead."

He laughed. "You can't call me that. I just agreed to keep it all in my cupboard for another god knows how many years."

"Fine. You're a saint and an angel and I don't deserve you. How did it even escape your notice for so long?"

Michael scooped up a handful of assorted debris and dumped it back in the box. "It was in the very back of the cupboard, behind some of my old uni stuff. I needed a bit of camera kit from there and found the box."

Cleo's eyes lit up. "Ooh, what were you doing?"

He stifled a sigh. The enthusiasm on her face was making him feel ... well, kind of shit, to be honest. She was only excited for him, trying to be encouraging. He knew that. So he could never bring himself to admit just how fucking difficult keeping his promise to her, to try to make it as an artist now he'd quit the paparazzi stuff, really was.

"Some landscape shots," he said vaguely. "Trying something different, you know." In reality, he'd got all his old filters out in the hope that it would remind him what he used to do, who he used to be, that naive student who thought he would one day set the world alight with his photographs. Instead of just some guy armed with an ever-dwindling list of galleries who hadn't knocked him back yet.

"That's cool." Cleo looked as if she wanted to say something else, so he changed the subject to one of the few he knew he could always, always distract her with.

"My mam says hi, by the way."

Her face softened. "She texted me the other day. Seems like she's doing well."

"So well." The relief that had taken residence in his heart hadn't shifted one iota in the weeks since his mam had got to ring that bell for what would hopefully – please, god, let it be – the last time. The ever-present fear that the cancer could come back marred the edges of it, but for now he was trying to live in this moment, where his mother was doing just fine. "Thank you," he said to Cleo.

"What for?" she said innocently.

He narrowed his eyes at her. "I know you did something. The money I gave her from those photos certainly didn't fund the whole of that last round of private treatment, no matter how hard you all try to pretend it did. And I don't think it funded the fancy spa break either."

Eighteen ludicrous months ago, Cleo and her now husband, movie star Devon Grant, had allowed Michael to sell the exclusive photos of Devon's proposal to a glossy mag, on the condition that he gave up the paparazzi shit. The money hadn't been what it might have a few years ago, but it had been enough to clear some of his mother's debt, pay for some treatment, and give them a little bit of breathing space. And apparently Devon and Cleo had given his mam more.

"OK, the spa was me," Cleo said unrepentantly. "And you can stop having a face on about it. I earn a ton of money now, and Devon earns several tons more, so if I want to spend some of that on making sure someone I love gets a bit of pampering, I bloody well will." She stuck her tongue out at him to soften the statement, but he could tell she meant it.

"And the considerably more expensive treatment?"

She said nothing for a second.

"Cleo ..."

"Devon paid for some of it," she admitted. "I did tell him that you would probably kick off, but he made the very good point that he cared about Liz, had the means to do something to help Liz, and that – his words – 'Michael's stupid pride won't cure fucking cancer'." She stared directly at him.

Michael shifted uncomfortably. He'd always known he was a being a bit of a dick about the money. Devon and Cleo had it; he didn't. Cleo loved his mam, who had shown her way more love and affection than her own mother ever had. She and Devon wanted to help and could do so without breaking a sweat, and it wasn't as if Michael wanted to see his mother suffer. He would have moved heaven and earth to get to this moment. But he hated how small it made him feel to accept their charity.

He swallowed down that awful, bitter, shameful feeling. His mam was better, and that was all that mattered. Although ...

"Wait. He paid for some of it?"

Cleo looked away.

His chest tightened. "Who paid the rest?"

Surely not. Surely hell had frozen over first. And surely this couldn't have happened without any of them breathing a word.

"That's for your mam to answer," Cleo said softly, and Michael knew.

His grandmother.

The woman who, last time he saw her, had sworn she would never speak to any of them ever again, that they were all nothing to her. Michael had taken her at her word and cut off contact without a second thought. After a lifetime of tolerating her barbs and her cruel condescension, and after years of pretending that he and Cleo were still happily married to prevent her disinheriting Liz, it had been a relief to walk away.

He should have known his mother wouldn't have been able to do the same forever. But how had they got to the point where Margaret would pay for Liz's treatment, after so long spent acting as if it were none of her business that her only daughter was suffering? That was a conversation he'd have to have with his mother, and he'd look forward to that about as much as he'd look forward to a root canal. Possibly less.

Cleo broke the silence that had fallen. "I'm sorry, mate. I told everyone it would be better to tell you from the start. But you've been a bit ... up and down lately. No one was sure how you'd react."

He grunted in response. That was fair, he supposed.

Up and down was certainly right. He had no idea how he felt about anything anymore. He was happier than he used to be, wasn't he? At least he no longer had the pap work sucking his soul dry. He didn't have to traipse around London, getting elbowed and shoved and trying not to think about the fact that his job was essentially to invade people's privacy. Life was better now that his job was ... lots of things. He picked up odds and ends of work here and there, through the "contacts" he was atrocious at making but recognised as a necessity – a wedding or two, a couple of commercial shoots, selling prints. He was making a living, just, from his photography, in a way that didn't make people think he was the scum of the earth. He had a website and two Instagram accounts and all the other things you needed when you were trying to get your name out there. He'd had one extremely unsuccessful exhibition at a "gallery" that was, in truth, a semi-deserted coffee shop with a lot of wall space, and he had to keep believing that he'd find another opportunity soon.

But there had been a hole in his life for the last six months, and it was Cleo-shaped. He was thrilled for her, with her nauseatingly happy marriage and her dazzling new career in the States. But she was his best friend – his only true friend, if he was honest – and he missed having her around so much it hurt.

"Michael? You OK?"

He gave his head a shake. He shouldn't be wasting this time feeling sorry for himself. "I'm fine. I'll talk to my mam. And I'll put all this stuff away until next time you're over here. Tell me about what you've been up to. I see Devon's out filming in Colorado or somewhere?"

"Erm, yeah." She sounded reluctant to change the subject, but she let it be. She knew him well enough not to push. "He's happy. He's close enough to Jesse that they're able to have some quality father–son time. I'm going out there in a couple of weeks. And I'm interviewing Courtney White next week about her whole return-to-music thing, so that'll be fun ..."

Michael listened as she chattered away. He was genuinely interested in how her journalism career was going over there, and he was glad she was still coping with the frequent separations from Devon. But fucking hell, he couldn't stop the gaping emptiness that was growing in the space his heart should be. She had a whole glamorous life to occupy herself with. What did he have? Meals for one and failed attempts to pull together something that wouldn't make a gallery's customers complain about "creepy portraits staring at them while they had coffee. What happened to those nice seaside pictures?"

He could feel his camera glaring at him from the kitchen table, asking him why he couldn't get his shit together. He turned his back on it.

"Listen, Cleo," he said, even though his friend was in the middle of a sentence about how ridiculous LA was. "I'd better go. I'm meeting Ed in a bit and I need a shower first." It was a lie. He wasn't meeting Ed. He hadn't seen any of the few people who just about counted as friends in weeks.

"Oh, OK," she said, looking surprised. "Say hi to him for me. Are you sure you're–"

"I'm fine. Totally fine. I'll speak to you soon."

Another lie. He wasn't fine. He was a miserable twat, and he didn't need to bring Cleo down. After ending the call, he tidied all her things back into the cupboard, restoring his flat to perfect order.

And then, avoiding the phone call he didn't want to make, he took himself out for a walk, hoping today, finally, would be the day inspiration struck.

2

MIRANDA Janes was wearing ... damn, she couldn't remember. She twisted her beaded dress around until she found the label. That was right, Zachary Davies, the darling boy she'd met at last month's St Martin's event who'd then sent her a dress that fit like a glove. She'd make sure to mention him to as many people as she could tonight, because this kid deserved to go far. It was a fashion awards thing, so there should be plenty of people who would be interested.

She was so glad she'd moved to London. It seemed as though every night there was another party, full of interesting people for her to talk to. It was the ideal place to be when you were between movies, which Miranda was right now. She bit her lip. Should she have said yes to the video game adaptation? No. She should not have. There were only so many beautiful but uninteresting love interests she could play. Miranda had her eyes on a different prize.

She checked her makeup and the time. The former was flawless, and the latter was early. Her car wouldn't be here for a while. She picked up her phone and called her agent.

"Miranda, what's up?" Nora answered briskly, as ever. Nora Delaney was not one to waste time on niceties, but she was an absolute powerhouse, and surely the only woman in Hollywood who'd be able to pull off what Miranda was asking of her.

"Hey, Nora. I was calling to see if you made any progress yet." Miranda crossed her fingers. *Please, please let there be good news.*

"I got a meeting with AJ."

Miranda's heart beat a little faster. "You did?"

"Yeah. Next Wednesday. But I've got to be honest, sweetheart, I'm still not holding out much hope. He seems to have a pretty set idea of what he wants."

And it's not you. Nora didn't say it. She didn't have to.

AJ Hollinger was the hottest director in the world right now. Hot enough that a studio had green-lighted a staggeringly ambitious adaptation of a complex world-and-time-spanning literary fantasy novel for him to direct. And Miranda wanted to be in it.

"He still wants Elia?"

"I think so. She fits his vision. Very waify. Angles. You know."

Miranda did know. Elia Stone was a stunning, ethereal beauty, and a delightful person by all accounts. But she was primarily a model, not an actress. She'd had a small part in a heist movie last year, playing a model, and the critics had said she hadn't been great. But it seemed she was now up for the lead in one of the most hotly anticipated movies of the decade. Miranda was not a bitter or jealous person, not in the slightest. But it burned. *An Ocean of Fallen Stars* had done something to her when she'd read it. It was a beautiful book, and the lead character, Damia, had spoken to her soul. Miranda *had* to play her.

"And I'm just the pretty, wholesome blonde next door." Miranda sighed.

"Honey, not many people live next door to someone who looks like you. But yes, your image is an obstacle, I won't lie."

Her image. Miranda had never cared about that. She did what she wanted and she wore what she wanted, and it just so happened that the things she wanted to do and wear fit neatly with people's ideas about women like her. Could she do anything about that? Should she want to? She was an actress – send her through hair and makeup and wardrobe, put her in front of a camera, and she could be anyone. She'd trained hard to make that so. But it seemed no one really wanted to know that. She was Miranda Janes, and she needed to stay in her little Miranda Janes–sized box.

"Hey," Nora said, and Miranda realised she'd fallen silent. "I'll do my best for you, you know that. You never give up, and neither do I."

"I know. You're the best." She meant it. Becoming a major talent agent was not easy, and to do it as a Black woman must have been ten times harder still. Nora was a force to be reckoned with, and Miranda couldn't ask for anyone better in her corner. "I'll let you go. I'm sure you're busy."

"Keep your head up, Miranda. We'll get you something excellent, I promise. Speak later." Nora hung up.

But I don't want something excellent. I want this.

Miranda checked the time again. She still had fifteen minutes before she had to leave. She opened Instagram, and for the hundredth time that week, clicked on Elia's profile. Dang, she was exquisite. Her latest post was a picture of her on a wisteria-covered balcony, a halter dress that seemed to be made of crystals and wire draped over her slender, elegant body. Miranda wanted to hate her, but she wasn't that kind of girl. Her friends were always telling her that she'd get much further in Hollywood if she didn't feel so compelled to be nice to everyone all the time.

But although she couldn't bring herself to feel an ounce of personal animosity towards Elia, something inside Miranda hardened a little as she stared at the gorgeous pictures. Elia was so young, and she had no serious acting experience. Damia was going to be a sophisticated, challenging role. It needed depth, and Miranda was more than ready to show the world that she had that.

But how, if no one was willing to look at her that way?

Blowing out a frustrated breath, Miranda forced herself to leave Elia's grid and look at her own feed. She pressed Like on her friend Cleo Carrigan's picture of her gelato from Bacio di Latte, and smiled when she saw that Henry Deng – the husband of another one of her closest friends, country singer Courtney White – had posted a picture of Heathrow arrivals with the caption "Home". Fabulous. She loved Henry. Perhaps she would try to catch up with him while he was here.

She was about to send him a message when another picture caught her eye. The sun, low in the sky, shining over a small deserted churchyard, probably one of those funny little ones you found all over central London in the oddest places. Even in a picture, the quiet stillness of the place took Miranda's breath away.

The caption read "Peace", and the poster was @miched42. A private account she'd almost forgotten she was following, so rarely did he post on it.

Michael Hedley, Cleo's ex-husband. The former paparazzo who had taken some great pictures of her in the past. Her sister even had the one he'd taken all those years ago at the BAFTAs – when she'd been heart-broken but determined that no one would see it – in a frame on her wall.

The doorbell buzzed. Frank, her security guy, was here with her car. It was time to shake off her mood over the movie and go have some fun.

But the wheels of her brain kept turning with the glimmer of an idea.

3

MICHAEL cast an assessing eye over the photos in front of him. They were fine. They were good, objectively speaking. Pictures of Regent's Canal, the morning sun sparkling off the water. He could put them on the Etsy shop Cleo's friend Priya had helped him set up, where he sold art prints for a few quid.

But fine was all they were. He knew in his heart that this wasn't what he was made for. He took nice enough pictures of landscapes and street scenes that looked good on people's walls in cheap black frames. But he needed something more. He needed people.

That was what Michael loved – capturing human beings in all their messy beauty. There'd always been magic in it, for him. A picture could either show the world what someone looked like, or show it who they *were*.

It was hard, though, to take portrait shots when your social circle consisted of about four people and it was hard to admit to anyone else that you were trying to become an "artist". The very word made him shudder, even though it was what he'd dreamed of being his whole life, what he'd come to London to study for, what he'd promised the people he loved he would become. He'd been trying – he'd hung out at galleries and studios and artists' collectives, but he'd never been able to find the opportunities, make the right connections. Or any connections really. Everyone else on that scene seemed so sure of themselves, seemed to belong there, and he didn't know what to say to any of them. Like, who the fuck did he think he was? Some lad from a shitty little town in Northumberland who'd spent the best part of his twenties traipsing after celebrities. The idea of him as a serious artist was laughable. He should just go and get a normal job in Aldi or something, sell his pretty little landscapes on Etsy, and stop being such a pretentious dickhead.

Yet he couldn't. Something – was it passion, or was it stubbornness? – wouldn't let the dream die. That was why he still had a list of galleries to approach saved on his laptop, even though he'd been told time and time again that portraiture, especially his style of it, was a hard sell. Why his search history was full of courses and mentorship programmes that all seemed too good to be true and too expensive to be feasible. Why he spent every day racking his brains for ways to expand his dismal portfolio.

You could go home and take some pictures of your mam, said an annoying little voice in his head.

And have the conversation he'd been avoiding? God, no. He needed more than a day, which was how long it had been since Cleo's revelation, to get his head in order. Even though he desperately wanted to know what was going on between his mother and his grandmother, if only to check Mam wasn't being manipulated as she had so many times before, the last thing he needed was to lose his shit with her. She'd been through so much.

His phone pinged. Thankful for the diversion, he picked it up. It was an Instagram message.

From Miranda Janes.

Michael almost fell off his chair. Miranda Janes was messaging him? Of course, he'd known that she was following both his business and personal accounts, because it wasn't as if you didn't notice when Miranda fucking Janes sent you a follow request. But she was one of the most beautiful, charming movie stars in the whole world. Yes, they had mutual friends and had met once and had a brief conversation that Michael had thought about at least once every day for the last six months, but what the hell did she want with him?

He should probably open the message and find out, but his stupefied brain had apparently stopped sending signals to his hands.

Eventually, he regained control of himself and read the message.

> Hi Michael!
> We met at Cleo and Devon's wedding.

As if he needed reminding who she was.

> I hope your photography is going well.
> What's your schedule like right now? I have a project I'd like to discuss with you.

Bloody hell. Miranda Janes wanted to discuss something with him. What on earth could that be? He didn't care, obviously. She could ask him to take pictures of her draining board and he'd say yes. He had literally nothing better to do, and why would anyone turn down the chance to work with a world-famous actress?

> My schedule is pretty open at the moment, so happy to discuss whatever you have in mind.

Pretty open. Ha. If it got any more open it'd be a field. He added his number to the message and pressed Send.

* * *

Two hours and seventeen minutes later, not that Michael was counting, his phone rang with a withheld number. He took a deep breath.

"Hello?" He hadn't meant to sound that nervous, but there was nothing he could do about it now.

"Michael, hey." A honey-rich voice poured down the line. "Miranda Janes here."

"Hi, Miranda." That was better. He sounded like a grown man now, instead of a frightened schoolboy. "How's things?"

"Things are ... hmm. Well, generally they're good. Life's good, you know?"

Michael didn't know, but he nodded anyway, which was stupid, because he was on the phone, and shit, he was handling this conversation as if he'd never come across a famous person in his life. Had he always been this useless at talking to people? He'd been best friends with Cleo for so long that perhaps he'd given up and let her do all the talking for him. He managed what he thought was a suitably non-committal noise, but Miranda seemed unbothered by his inadequate response and pressed on.

"But I do have this problem, and I think that maybe you could be the solution."

Michael didn't think he'd ever been that in his life. He'd always been the problem.

From somewhere, he conjured up a short laugh. "I'm intrigued. What can I do for you?" How many people in the world had dreamed of saying those words to her? He'd certainly been one of them on more than one occasion. He pictured her, sparkling blue-green eyes, long blonde waves, legs that seemed to go on forever ...

Fuck's sake. Be professional, Hedley. No wonder women think men are trash.

"I need some pictures," she said. "Although you probably figured that, being a photographer and all."

"Well, you know, I did wonder if Cleo had told you I make a mean sausage and mash."

Miranda laughed. "She did not, but let's talk about that another time. I am obsessed with British food that I have to go to the gym for two hours to work off."

Michael blinked. This woman was full of surprises. She launched into an explanation of the film role she was after and the director's desire to hire a model.

"So you see, Michael, he wants someone *interesting*. Someone who looks the part. And while I'm aware that there are much harder things to be in this world than a pretty blonde white woman, I am kind of sick of people thinking they can pigeonhole me because of that. I want to show AJ – and maybe everyone – that I can be much more interesting than they think. And I think that you might be the person to help me do that."

"Oh. OK. And how ...?" He didn't understand what she wanted him to do, but his heart was already beating a little faster at the idea of photographing her again. She'd been one of his favourite subjects in the old days, and at Cleo and Devon's wedding he'd had to tear his camera away from her more than once. There was a grace to her that was almost impossible to do justice to in a photo, although he thought he might have come close on a couple of occasions.

"I am launching," she said, and he heard the determination in her voice that those who knew her often hinted about, "an Instagram campaign. Nothing formal, of course, but it's the part of my image over which I have total control. The world has fallen in love with Elia Stone via her Insta. I'm going to remarket myself on mine. I'm thinking a number of photo shoots in various locations. I want a stockpile of pictures that will show them all who I am, what I can be."

"You really want this part, don't you?"

"I really want this part," she replied. "And I'm going to get it."

There wasn't a single cell in his body that didn't believe her.

His mind was already racing with possibilities, but

he had to ask. "Why me?" He thought he knew at least part of the answer, but he wanted to hear her explain.

"Partly it's because I want to keep my motivations off the radar. This industry gossips, so if I reached out to more established photographers, there's a chance they'd talk, so I wouldn't be able to spell out exactly what I need and why. I know you're no stranger to keeping a secret."

Did she mean his marriage to Cleo, Devon and Cleo's relationship, or Devon's plan to propose? Maybe all of them – it was true that Michael was pretty practised at deception.

"But mainly," Miranda continued, "it's because of that picture. You know."

That picture. The one he was probably most proud of, the second he'd captured a post-breakup Miranda on the BAFTAs red carpet, squaring her shoulders and drawing on all her inner strength as she prepared to encounter her ex and the woman he'd dumped her for. She'd been more than beauty in that moment, and Michael knew the second he hit the shutter that something special had happened.

"Yeah," he said softly, half of him still lost in that long-ago moment. "I know."

"You seemed to see something in me then, something I never even saw in myself. That's what I want." She gave a little laugh. "Or maybe it was just luck, I don't know. But I feel like if there's anyone in this world who can help me pull this off, it's probably you."

Well, fucking hell. Someone had confidence in his

skills? Someone who wasn't his mam or Cleo? Michael was pretty sure that hadn't happened in a very long time.

How could he refuse?

"I'd love to help," he said. "Whatever you need."

4

MIRANDA looked around the hotel suite with satisfaction. It was exceptional. From Henry Deng's hotel group, you could expect nothing less. The elegant antique furniture contrasted beautifully with the contemporary jewel-toned walls, and the morning sunlight streamed in through huge windows. It was the epitome of understated glamour, which would be just fine as a starting point. Later, there'd be room for quirkier, edgier, more interesting. That was the plan. Miranda always had a plan.

She walked over to the huge mirror on the wall and scrutinised her appearance. She'd let her hair dry naturally into soft waves, and she wore what most men would think was no makeup but in fact had taken a full hour. Her eyes looked huge, and her skin looked fresh and youthful. The white linen dress had a simplicity that belied its seven-hundred-dollar price tag.

She looked innocent, pure. Delicate against the bold room around her.

Perfect.

The Damia at the beginning of *An Ocean of Fallen Stars* was little more than a teenager, a naive girl thrust into a world she didn't belong in. The actress who got the part would have to play her as well as the thirty-five-year-old warrior queen she would become. So today, Miranda would be soft and luminous. She hoped.

Oh god, she really hoped. But what if she was wrong about Michael? Should she have chosen someone with more experience, a proper fashion photographer used to shooting the Elia Stones of this world? Perhaps that BAFTAs moment had been pure luck. Perhaps reaching out to him was a mistake.

But then she thought about the engagement photo, the shock and joy on Cleo's face, the hope and adoration on Devon's. She thought about the wedding pictures, and how she'd almost felt uncomfortable looking at some of them because they felt so intimate, the love that Devon and Cleo had found captured so perfectly.

She thought of the curiously intense man she'd seen behind the camera that day, a sandy-blonde curl dropping over his forehead as he turned the lens on her. She'd felt the weight of his gaze on her as she danced, and though she was used to men's stares, something about his had felt different. She'd felt that whatever he was seeing, whether through his lens or with his own eyes, was something no one else did.

And then there was no time to think about it any more, because there was a knock on the door.

"Come in," she called, and in walked Frank, followed by Michael Hedley, laden with equipment and looking endearingly nervous.

"Michael." She stepped towards him, extending her hand. "Good to see you again."

He put down a bag, and a cool hand closed around hers. "You too."

She leaned closer and kissed the air next to his clean-shaven cheek. He looked a little taken aback. Oops. Miranda was so used to greeting anyone and everyone this way that it hadn't occurred to her that he might not be. She stepped back and gave him a friendly smile. "Thanks for coming."

"Of course. Thanks for asking me." He looked around him. "Nice room." She could see his eyes taking in the space, the light, and the last vestiges of apprehension melted away. Michael was a professional, and a trusted friend of people she cared about. This was going to be great.

She looked at her security guy, who stood near the doorway, awaiting instructions. "Hey, Frank, you can take the next few hours off. I'll call when I'm ready to leave, or if I need you before that."

Frank nodded. She knew he'd linger outside the door for a few minutes, just to check no one else approached it, and that he'd more than likely skulk around the hotel until she called. She always chastised him for not taking his time off properly, and he always ignored her.

He closed the door behind him, leaving Michael and Miranda alone. She felt oddly nervous, as if she were somehow unused to being around strangers, which was ridiculous. It was corny as hell, but Miranda liked the idea that there were no strangers, only friends you hadn't met yet.

"So." Michael cleared his throat. "I guess we should chat a bit, figure out what you're after from today."

She shook her head and recovered her composure, something she was not all that acquainted with needing to do. "Yes, absolutely." She gestured to two peacock-blue armchairs next to a low oak table. "Have a seat. Coffee?"

"That'd be nice, thanks."

Miranda poured two cups from the pot she'd had sent up earlier and settled into the chair opposite him. Michael's gaze never stopped moving, darting from one feature of the room, to her, to another, to her, to a window, a wall, to her. From another man it might have been creepy, but she could practically see his brain working, assessing the possibilities, ideas forming.

"Would I be correct in assuming we're going for a kind of innocence-among-opulence vibe today?" His gesture towards her dress was polite, and she couldn't help feeling a tad disappointed at the way his eyes scanned her body in a way that screamed professional detachment.

Get a grip, Miranda. Not every man in the world is going to want you, you know. She clearly wasn't his type – he'd been married to short, curvy, dark-haired Cleo, for crying out loud, her opposite. Not that it mattered, of course. He might be her type – she'd always been a sucker for an aloof, artsy guy – but that wasn't why they were here. She needed his skills, not his admiration.

"You got it. Sweet, delicate, young." She was impressed that he'd caught on so fast. They were clearly on the same page, and she needed that or this would never work.

"Cool. And is there anything in particular you want – any pose or any part of the room, anything like that?"

"Not really. Just whatever you think will convey that mood best. I put myself in your capable hands."

OK, fine. She'd said that on purpose to see how he'd react. And the ever so slight flush that tinted his neck was gratifying, but she also felt kind of bad now. Her natural flirtatiousness evidently wasn't right for this situation, so she'd better try to keep a leash on it. She didn't want to piss him off or make him uncomfortable.

He still hadn't replied, so she fixed her gaze on him until his eyes returned to hers. "I trust your judgement," she said softly. "I'm not sure why, given that we barely know each other, but I have good instincts about people. So just tell me what you think I should do, and I'll do it. And if I have something I want to try, I'll tell you. How does that sound?"

He smiled, and for the first time since he came into the room, he seemed to relax a little. "That sounds good." He knocked back the last of his coffee and got to his feet. "Let's do this."

5

CHRIST, she was beautiful. Michael had seen her in lavish gowns and daring dresses, hair in a complicated updo and face professionally and flawlessly done. But today, in a simple white dress and the barest touch of subtle makeup, Miranda Janes took his breath away. Could he possibly take a picture of her that showed the world this luminous glow? He'd already taken a few in the last two hours that were breathtaking – some of the ones on the balcony looked good, and at least one of the mirror shots – but he didn't think he'd got it quite right yet. Something still wasn't perfect, and Michael wasn't stopping until it was. Or until she got bored and kicked him out, whichever came first.

It wasn't on him, and it wasn't really on her, either. Miranda was an excellent model – finding the light with stunning accuracy, moving her body with effortless control, waiting with endless patience as he sat her down in a chair, checked the light, asked her to get up again, moved the chair a fraction, lather, rinse, repeat. She looked gorgeous in every single picture, sweet and young and delicate as planned. But underneath it all, beneath the silky hair and soft smile, he could still see a trace of some steel core within her. He was fairly sure most people never saw it, maybe never would see it in these shots.

But Michael could – it was that determination that had made her look like a queen in that BAFTAs photo even though her heart was broken. The confidence and persistence that had driven her to message some random bloke with a camera and rope him into her grand plan to land the role of a lifetime.

He needed to get her to soften all of that, just slightly. But how, when it seemed to be such a fundamental part of who she was?

"Hey, Miranda? Shall we try on the bed, maybe?"

Oh Jesus, that had sounded wrong. He firmly shut down the part of his brain that was now wandering in a foolish direction and forced himself to keep looking at Miranda, who looked like she was biting back a smile.

"Sure," she said, hopping up off her armchair. "Where do you want me?" She laughed. "So to speak."

Michael hoped his face wasn't as red as it felt. "Sitting up against the pillows, I think. Just get yourself comfortable."

"How's this?" She sat on the gold brocade bedspread, tucked one leg underneath her and pulled the other knee into her body, smiling up at him.

"Brilliant," he said, a little more earnestly than he would have liked. For crying out loud. You'd think he'd never been in the presence of a beautiful woman before. He took a few shots, pleased with the way her hair caught the sun. The bed was enormous, making her look a little lost, vulnerable. "Hey, Miranda, tell me about something or someone that makes you happy."

"Makes me happy?" She gazed at some spot somewhere

behind him. "A good party makes me happy. Such an unsurprising answer, right? So superficial, so shallow. That's what they all say." She waved her hand, presumably to indicate who "they" were. "But I don't care. It's true. I love meeting interesting people, the more the better, and if I can meet many at once while wearing something fabulous, why shouldn't I?"

Michael, who would rather sit on a rusty fork than attend one of the glamorous parties he used to hang around outside of, made a sound he hoped conveyed encouragement, keeping his eyes glued to his camera. "Anything else?"

"Sure. I love my family, obviously."

He lifted his head. A note of wistfulness had entered her voice. "Tell me about them."

"They – my mom and dad, my sister and her husband and kids – live just outside Seattle. They're the best."

"What do they do?" he said, moving closer. "Are they involved in showbiz too?"

She shook her head. "Oh no. My mom's a college professor. My dad's an orthodontist. My sister's a software developer. They're all very normal. They're proud of me, of course, but totally bemused by my life."

This was it. This was what he'd been looking for. As she spoke, the last scraps of that toughness were melting away. Her shoulders, her jaw, her eyes, everything about her seemed to soften at the edges.

"Just lift your chin a tiny bit for me. So you have nieces and nephews?" He kept his voice soft, as if regular conversational volume would break some kind of spell.

"One of each. Seven and five years old. They're awesome. I wish I got to see them more often, but at least there's FaceTime. It's hard, to be away from the people you love. But you know that."

Those blue-green eyes were on him now, direct and sympathetic. "Yeah. My mam's only a few hours away by train. But I miss Cleo. It's weird, her being halfway across the world. Don't get me wrong, I'm so happy for her ..."

"But you can be happy for her and still hurt a little yourself."

For a second, all he could do was stare at her. Something in her voice told him that she wasn't just talking about him and Cleo. He wanted to ask her more, ask what made her hurt, but then he remembered he was here to do a job and right now he was emphatically not doing it. He put his finger back on the shutter and took a few more shots as some kind of weight hung heavily in the air between them, and when he couldn't stand the strangeness of it any longer, he stepped away and flicked through the last few shots on his display screen.

"You got it, didn't you?"

How could she know that, from his back? He turned around. "Yeah, I think so. I mean, we can try some more, if you want. We didn't use—"

"No. I can tell you think we have it, and I trust you." She grinned at him, and if there'd been any of that weird heaviness still in the atmosphere, it was dazzled into oblivion by her smile.

"Great. I'll, er, I'll get going then." He started gathering his things.

"Why don't you stay a while? We could order up some lunch. The chef here is excellent."

She sounded friendly, genuine, but surely she was only being polite. She must have way better things to do than hang out with him. Besides, as much as he'd enjoyed her company, as much as he would have liked more of it, he was itching to get back home and start looking through these pictures. There was something special among them, he just knew it.

"No, thanks, really, but I'd better go. Start working on these." He held up the camera before putting it carefully back into his bag.

"Oh. OK." Her gaze dropped to the carpet. She wasn't disappointed, was she? Had he been rude, not accepting the invitation? But then her smile returned and she strode forward confidently, hand outstretched. "Thanks for today, Michael. I can't wait to see what you've got."

He took her smooth hand in his and shook it. "Yep. Sure. I'll send you an email when I'm done. Until next time, then."

"Until next time."

6

"OH my god, is that the first time a man's ever declined an invitation from you?" Jen threw her head back in laughter.

Miranda scowled at her phone screen. "Surely you remember me asking Freddie Sloan to the seventh-grade dance and him saying he'd rather dance with a man-eating shark?"

Her big sister rolled her eyes. "You had to go all the way back to middle school for that. And everyone but you seemed to realise Freddie was gay."

Miranda made herself more comfortable on her living room sofa. "I genuinely thought he admired Justin Timberlake as an artist."

"You were too cute, Rand."

"Not cute enough, apparently," Miranda said with a melodramatic sigh. "Anyway, it wasn't like that today. It was work. Michael wanted to go get started on editing the pictures or whatever."

"Like he'll need to do a single thing to them. But wait … so he's an artist, he's British, and he's intense about his work?"

Miranda shrugged. She knew where this was leading and there was no point trying to dodge the subject. "Kinda sums him up, yeah."

Jen shook her head. "Oh boy. You're in trouble."

"Shut up, Jennifer." Her sister hated being called that. She'd been Jen for years, ever since she'd married someone with a less awkward last name than Janes, and Miranda knew it. But no matter who you were or how old you got, annoying-little-sister habits died hard.

Jen didn't take the bait. "Rand, that is your kryptonite and you know it. Is he skinny?"

"Lean, I'd say." And surprisingly toned, she couldn't help but notice when he'd reached up to angle a lamp earlier. But she wasn't about to tell Jen that.

"Into that whiney indie music you like?"

"It's not whiney. It's emotional. And I have no idea. I've had like three conversations with him ever." And every single one had made her want another. Why was that?

Jen was moving through the house now. It looked like she was heading for the kitchen. "I give it two weeks before you're madly in love with him, and three months before you decide he's not The One."

"Ha ha. Not all of us can meet our soulmates at nineteen and live nauseatingly happily ever after, you know." Miranda said it with affection, but she wondered for the thousandth time if Jen had the slightest idea what it was like outside her loved-up little bubble. It wasn't as if Miranda wanted to be almost as famous for the long list of failed relationships trailing in her wake as she was for her acting.

Jen walked into the kitchen. "I know, and ... oh, for

Pete's sake. Izzy! Tommy! Why is there pasta all over the kitchen floor?"

"It's Tommy's fault, Mommy. It wasn't my idea at all! Is that Aunty Rand? Can I tell her about Mrs Ostrich?" A gap toothed-smile, shiny brown braids, and one of the two most gorgeous faces in the world appeared on the screen.

"For the last time, Izzy, her name is not Mrs Ostrich. Where is your brother?"

"He's under the table, crying. Like a big baby." Izzy plucked the phone from her mother's hand. "Hi, Aunty Rand! My flute teacher, her name isn't really Mrs Ostrich but it sounds like it, says I'm doing real good now! And I have a new best friend, Lulu. She has a big dog. Have you made a movie today?"

Miranda, used to having that much information flung at her in the space of three seconds, smiled at her seven-year-old niece. "Not today, sweetie. Sounds like you're having an exciting time, though. Keep working hard on your flute, won't you?"

"I will. Then maybe someday I'll be as famous as you."

"I'm sure you will."

Izzy chattered some more, and eventually Tommy stopped crying and emerged from under the table to show Miranda that he had his first loose tooth. Jen gathered them both into her arms and dropped kisses onto the tops of their heads, and Miranda's heart scrunched up with a now familiar mixture of love and envy. Miranda might be the one with the fame and fortune, but Jen had what truly mattered. She had a husband who adored her, two fantastic kids, a job she was good at, friends and family who lived nearby. The perfect life had all just fallen into place for her. Not that Miranda begrudged her any of it – her sister was the best. Jen was always there for Miranda, always had been, their whole lives. She was a wonderful person, and Miranda wanted nothing but happiness for her sister. But she wanted it for herself too, and sometimes, in the dead of night when she couldn't sleep, she thought she might never find it. Miranda had been in love more times than she could count, and no matter what she did, no matter how hard she tried, it always slipped away in the end. She moved on, or he did, and she was left alone again.

"Miranda?"

Oh. She'd drifted away and Jen was still talking to her.

"Sorry, I was miles away. What was that?"

"I said, you're still coming home for Dad's birthday, right?"

"Try and stop me. We decided on that lodge out by the falls, didn't we?"

Jen nodded. "Yeah, but ..."

Miranda held up her hand. "Don't make me have this conversation again, Jen. I am a literal millionaire. I will not take a penny from you for it. You can buy the cake and the decorations."

"OK, fine," Jen muttered. "It is very galling, you know, to have a baby sister who is so much richer than you are."

"Yeah, yeah, I know. Blame Hollywood for its ridiculous remuneration packages. But whatever. I'll get Aisling to book the lodge and the caterer."

Jen looked affronted. "I may not have as much money as you do, but I have a phone and working vocal cords."

"And I have an assistant who I pay well to do things like this. You have enough on your plate looking after those two."

"Tell me about it. Did you know they're having three separate costume days at school next month? Why? Why must there always be costumes, for crying out loud?"

Miranda made the appropriate noises while her sister ranted about the ever-growing list of things Izzy and Tommy apparently required to attend elementary school. But her mind was drifting again. When would Michael have the photos ready for her to see? She knew they'd be great; she just knew it. There were a few days left before Nora's meeting with AJ, so if Miranda could post one of those pictures, perhaps that would help. Nora just had to keep the door open long enough for her to barge – beautifully, stylishly – through.

7

"LYING to my face all this time? How dare you? After everything I've done for you."

"What have you done? Manipulated two teenagers into a marriage they never should have entered? Bribed us into doing whatever you wanted? Treated your daughter like shit for years? Refused to pass on any of her own father's money or possessions unless we danced to your tune? Hoarded them for yourself because you didn't approve of the choices she made? Yeah, we lied to you. And now we're done."

"You will never see a penny from me, and neither will your mother. You're a disgrace to this family. Get out of this house, both of you, and never come back."

"Gladly."

The Northumberland countryside outside the bus windows was as comforting and familiar as ever, but Michael had no attention to spare for it today. His brain was back in that day eighteen months ago, when he'd finally shaken off the deception and walked away from his grandmother.

He should have done it sooner. He was ashamed now at how long they'd kept up the charade that he and Cleo were still together. But he remembered his mother's face as he'd practically had to drag her away from the chilly old house. Covered with tears, crumpled in despair. She'd accepted that the time was right for honesty, that she could no longer ask Michael to play nice with the woman who clearly despised him. But it was never about the inheritance for his mam. It had been about family, and it had broken her heart that Margaret had cast her aside too.

He'd gone back home for while after that. His mam was lonely and preparing for a new course of treatment, so it had been a no-brainer. And in those weeks, she'd come around to the way things were. Margaret was toxic and cruel, and no matter how much Liz loved her, she didn't deserve to be treated that way.

But now things had changed. He didn't know why, or when, but at some point his mam and grandmother must have reconciled enough for Margaret to pay for the treatment. How the fuck had that happened, and when had anyone been planning to tell him?

Shit, this was his stop. He got off the bus on the high street and started the walk to his mam's house. Home. It always would be, that tiny little house he'd grown up in, even though he couldn't ever imagine coming back for good. He'd tried to picture it so many times, in those months he was here, and even before that, when he'd despaired of the life he was living and his mam was ill and every sensible part of his brain was telling him to move back home and be a wedding photographer or something. But he'd never been able to shake the feeling that London was where he needed to be. His life was there. The only chance he could see for a future was there. He knew it had been selfish of him to stay.

But sometimes it felt like the only thing he'd ever done for himself in his whole life.

Finally, his mam's front door came into view. She greeted him with a huge hug, and as his arms went around her he let himself relax a little bit. She was here, she was well, and in the grand scheme of things, what else mattered?

"Oh, I've missed you. You look shattered, pet. What have you been doing with yourself? Sit down and I'll fetch you a brew. A proper cuppa with decent water and everything. I've got mac and cheese and garlic bread for tea – is that alright?"

"Sounds great, Mam." He let her bustle about, chattering away and putting the kettle on. A cup of tea wouldn't hurt. His questions could wait for a few minutes.

When he was settled on the couch with a mug full of hot tea and a plate of chocolate digestives on the coffee table between them, Michael took a breath.

"So. Mam."

She winced. "You know, then?"

"I know that Gran paid for some of that last round of treatment, yes. What I don't know is how on earth that came about." Michael was trying very hard to keep his voice even and calm. But his mother, of course, was not buying it.

"Oh god, you're pissed off. I knew you would be. This was why I didn't tell you, but I suppose I should have done."

"Please. Just tell me now."

"OK. Well, it was about eight months ago. I didn't speak to her until then, not at all. Although I did know that Maureen, you remember Maureen, was going in to clean for her, so I knew how she was doing. And she was OK, but then she had a bad fall, and she phoned me. And Michael, what was I supposed to do? She was hurt, and she needed help, and she's my mother. So I went to hospital with her, and when she got out I started checking on her again, just once a week. And it was ... different. Something had changed. She was still a bit, you know, like she is, but she wasn't anywhere near as cold. Stopped complaining, stopped criticising. I still wasn't hoping for anything, so you needn't worry that she was wrapping me around her finger again or anything like that. I was just making sure she was safe. And then I went away for Cleo's wedding, and when I came back ... she apologised."

Michael nearly spilled his tea. "She did what?"

His mam let out a small giggle. "I know. I almost fell off my chair. I don't think I'd ever heard her say the word 'sorry' in my entire life. But she did. I could see it wasn't easy for her, but she said she was sorry about all of it – you and Cleo, the will, kicking me out when I got pregnant. Everything, all these years. She said she didn't want to spend her last years on this earth at odds with her only daughter."

"And I suppose you forgave her right away."

"I didn't, actually." She folded her arms. "You'd be proud. I said that she'd done and said some terrible things, and that she'd missed out on so much because of her pride, and that I would always love her but I would need time. I said I would go and see her more often and we could try to mend our relationship, but that none of us would ever let her treat us like that again."

She was right; he was proud. How about that? His mother had, for the first time, stood up to his grandmother's crap. Still, he couldn't help but be sceptical. That woman had been monstrous for as long as he could remember.

"And she accepted that, did she?"

"She did. I know you won't believe it, but she really made an effort. We talked, more than we have since I was a child. She showed me photos of my dad when he was younger. She gave me some of his books and other bits. She finally shared all the things she'd held back from me. Then she told me she'd changed the will, and that she wanted to pay for the treatment. And she hasn't brought the money up even once since then. You know she always would have done in the past."

This was true. Every single penny she'd ever given them, every single time she'd bothered herself to help out her own flesh and blood, she'd lorded over them whenever she needed to score a point. That she'd managed not to do that for what seemed like months was ... unexpected.

He took a mouthful of his tea, then another. He drank the whole cup, because he couldn't think of anything else to do. His mam just sat and watched him.

"Are you angry with me?" she finally said.

"Of course not. I could never be angry with you. None of this is your fault."

"Don't let me off too easy, pet. Some of it is. I should never have made you deal with her for my sake. I should have been firmer with her, and with myself, a long time ago. I let her hurt you, time and time again, and I'll never forgive myself for that." Tears welled up in his mam's eyes, and time was he would have done anything to make them stop. But she was right, to a degree, and he knew it. "I'm so, so sorry."

"I love you, Mam. I chose to put you first. That was my decision, and Cleo's."

She shook her head. "It was wrong of me to let you for so long. I won't make that mistake again, I promise. It's you and me, love. Always has been, always will be."

He cocked his head. "Come here."

She came and sat beside him on the sofa, and he put his arm around her and gave her the biggest hug he could manage. And as he did, he felt something inside him lift. It didn't matter that his mam and grandmother were on speaking terms again. It wasn't about him. They'd all learned their lessons, and he didn't have to worry about his mam being manipulated again; he believed that now. It wasn't like he had to have anything to do with her ever again.

"She ..."

Michael narrowed his eyes at his mother.

"She what?"

"She's written you a letter. I said I couldn't promise to give it you, and I certainly couldn't promise you'd ever read it. She understood that. She said that she owed you an apology anyway, even if you never accepted it."

He managed to stop himself gaping like an idiot. "Has she had some kind of bloody personality transplant or something?"

His mam chuckled, a little bit sadly. "No, pet. She's had a very real shock to the system. This hasn't happened overnight. It's taken a year and a half of having no one, and a health scare. And she's still very much herself – she was very haughty when she handed over the letter. But I do believe she's done some genuine reflection." She shrugged. "It's enough for me. It doesn't have to be for you."

Maybe he was being overdramatic, but the world felt as if it were turning upside down. All his life, the cold, arrogant, unyielding condescension of his grandmother had been a constant. The sun would rise, DFS would have a sale, and his grandmother would be a terrible person. It was all he'd ever known. When he'd walked away, he'd put her in the box in his head marked "Shit I'm done with", and that had been that. Did he want to get all that back out again?

He didn't, no. Not right now. But ...

"You can give me the letter. I don't know if I'll read it."

He knew his mam was trying very hard not to let hope bloom in her eyes, but she was absolutely useless at hiding her feelings. An open book, she was. A big-hearted, soft-as-clarts open book.

She went to the dresser and took out a thick cream envelope. She handed it to him, and although he put it face-down on the coffee table to put in his bag later, he couldn't help catching a glimpse of the writing on the front. His name, in a shaky, spidery script that was worlds away from the elegant cursive he knew.

"So," his mam said brightly, as if she could see he needed to change the subject before his brain exploded. "What have you been up to?"

"I've been working with Miranda Janes." Oh. He hadn't thought he would say that. It'd just slipped out, probably because his head was still in a spin from the revelations of the last twenty minutes. Shit. He wasn't supposed to say anything, was he? "I don't think anyone's supposed to know that, though, so keep it quiet, yeah?"

"Ooh, are you? And of course I will. Not that I've anyone to tell. Maureen and the other ladies at Pilates are all older than me and haven't heard of any actor born after 1976."

"Yeah. We've just done the one session so far, but I think it went well." That was an understatement. He'd spent all yesterday afternoon poring over the shots he'd taken, looking for things to adjust and failing to see anything but her radiance. He couldn't remember the last time he'd taken anything quite so stunning. He'd done some basic cropping, tweaked some saturation and balance here and there, but he knew that almost no one would notice any of the details. All they'd see was her.

His mam beamed at him. "That's brilliant! A right

feather in your cap. She was ever so lovely at Cleo and Devon's wedding, too. We had a nice old chat."

"Did you?" Michael had, of course, seen Miranda talking to everyone at the wedding, including his mam, but he'd assumed it was just small talk, the kind that celebrities and socialites were so good at filling the air with.

"Aye. We were talking about cleaning."

"Cleaning?" His eyebrows couldn't get any higher if they tried.

"Yes, surprised me too, but she was a cleaner once, when she was a teenager. She wanted these fancy acting lessons, but her parents said they'd pay for half only if she could raise the other half. She said she was pretty sure her parents said that because they didn't really think she'd do it, so she spent a whole summer cleaning houses and working in a milkshake bar until she had enough to pay for the whole thing herself." Liz laughed. "She strikes me as the kind of girl who always gets what she wants. But not in a bad way."

"Yeah, that just about sums her up, I reckon," Michael murmured.

His mam was looking at him weirdly, one eyebrow slightly raised.

"What?" he said.

"Nothing," she replied innocently. "Shall I get this mac and cheese started, then?"

8

UGH, Miranda hated thinking of Instagram captions. How did everyone else do it? More to the point, how did they post things like "Girl of your dreams ..." without cringing themselves to death?

Besides, how could she ever come up with anything that would match the sheer perfection of this picture? Michael had sent her a link to all of them, but he'd attached three to the email itself, and she'd known instantly that this one was the one. It had been taken towards the end of the shoot, when she'd been sitting on the bed. The sun streaming in through the window seemed to give her an almost unearthly glow, and the expression on her face made her look much younger than she was. She looked soft, sweet, innocent, vulnerable. Exactly like she'd wanted.

Michael Hedley was a genius.

She, however, was not, especially when it came to this caption. She simply had to get this posted before Nora's meeting with AJ tomorrow. The only thing that kept coming to mind was a quote from *An Ocean of Fallen Stars* – "And when all she had left was hope, that would still be more than enough" – but that would be a little too obvious.

Leaving half her brain to ruminate on that a little

longer, she picked up her phone to message Michael. She had already, of course, thanked him for the pictures and enthused over how fabulous they were, but she'd forgotten to check something.

MIRANDA: Should I tag your business insta when I post this or just put your name?

MICHAEL: It's ok, you don't have to credit me.

MIRANDA: Of course I do! They're your pictures. I give credit where it's due. And it's more than due. The world should know who you are.

MICHAEL: I thought you were keeping this quiet though.

MIRANDA: The exact whys and wherefores, yes. But I don't need to hide the fact that these are pro photos. It's not an unusual thing to do.

MICHAEL: Credit me later. Don't want to divert attention away from what you're trying to do. Happy to stay in the shadows for this one :)

Miranda couldn't figure him out. Most creatives would be happy to get their name out there, especially on work as good as this. Was he really doing it to let her get on with the business of attracting AJ's attention? Or did he genuinely not want the exposure? Another thought struck her. Was he embarrassed to be working with her? She knew from Cleo that Michael's dream was to be a fine art photographer. Could it be that he didn't consider what they were doing art in any way? Was he yet another person incapable of taking anything she did seriously?

The idea brought a sour taste to her mouth, but she swallowed it down. What did it matter what he thought? He'd taken the picture, he'd done a fantastic job, and now she had what she needed. His opinion of her wasn't important, and she was only making assumptions anyway.

She needed to focus. *Just pick some words and post it, Miranda. Get it done.*

A half-remembered quote drifted into her brain. She quickly googled it, then posted the picture to her grid with the caption "One drop in a limitless ocean" – a quote from *Cloud Atlas*, a book she'd loved and which had reportedly been one of the inspirations for *An Ocean of Fallen Stars*. It was still maybe a little obvious, but Miranda was past caring. She didn't have time for too much subtlety.

Her phone buzzed with a message.

> MICHAEL: Looks great. Here's hoping it catches the right eyes.

A warmth bloomed in her chest. That was fast. Did he have a notification set up for her posts or something? And it was also sweet. Perhaps she'd jumped to unnecessary conclusions about how seriously he was taking this. Taking her.

> Fingers crossed, she sent back.

MICHAEL: I had an idea for the next one.

Miranda opened the link he'd sent and gasped to her empty living room. Pictures of the Barbican Conservatory filled her phone screen – brutalist concrete and lush greenery mingled together to create a stunning dystopian playground.

MICHAEL: I started reading that book and pictured this place as soon as I read the part where she gets taken to the Court.

Goodness. Had he started reading *Ocean*, for her? Miranda had never known anyone get so invested in one of her plans.

MIRANDA: It's PERFECT. I'll get my assistant right on it. What's your availability?

MICHAEL: Nothing I can't shift.

The warmth spread from her chest up to her face, and Jen's words rang in her head.

"Oh boy. You're in trouble."

Well, this was inconvenient. Just because he was exactly her type – talented, somewhat aloof, intense but with a sense of humour, quietly good-looking – didn't mean she should go developing one of her ill-advised crushes on him. She was hiring him, for one thing – she was essentially his boss. That wasn't a dynamic she should mess with, not if she wanted to keep him around professionally. And she did, very much so. She would just have to keep her ridiculous romantic impulses under control this time. It wasn't as if it ever worked out well when she didn't, anyway. It had been a year since her last failed relationship, the longest she'd ever been single for, but she was in no hurry to rack up another heartbreak, his or hers. The only thing she wanted to be attached to right now was this movie. Any feelings of attraction, or whatever might be going on, could be pushed aside in favour of that.

Miranda tore her thoughts away from Michael and looked at the likes and comments racking up on her post. More than usual, she thought, although that could be wishful thinking. Cleo, Courtney, her former co-star Shaun Silver, and supermodel Holly Harkness had all left appreciative comments already. Miranda replied to say thank you. But as grateful as she was, as wonderful as her amazing friends were for leaving those comments, she knew she wouldn't know until tomorrow whether the picture had hit the mark.

Please, Nora. Please make AJ keep the door open a little while longer.

They hadn't seen anything yet.

9

MICHAEL looked around in satisfaction. Two hours after his text conversation with Miranda, he'd had an email from the ruthlessly efficient Aisling informing them that the Barbican Conservatory had been booked out for their next shoot. This was one of his favourite places in London to take photos, but the tour system they had in place didn't normally leave much time to explore the possibilities. Now the place was theirs for three whole hours.

He'd had it in mind for a possible location since the moment Miranda had first got in touch, but then he'd started reading that book, the one that the movie was based on, and the dystopian setting of the novel's middle section had reminded him so strongly of brutalist architecture that he hadn't hesitated to suggest it to her. He was quite enjoying the book, actually. It wasn't his usual thing – he was much more of a non-fiction guy – but the novel was beautifully written. And of course, he'd pictured Damia as Miranda. Which made a few scenes ... interesting.

He forced his mind away from all that and towards figuring out where he should start. Maybe there, by whatever that dangling bit of greenery was. The light was good there, although he might need to supplement it a bit. Would the reflector be enough? He pulled it out of his bag, and then almost dropped it, because there she was.

"Michael, this is perfect, so perfect. Thank you for suggesting it – I can't believe I never even knew this was here! It's beautiful, and so surreal."

She looked phenomenal in a ruby-red wide-legged trouser suit. The cut was impeccable, and the fabric so luxurious and rich that he had to fight the urge to reach out and feel it beneath his fingertips. Between the satin lapels of the jacket was nothing but smooth skin. With her tousled hair and smokey eyes, she kind of reminded him of Debbie Harry in her younger days. Her smile almost dazzled him, but he shook his head and got a bloody hold of his senses.

"You look incredible. That director's out of his mind if he can't see you differently after this."

"That's the idea. And I think – I hope – it might be working a little already. My agent met with him on Wednesday, and I don't think he mentioned the picture, but she said he seemed a little more receptive. He made noises about auditions, at least, which means he's no longer set on Elia. AJ's the only one who'll make this decision – he insisted on it – so he's the only one I need to convince."

As she spoke, her expression lost its sunshine and morphed into something harder, tougher. Her eyes glinted with that steel he'd seen in her before.

He lifted his camera and took a picture. She gave him a quizzical look.

"Sorry," he said with a nervous laugh. "Just ... your face did something that I wanted to capture. Come and see."

She stepped closer to look at the display screen on his camera. She smelled of something seductive and expensive, and he breathed it in as subtly as he could.

The composition of the shot was all wrong – there was nothing interesting in the background, and the proportions were off, but her face ...

"Oh yes. I see it," she breathed.

She was the furthest thing from a slab of concrete Michael could imagine, but the strength of her expression was a perfect match for the unforgiving walls around them, softened by all the lush colour.

"Maybe try to keep that thought in your head, how much you want this."

"That shouldn't be hard at all." She stepped back to a more normal distance. "Are we ready to go?"

He smiled. "Absolutely."

* * *

Two and a half hours later, Michael was pretty sure they had at least a hundred photos that should, if the man had any sense, have AJ Whateverhisnamewas begging Miranda to play Damia. Amongst the stark concrete and lush foliage, she stood out like a tropical bird. A terrifyingly beautiful one that might eat your heart out given half the chance.

He took a quick breath and made himself ask the

thing he'd been trying to work up the nerve for for at least twenty minutes. "Miranda?"

"Yeah?"

"I wondered if you'd mind ... if it's OK with you ... we've definitely got some good shots for your Instagram now, so I was hoping, thinking ... would it be OK if I maybe tried a few more, well, sort of arty kind of things, maybe?"

It was probably the least coherent sentence he'd ever said. It may have been the least coherent sentence anyone had ever said. But Miranda didn't seem to notice.

"Sure," she said brightly. "For your portfolio? Cleo told me you were an artist."

Michael shifted from foot to foot. "Trying to be. Something like that, anyway. And yeah, but only if it's OK with you. I'm here to do a job for you, and this stuff might not be right for that, so ..."

She pushed away from the balcony she'd been leaning against. "If you think we've got what I need, then I'm more than happy for you to take advantage of being here. On one condition."

"What's that?"

"You come for lunch with me instead of running off this time." She softened the accusation with a wink, but he couldn't help but wonder if he'd actually hurt her feelings last week.

"I'd love to," he said, with as much sincerity as he could put into his voice without cringing. Not that he was being insincere, by any means, but it didn't come naturally, this being-open-with-people thing.

"Then I and this beautiful place are entirely at your disposal, Mr Hedley."

For thirty glorious minutes, he let himself play. He was in one of the most amazing locations in London, with one of the most beautiful women in the universe, so if he couldn't get at least one decent shot, he didn't deserve to be a photographer and would go and find a job in Greggs, where at least he'd get cheap doughnuts for the rest of his days. He tried every way he could think of to capture the splendour of his surroundings and of his model. Everything he asked of her, she did without question, and he got the feeling she was enjoying herself, moving her face and her body in ways she maybe normally didn't get to. He captured the curve of her jaw, the shadows on her face, the line of her throat, and every single part of her seemed to display a grace he would never be able to describe if he had every dictionary in the world at his fingertips.

All too soon, their time was up, and as Michael reluctantly but quickly packed his things away, he found he was buzzing with a joy he hadn't felt in so, so long. As much as the weddings and the pretty landscapes had been a welcome and much needed change from what he'd been doing, none of it had ever quite given him the high of creation he'd just felt. That feeling that he was *making* something, pulling something out of a world of fleeting moments and into a more durable one. Something he could give to the world that someone somewhere might actually love.

He could be wrong. Maybe it was all shit and he would discover that when he got home. But that wasn't the point. Sometimes the doing mattered more than the end result.

Again, he felt that urge to run home and start going over his work. But he'd promised her he'd stay, so he'd stay. If that moment where he realised he'd been wrong was coming, there were far worse things to delay it with than more time with Miranda Janes.

10

"DO you think you got something you can use for your portfolio?" Miranda asked, once they'd ordered lunch. They were seated in a quiet, private corner of the restaurant in another one of Henry's hotels. The food here was superb, she'd heard, and she didn't doubt it. Henry never did anything unless he could do it to perfection.

Michael nodded. "I think so. If that's OK with you, of course. I would never show any pictures of you to anyone if you weren't happy with it, and we were technically on your paid time, so ..."

She waved her hand. "It's fine. I'm happy to help. And I had fun. I've been playing 'pretty' for so long it was refreshing not to worry about that at all."

"You were still pretty." He was blushing. How cute.

"Why thank you," she said casually. "I mean it, though. It was fun." She leaned back in her chair a little, assessing him. "You're different when you're in that mode, you know."

He raised his eyebrows. "I am?"

"Sorry. That's pretty presumptuous of me, isn't it? I don't even know you, really. Not yet." Oh dear. She was doing it again, the flirting. She had to stop doing that. The poor guy looked so awkward. "You're great when we do my stuff – you're so easy to work with, professional, open-minded, all of that. But it seemed as if you came alive when you were doing your thing. It was a privilege to be a part of that."

If she thought he was blushing before, he was practically on fire now. His face, normally so carefully neutral, seemed awash with a mix of emotions – he looked a little pleased, a little uncomfortable, sort of embarrassed but at the same time proud.

"Thank you, so much, for doing it. Building my portfolio has been ... challenging. The whole getting-back-to-art thing – I promised Cleo I would, but it's been more difficult than I thought it would be. In so many ways."

"Oh?"

"Yeah."

"In what ways?" She sensed he didn't really want to talk about this. But she also sensed that maybe he needed to, too. So if she had to take advantage of the fact that he probably wouldn't want to be rude to her, she would do so shamelessly.

Michael exhaled. "Well, obviously trying to make it as any kind of artist is a lot of work. You'll know that." She nodded, pleased beyond measure that he seemed to be referring to her as an artist. Not many people afforded actors that honour. "Finding those opportunities is a slog, and the art world can be ... exclusive, I suppose. It's difficult when you don't already know the right people. Like, it's hard to get a gallery show if your name isn't out there. And it's hard to get your name out there if nowhere wants to show your work."

"I can imagine. Contacts matter in any industry."

"Yeah, and I'm terrible at making them." He looked off at some indeterminate point in the distance. "And it's also been hard, emotionally, I guess? Is that the right way of putting it? Mentally, getting back into this thing that I used to love after so long doing the soul-destroying stuff. Figuring out what I want to be doing, what I want my work to say. If I even have anything to say. It's a lot."

"I bet," she murmured. His brow had furrowed so far she wondered if it was giving him a headache. She wanted to reach out and smooth the tension away.

Thankfully, the waiter saved her from herself, placing perfectly cooked, fragrant scallops in front of her and tuna ceviche in front of Michael.

"This looks incredible," he said, and they were silent for a few minutes as they savoured their food. The silence warped into something that felt warm, comfortable, as if in that brief exchange he'd let her in to some place not many people got to go. The thought was indescribably thrilling.

They ate the rest of their fabulous lunch either in that silence or chatting about nothing in particular – their favourite places in London, the music they liked – until Miranda asked, "So, have you been out to LA to see Cleo since she moved there?"

Even from across the table she saw his jaw tighten. "Yeah," he said shortly. "It's nice." He took a long drink of water. "LA's very different to here, though. Not sure I could live there."

"Oh, for sure. It's an overwhelming, kind of ridiculous place. I guess I'm used to it now, but ..." Her mouth took over, sending forth a stream of easy chatter about LA, because she'd received the message loud and clear. But her brain kept turning over his reaction. How odd, for him to not want to talk about Cleo.

She guessed it was because he missed her, which Miranda could understand. Although she and Cleo hadn't known each other nearly so long or so well, Miranda had liked her the moment they met, and through Devon they had become firm friends. Cleo was a joy to be around, and Miranda got the impression that she was perhaps Michael's only real friend. She would have put money on the fact that he was lonely now, and even more money on him never admitting to anyone how much.

The conversation moved on, and she was listening so intently to Michael that she didn't notice somebody approaching their table until Michael's eyes flicked towards them.

"Miranda! Why didn't you tell me you were coming?"

Miranda rose to meet the familiar figure. "Henry! So nice to see you." She kissed him on both cheeks. "Last-minute decision. But a good one, as ever. Everything was delicious. You remember Michael Hedley?"

Henry turned and extended his hand. "Of course. Your photos from the wedding were wonderful."

Michael blushed, just the tiniest bit. "Thank you. Your island made an amazing setting."

Miranda saw an opportunity and took it without hesitation. "Michael and I have been working on some of his more artistic photos today. He's wonderfully talented. You could commission him for artwork for your hotels."

Michael shot her a look. "Are you always this unsubtle?"

"Absolutely." She grinned at him.

"Can confirm," Henry said with a chuckle. "But she knows I'm always on the lookout for new things. And it reminds me, I've been meaning to get a print of one your photos of me and Courtney. Cleo sent me the file but I might need a higher-res version for what I have in mind."

"I can help you with that, no problem."

Miranda smiled as Henry took Michael's email address. This day was getting better by the minute. Running into Henry was a delight, because he was one of the nicest men on the planet, and now Michael could solve a problem he'd forgotten he had. Wasn't it wonderful when life worked out?

"Great," Henry said. He smiled at Miranda. "I'd better get back to work. But it would be lovely to see you again while I'm in the country."

"I would love that."

"I don't suppose you're free tomorrow? There's a fundraiser at our Mayfair hotel that might be fun. You should come too, Michael. It's a very artsy crowd."

She could see Michael opening his mouth to decline, and she'd be damned if she was going to let him.

"Sounds wonderful, Henry," she said quickly. "Doesn't it, Michael?"

He'd mentioned how hard it was to get a foot in the door. Well, here was a door, and she was going to guide his foot in the right direction.

11

YOU *can do this*, Michael told himself. It was just a party. All he had to do was ... walk into a room full of posh arty people and find something to say to some of them. While on the arm of a famous actress. Where the only other person he'd know there was a billionaire hotelier.

Oh god. What the hell was he doing? Why had he said yes to this? This was stupid. He could have been ... well, sitting in his flat on his own, like every night. He sighed. He knew he needed to get out more, but this was not exactly easing himself into it.

Miranda reached over from her side of the back seat and placed a gentle hand on his arm. "Hey. It'll be OK. I won't abandon you, I promise."

He managed a smile. "Am I that obvious?"

She winked. "Kinda."

"It's not my usual scene, this kind of thing."

"And what is your usual scene?" she asked, with a shake of her head that made her long earrings sparkle.

He let out a dry laugh. "I'm not sure I have one. My social life only ever used to involve Cleo, really. A couple of other mates I'd go to the pub with now and then. But I worked evenings, mainly. I'm pretty used to these kind of events – I was just always standing on the pavement outside."

She nodded. "Your life's changed a lot. I remember what that's like."

"Yeah?"

"Yeah. When *Iris Jackson* came out, that totally changed things for me. All my roles before that had been small, so I was still pretty much under the radar. Then that movie changed everything, and my life became ... what it is now, I guess. I loved it, but it was a lot to deal with, too. Takes some getting used to."

"You've got that right. All the other stuff has been weird enough – you know, Cleo suddenly becoming famous, changing my job, all that business with my family. I can't imagine what it would be like if this" – he waved his hand in a way he hoped encompassed the fancy car, her silver dress, the crisp new shirt he'd panic-bought that afternoon, and the night in general – "was my everyday reality."

"It's different, for sure." Her tone was light, but Michael thought there was a touch of tightness at the edge of her smile. Shit. Had he just insulted her lifestyle? They weren't even bloody there yet and he'd already put his foot in it. God help him.

But she continued. "But you know, a big part of getting used to any situation is to remember that people are people. You can find kind, interesting people anywhere, and I make it my business to seek them out. And the rest of it is just telling yourself you belong there." She shrugged an elegant shoulder. "No one has any right to make you feel otherwise."

He snorted. Like it was that easy. "I've spent my

whole life wondering if I belong in places. And a major chunk of it being told I'm definitely not welcome. It's not easy to shake that off."

"No," she said thoughtfully. Then she squeezed his hand, just quickly, and he felt a fraction of his tension leave him. "But we're not going to think like that tonight. Tonight, we're going out for a drink, you and me, OK? We've been invited to our friend's place, and we're going to catch up with him. If we happen to meet some other interesting people there, that will be a nice bonus."

She was definitely stretching things to include him as a friend of Henry's – they'd had a total of two and a half conversations ever – but he didn't bother arguing with her. She made it sound so easy. And maybe it could be. Miranda had a way of making him feel like anything could be possible.

The car pulled to a stop.

"Ready?" As she prepared to get out, she turned and looked over her shoulder, and Michael had never wished for a camera in his hands more. Her neck was a thing of beauty.

"No," he said. "But let's go anyway."

He followed her out of the car, tilting his head at an angle that he knew would make it difficult to get a decent photo. There wouldn't be many paps here – not that he was about to look up and check – because it wasn't a star-studded event, present company excepted. But the high-end glossies sometimes covered things like this, especially if they'd caught a whisper someone like

Miranda might show up, and Michael had no desire to feature in one. Thankfully, Miranda gave one graceful wave and kept walking for the door, where they were ushered through without a word. No one needed to see Miranda Janes's invitation, it seemed.

The hotel was just as quietly luxurious as the one they'd eaten in yesterday and the one they'd shot in the other week, all sleek lines, rich colours and inviting textures. Henry Deng – or the people he hired – had impeccable taste.

As they accepted champagne from a suited waiter, Michael tried not to feel self-conscious. He didn't do very well. Looking around at the mingling crowd, he could see that his shirt probably cost about as much as everyone else's socks.

"You look great," Miranda said in a low voice.

"Can you read my thoughts or something?" He took a gulp of his champagne.

"I can read your body language." The thought of her looking at his body temporarily chased all his other thoughts away. "And clothes are the first thing most people worry about in situations like this. But honestly, you look good. That shirt fits you perfectly."

Were her eyes lingering on his arms? Maybe. She was assessing the shirt, after all.

"Thank you," he said. "You look spectacular, of course." The silver lace dress was relatively simple, but she was still breathtaking. He took out his phone. "May I?"

She took the phone from him, flipped the camera,

leaned closer, and before he knew it, she'd snapped a selfie of them. She handed the phone back with a mischievous smile. "Not up to your standards, of course."

He looked at the photo and burst out laughing. "I look so puzzled."

"Do you? That looks like your normal expression to me." She took a sip of her champagne. "Or the one you wear around me, anyway. Perhaps you find me very puzzling."

Before he could work out the extent to which she was joking, they were interrupted by Henry Deng.

"Michael, Miranda, so glad you could make it." He seemed genuinely pleased to see them, both of them. Michael felt himself relax a tiny bit. Perhaps Henry was just so good at networking that making people feel welcome was his thing, but he did seem like a nice guy, and when they'd chatted at the wedding – about nothing in particular, maybe football? – they'd got along well enough. So there were two people in this room he could exchange more than three words with, at least.

"Thanks for inviting us," Michael said, then wanted to kick himself. He should have let Miranda speak. Now it looked as though he was speaking for her, like they were an "us". They weren't an "us". He was basically her employee, and she was dragging him around with her for reasons best known to herself.

Neither Miranda nor Henry acted like anything was amiss, just carried on the conversation as if he wasn't an absolute social liability.

"How long are you in England for?" Miranda asked. "Is Courtney coming out to join you anytime soon?"

"I'm here for a month or two, I think. Sorting a few things out. And no, Court's staying in the States. She's got a lot on, with her return to music after so long in movies. She's still working on the album, doing some interviews, that kind of thing." Henry's chiselled face seemed to glow with pride.

"It's so exciting," Miranda said. "I love Courtney as an actress, but I can't wait to hear her new stuff."

"Yep." Henry looked thoughtful. "Big changes."

"Cleo said she was doing an interview with Courtney about it all," Michael said, ignoring the tiny pang of guilt that accompanied his mention of Cleo. He hadn't really spoken to her since she'd told him about Margaret, so maybe he shouldn't be dropping her name just so he could have input into the conversation. This was all making his head hurt. How did he find himself surrounded by the rich and famous? Pap stuff aside, his greatest claim to fame had previously been that he once bumped into Alan Shearer in Alnwick.

Henry smiled fondly. "Yeah, they did that the other day. Court said they were having so much fun together they kept forgetting to do the interview part."

"Oh, I'm so jealous that they got to hang out without me!" Miranda turned to Michael, putting her hand on his arm. He was starting to get used to the idea that she just touched people all the time, without thinking. "We have a group chat, the three of us. We started it just before the wedding. I'm going to use it to yell at them for having fun together while I'm on another continent."

"How dare they?" Henry laughed.

"Henry, there you are, I was– Oh, I'm sorry." The tall, green-suited man who'd wandered over seemed to suddenly catch sight of Miranda and almost fell over himself. "I didn't mean to–"

"No, no," Henry said cheerfully. "Join us. Hugh, this is Miranda Janes and Michael Hedley. Miranda, Michael, Hugh Humberstone-Ridley."

"Ridiculous name, I know. I blame my parents." Hugh extended his hand. "Miranda, a pleasure to meet you. And Michael, nice to meet you too." Michael heard the faint question in his voice. *Are you a somebody?*

"Michael's a photographer," Miranda said smoothly. "We've been working on a project together."

"Oh? What kind of photographer? Fashion?"

Oh god. Was this the part where he was supposed to try to make himself sound like a proper person with a proper career? Miranda gave him a subtle but encouraging nod.

"No, I ... I guess you could say I've dabbled in a few things over the years. But portraiture is what I'm interested in. I studied as an artist and I'm trying to get back to that right now."

Henry waved his glass in Hugh's direction. "Hugh's actually ... well, Hugh, what would we call you these days? An artist? A former artist? An agent? A collector?"

"Yes," Hugh said, with a somewhat short laugh.

"Some or all or none of those things, among others, depending on what day it is."

Henry smiled. "Hugh knows more about the art scene than anyone else in London."

Michael sipped his drink. Shit. Should he have been trying harder to impress this guy? He sounded like someone it would be useful to know.

"Well, I don't know about that, Henry." Hugh looked a little uneasy, but Miranda, as ever, didn't allow the awkwardness to settle for even a moment. She turned her dazzling smile on Hugh.

"But it all means your life must be spent hearing 'Oh, my friend is an artist, you should see his work!'"

Hugh let out a relieved chuckle. "Something like that."

"Well." Miranda threw Michael a sly wink. "Michael *is* a fabulous artist, but you've probably already seen some of his work. Did you see Devon Grant's proposal photo?"

"Darling, everyone in the world saw that photo." Hugh raised an eyebrow at Michael. "That was you?"

"It was."

"Hmm." His expression was unreadable, and Michael couldn't think of a single thing to say. This was the opportunity to talk to someone about his work, which was meant to be why he was here, but he was so intimidated he couldn't speak.

Miranda rescued him yet again. She made a tiny gesture, and a waiter sped over with a tray of fresh drinks. "Tell me about this suit, Hugh. So few men can pull off green."

The other three chatted away, while Michael sipped his champagne and wondered how the hell they did that. Did they teach that at rich-people school, the art of talking about nothing much with people you didn't know? A woman in a mustard trouser suit came over and joined them – her name was Julie, maybe? And she was something to do with film – and then Hugh left, and then Henry left, and then there seemed to be an ever-revolving cast of people around them. Sometimes he managed to think of a few things to say to some of them, but mostly he just stood there while Miranda sparkled.

What was he doing here? He should have stayed at home. He could have been sat in front of the TV with a beer, rewatching *Breaking Bad*. This was too much.

"Excuse me," he murmured to Miranda, then made for the loos.

Washing his hands with expensive-smelling soap, he looked his reflection in the eye. *Get it together, you twat. You want to be an artist, these are the people you need to schmooze with. She did you a favour. This is an opportunity, so treat it like one.*

He walked back towards the party and stopped before the door to take a fortifying breath. As he was about to re-enter the breach, someone stepped out, practically onto his toes.

"Oh, sorry ... Michael, right?"

It was Hugh, the art guy of unspecified job title.

"No worries. And yes." What to say, what to say ... "Are you leaving?" A bit daft, because what business was it of Michael's, but at least it was something.

"Yes." Hugh grimaced. "Just ran into an ex. Far too regular an occurrence in the arts scene, of course, but this one in particular was not pleased to see me."

"Time for a tactical retreat, then."

"Exactly." Hugh gave him a curious look. "I texted my fiancé to tell him I'd just met Miranda Janes, and he got very excited and sent me her latest Instagram picture. Your work?"

"Yeah," Michael said, trying to sound casual.

"It's very good."

"Thanks."

Was that the conversation over? Should he go back into the party now, let Hugh leave? Just when he'd decided the bollock-shrinkingly awkward moment had gone on long enough, Hugh seemed to make a decision.

"OK." He handed Michael a business card. "There might be some things I can help you with. Let's have lunch."

"Oh. Yes. Great. Thank you." Michael had no idea what kind of help Hugh was offering, but it was the first time anyone had, and he wasn't about to say no.

"See you soon, then."

"Night."

Michael just stood there, holding the card, like a total fucking lemon.

"There you are. I was worried you'd decided this whole thing was too awful and bailed on me." Miranda was suddenly right next to him, looking at the little piece of card in his hand. "Is that Hugh's?"

He nodded slowly. "Yep. Says he might be able to

help me. I'm not sure how yet, but it's something, right? It's the only hint of an opportunity I've had in ages, anyway."

She threw her arms around him. "Of course it's something, Michael. It's fantastic!"

And for once, he let his arms do what they wanted to do and close around her waist.

"Thank you for doing this," he said softly. Inadequate words, but all he had.

She squeezed him a little tighter, then released him and stepped away, and some foolish part of him felt disappointed.

"I did nothing that I wouldn't do for any of my other friends. And all I did was drag you here and start a conversation. You're the one with the talent."

Friends. Miranda Janes had decided they were friends. This was supremely weird. But her words sparked a glow in him that he hadn't felt in a while.

"Come on." She tucked her arm through his. "Let's have another glass of Henry's excellent champagne in celebration."

12

"THE lodge is all booked for your dad's birthday weekend, and your sister emailed with some recommendations for caterers, so I'll get onto those next week. I still need to book your flights, but we have plenty of time – do you want to go Thursday or ... Miranda?"

Miranda blinked a few times. "Sorry, darling, did you say something?"

Aisling cocked her head. "I've been saying things for about ten minutes. Are you OK?"

Miranda had not been listening in the slightest to any of it. "I don't know what's wrong with me. I'm on another planet today. I assume you were telling me how fabulously you have organised my life, as usual?"

Her assistant laughed. "Naturally. And I was asking what day you wanted to fly for your dad's birthday."

Miranda tapped a finger to her lips. "Leave that with me a while. I may go visit Cleo for a few days, if she's around. Can I get you another coffee, sweetie?"

"I can do that."

Miranda waved her away. "No, no. I've got it."

She went to her kitchen and set the coffee machine going, wondering what on earth was up with her. She'd asked Aisling to come over today rather than having their usual phone call because she'd wanted the company, and now she was spacing out all over the place. She felt restless, unsettled, and she wasn't sure why. True, this was the longest she'd ever gone between movies, but Miranda had never had a problem with boredom. She'd always found ways to fill her time.

She took the coffees back into the living room.

"Thanks," Aisling said. "Have you heard from Nora about AJ?"

Miranda sighed. "No. Not in a few days. I can't help but worry that time is running out. It seems to have been in pre-pro forever."

"I wouldn't worry. AJ is known for deliberating for a long time then making a lot of decisions very quickly. When I worked for Lauren Fox and she was cast in *Memory Thieves*, it happened that way. One minute he was still figuring it out, the next I was sorting out a Colombian visa."

"I just hope he changes his mind about Elia." Miranda chewed her lip.

Aisling sipped her coffee. "Me too. She was awful in that jewel-thief thing. He'd have to be stupid not to consider some proper actresses. And if it's the look he's after, I'm sure your photos will help. Those Barbican ones are unreal."

They were unreal. Miranda had squealed out loud when she'd seen them. She'd ended up posting four at once, because she couldn't decide which one she liked best. Michael seemed to have captured some mysterious strength in her face that she'd never seen there before. AJ had to see it too. He had to.

Aisling lifted her coffee cup again, but this time Miranda saw something that her distracted brain had completely failed to notice before. "Aisling, is that ..."

Aisling's pale cheeks burned bright red. "Oh, yeah. I meant to take it off before I came, because we're not telling everyone yet until Krish can get hold of his parents, who are on a cruise and won't pay for the Wi-Fi, but ... yeah." She held out her hand and showed Miranda the beautiful diamond-and-aquamarine ring. "We're getting married!"

"Congratulations, sweetheart!" She pulled Aisling to her feet and gave her a huge hug. "I'm so happy for you both."

She meant it. She was delighted for her assistant. Aisling was a wonderful person, and although she didn't talk much about her personal life, Miranda knew that she and Krish, a graphic designer, had been very happily in love for a few years now. She'd have to get them a congratulations present – perhaps a couple's spa retreat? Or maybe she could ask if Michael would do an engagement photo shoot. Miranda had heard those were a thing now. Her mind ruminated over gifts, and her mouth chattered to Aisling about the proposal and wedding plans, and both determinedly ignored the tiny part of her heart that was wondering why everyone else in the world seemed able to hold on to love.

When Aisling departed an hour later, Miranda let that tiny part take over, just for a second. She wanted to kick herself – she had a life beyond her wildest dreams, and it was full of love. She didn't need a man. But what she did want, what she had always wanted, was the kind of love her parents, her sister, her assistant had. She'd thought she'd found it so many times, but it never lasted. She was always either too much or never enough.

Her phone, thank goodness, pulled her out of her self-pity. It was a message from Nora. Could it finally be good news?

She opened the message to find a screenshot of a text. From AJ Hollinger.

> All right. She has my attention ...

Her melancholy evaporated. She'd done it. She'd put herself in the running for the role. She didn't care that he'd apparently seen straight through her ploy – the photos were intended for him, and if he'd figured that out, then he was evidently a perceptive man who wasn't put off by someone who went after what they wanted.

Another message came through.

> NORA: Hasn't committed to a screen test yet. But was also talking about meeting you. I suggested setting up a call but he didn't seem into that idea, at least not yet. He's so vague. I swear this guy is gonna drive me up a wall.

Miranda laughed. That was hyperbole, she knew; no one got the better of Nora. But if he was still prevaricating, it was time to step it up. Should she fly back to the States, try to arrange a meeting? She wasn't sure whether that was a good idea. AJ clearly liked to do things on his own terms. She'd attracted his attention, but he was already showing Nora that he wouldn't be rushed.

No problem. She'd keep doing what she was doing, for now. The Instagram thing was working out well. It was elevating her image, and that had to be a good thing in the long term, no matter what else happened.

And besides, she admitted to herself, she wasn't ready to stop working with Michael yet. They'd only done two shoots, and she already had hundreds of pictures of herself that she was in love with – not in a vain way, although she wasn't going to deny she looked great in them. But because they were *her*, in a way she rarely saw in photographs. She wanted more.

And she wanted to keep getting to know him better. He intrigued her. The way he was clearly passionate about what he did, yet so hesitant and shy about it. What was up with that? She was itching to find out.

More photos, then. Ones that would be impossible for AJ to ignore.

13

MICHAEL looked around Hugh's cool, comfortable home office. The walls were, naturally, hung with stunning paintings, sketches and photographs. Hugh clearly knew his shit. And right now he was looking at Michael's shit.

The best of the few portraits he'd managed to take and be happy with over the last eighteen months were being scanned by Hugh's assessing, careful eyes. One of Cleo. A couple of Priya and her most recent girlfriend, Ros. His mam. Miranda.

The room was silent. Michael could feel himself sweating. His palms itched. His skin felt too tight. He'd never wanted to get up and run out of anywhere more. But Hugh was the real deal. Michael had researched him, and the guy knew everything and everyone to do with the fine art scene in London. He'd been an artist, a curator, a dealer, a lecturer, everything – if anyone could help Michael find his feet in this world, it would be him. This was an opportunity, the only one Michael had managed to get in months. Maybe he only got it because of the glittering company he was keeping that night, but that was the way things worked. And none of it would matter if his pictures were no good.

Oh god, what if they were no good? He hadn't had any professional-level feedback in a hell of a long time.

What if this whole time he'd been fooling himself? Maybe whatever talent he'd had was now long gone, withered away through lack of attention over the years.

He was trying to remember which of the pubs round the corner had been advertising for staff the other day when Hugh said, "So."

Michael shifted in his seat.

"These are good."

A portion of the tension in Michael's shoulders drained away. Thank god. He wasn't totally shit. Even if nothing else came of this meeting, he'd take that.

"This one of Miranda is extraordinary." It was one of the ones from the Barbican. "I'm sure it's hard to take a bad photo of her, but still ... this is excellent, Michael."

"Thank you."

Hugh leaned back in his seat, a thoughtful expression on his face. "Tell me some more about yourself. When did you first become interested in photography?"

"My grandmother bought me a camera for my thirteenth birthday." The memory caused a strange pang in his stomach. His grandmother had always bought him birthday presents, and he'd received most of them as warmly as they'd been given, which was to say about three degrees above freezing. It was clear she never put any particular thought into the gifts, but this one had captivated him. "At first I wanted it to take pictures of my mates doing stupid things, but I found that I could do more than that. I could capture the world the way I saw it, and I could focus on whichever bits of it I wanted. I could make other people see what I saw. I could hide the things that weren't beautiful. For a kid like me, there was magic in that."

"A kid like you?" Hugh asked.

Damn. He'd got carried away in his memories and said too much. What answer could he give that Hugh of the ridiculous surnames would understand? The truth? A kid with no money, barely any family, and no idea how to make things better. A kid whose life was messy, full of ugly inconveniences. No. That wasn't an answer he felt like giving.

"Artistic opportunities were thin on the ground where I came from," he said instead. A truth, certainly. "So I came to London for uni and I loved it. I learned from some amazing tutors."

"It says on your CV that you've been freelancing since you graduated. What kind of work have you been doing?"

This was the question Michael had been dreading. Should he lie? The thought only crossed his mind for an instant before he dismissed it. For one thing, it was a daft idea. He had hundreds of photo credits to his name – not all of his pictures had gone through an agency. He was exceedingly googleable. And for another, he was tired of lying. He'd lied about his job – and his marital status – to his grandmother for years, and he had no desire to feel that weight on his shoulders again. So the truth it would have to be.

"Bits and pieces. But ... celebrity photography mostly."

"Editorial?"

"More ... ad hoc than that."

Hugh raised an eyebrow. "Michael, are you trying to say you were a pap?"

So much for trying to avoid the word. "Yeah."

"Interesting. It's an unusual route into the art world, that's for sure." Nothing about Hugh's voice or face changed, but Michael couldn't help feeling that the man was probably judging him anyway. Why wouldn't he? Michael judged himself for it every day.

"I'm sure you realise," Hugh continued, "that your portfolio is on the thin side. You could do with getting a bit more in there, show your range. You must have other work, surely?"

"I have ... some stuff." Was that even true? He must have some decent pictures stashed away, somewhere. "Some old uni work, but it's very old, and not the kind of thing I want to be doing now. They were much more traditional portraits, and as you might be able to see, I prefer a less formal style now. Probably a result of the way I've been working for the last few years." He meant a more fluid, spontaneous style. Not crouching on pavements for hours on end.

Hugh's thoughtful expression was back. He said nothing for a few moments.

"Listen, Michael, I have in the past taken on some mentoring work for artists at the start of their careers. Of course, they're usually a little younger than you, but ..."

Great. So he was too old now, as well as the hundred other ways he was all wrong for this scene?

"It can be tough out there, when you're trying to step in from such a different area, especially when it comes to networking, making connections," Hugh continued, telling Michael precisely nothing he didn't already know far too well. "Sometimes all it takes is a helping hand. I can offer that. But I need to know that you're serious about this." He stood up, and the thoughtfulness vanished from his face. "Add seven more pictures to your portfolio by Wednesday."

Seven? Fuck. Shit. No way. "OK. Sure."

He had no idea how he was going to pull seven decent shots out of his arse in the next two days, but he didn't want to let this chance, whatever it might be, slip through his fingers.

Almost as soon as he was back out on the pavement, he got a message.

MIRANDA: How did it go?

It was nice of her to remember. He'd texted her when Hugh had suggested they meet. He'd wanted to thank her again for drawing Hugh's attention to him in the first place, and if he was honest, he'd wanted to tell *someone*. His mam would have been delighted, but he hadn't wanted to get her hopes up when it could all still come to nothing. *And Cleo?* said the voice in his head. *Why haven't you phoned her lately?* He told the voice to piss off. He was busy. She was busy. And if he was going to fail, he'd rather do it in private, thank you very much. But Miranda had said they were friends, and it was thanks to her it was even happening, so he figured he'd tell her. He hadn't expected her to actually care.

> MICHAEL: Not sure. He mentioned some kind of mentoring, but he wants to see more pictures. He hasn't said yes to anything.
>
> MIRANDA: But he hasn't said no either. Sometimes not a no is all you need.

He couldn't help smiling at that. He wasn't sure he knew her well enough to say that was typical Miranda, but it certainly felt like typical Miranda from what he'd seen so far. After all, she hadn't had a no from AJ yet, and she wasn't giving up. Far from it.

> MIRANDA: Do you have enough pictures? Is there anything I can do to help? I need another session very soon, so you can take more of me if you need to.

His brain conjured up a whole portfolio of Miranda. Shot after shot of that exquisite face smiling, scowling, gazing up at him. He wasn't sure if that would be quite showing the range Hugh wanted, but—

The dinging of a bell warned Michael that he'd been just about to step into the road in front of a bike. He took this as a sign that he should stop wandering through London with a head full of Miranda and get a coffee instead. He went into the nearest cafe, took a seat with an overpriced cappuccino, and texted her back.

Michael: Time's tight, so I'll see if I have anything lurking anywhere that might do. But we can schedule your next shoot. When were you thinking?

Miranda: Wednesday?

Michael: OK. Do you have somewhere in mind?

Miranda: No. But I'm worried I'm running out of time.

Miranda: We can do it at my place.

Her place. Wow. Michael had been outside celebrities' houses – not often, but on occasion, to his shame – but to be invited inside? How things had changed.

Michael: Sounds good. Just tell me when and where.

14

"AND then the asshole said that he would consider it, but I know he didn't mean it. He's gonna promote that idiot whose dad he plays golf with, and I'll be left doing even more work with nothing to show for it." Jen paused, and Miranda heard her taking a gulp of her wine. "Ugh. Anyway, thanks for letting me rant."

"Anytime. You know that." Miranda hated that her sister had been passed over for promotion again, but also ... "I still don't understand why you don't quit. Go find a better job somewhere else. You know you have the experience for it."

Jen sighed. "I don't know that I do. It's a competitive field out there. If I quit, there's no guarantee I'd find anything else. Besides, if my boss gets transferred to San Francisco like he's always wanted, maybe then I'll get someone who appreciates what I do a bit more."

Miranda heard the hope in her sister's voice. "I wish I had your patience, Jen. I'd have told him where he could stick his job years ago."

"I know you would have." Jen yawned. "Sorry."

Miranda looked at the clock. It was morning here, but late in Seattle. "I should let you get to bed. It's what, almost midnight?"

"'Bout that. Way late for me. But I was too riled up to sleep. What are you doing today?"

"A photo shoot." Miranda cast her eye over the dresses she'd identified as the main contenders. Was the turquoise one too much? Or was there no such thing in this situation?

"Ooh, with the next love of your life?" Jen teased.

"Shut up. He is not."

"Hmm."

Miranda felt her neck heating up. "I mean it. I need to stop with this falling-in-love thing. It never works out, and I don't need the distraction right now."

Her sister laughed. "You totally have a crush on him though, don't you?"

"You're thirty-two years old, Jennifer."

"I'm aware," Jen said breezily. "And I'm right, too."

Damn it. "Yes, fine, you're right. But it doesn't matter. He's not even interested in me. Our relationship has been nothing but friendly and professional. I doubt I'm even his type."

"Beautiful, interesting, intelligent, talented and rich isn't his type?"

Miranda ignored the flattery. She knew she wasn't a hideous prospect as a partner, but she'd had more than enough experience to know that it took more than the attributes on paper to make someone fall in love. "He's so serious, likes the quiet life. No one gets that with me. Besides, his ex is this curvy little brunette – you know, Devon Grant's wife. If that's what he's into, I have no chance. So while I might have a teeny little crush on him, I plan to just be his friend. I think he needs one."

"Well, he could do a lot worse than a friend like you, babe."

"Aw, thank you. Now go to bed. Love you."

"I love you too."

Miranda hung up and turned her full attention to the dresses. Should she go with the silver? It had a kind of armour-ish vibe, which fit with Damia the warrior queen. But after the Barbican, that might be a little much. She thought Michael had managed to capture strength enough in those. So she'd done strength, innocence – what was left?

Sex.

It sucked in so many ways, but sex still sold. Miranda knew she was fortunate in her beauty, but her image had always been more pretty than sexy. Her glamour was all about fashion, not desire. But maybe it was time to change that.

She picked up the dress that Arla Grace, an up-and-coming New York designer, had sent her last month and let the silk run through her hands. It was a beautiful, beautiful thing. She wondered what Mi—

No. Stop it. You literally just told your sister you weren't going to let your crush get out of hand this time.

Miranda shook her head. This shoot should be about sex appeal, but only because it would attract the most attention. AJ's intentions for the adaptation weren't yet clear, but the book hadn't shied away from sex. This was an aspect of herself she needed to display, so she should do everything she could to maximise that. Michael was a professional, she was a professional, and the fact that she was a little attracted to him was neither here nor there.

Methodically, she laid out her makeup. Tina, her usual makeup artist, hadn't been available on such short notice, so if she wanted today to be flawless, she'd better get to work.

* * *

Two hours later, Miranda heard the gate beep and Frank's car turn in to the driveway. She'd had him go get Michael from near the Tube, just in case any paparazzi were lurking – unlikely at this hour, but you never knew. She pulled her robe on over her dress and went downstairs.

"Michael, hey," she said as he came through the door behind Frank. "Frank, I'll call you when we're done."

"Great." Frank turned and went back the way he came.

"Hi," Michael said, looking around as she led him into the kitchen. "You have a beautiful home."

"Thanks." She pointed to the box in his hand. "What's that?"

"Oh." He looked a little sheepish. "My mam always told me never to go to someone's house empty-handed."

How cute was this guy?

"But I didn't have time to go and get anything nice. You mentioned you were into fattening British food, so I took a punt and got some of my favourites. If you recoil in horror, don't worry." He threw her a quick, shy smile. "More for me."

He held out the box, and she recognised the blue and white logo. She opened it to find ... "Caramel custard doughnuts! Oh my gosh, I love these."

"You do?" He raised his eyebrows. "Didn't think you were a Greggs kind of lass."

"You'd be surprised. Jake, my ex, introduced me to these, and I became obsessed. They're the best. I think they might be one of the reasons I moved to London." They had the same taste in desserts. This was ... nothing, she told herself sternly. A sign that they'd be great friends. "Would you like a coffee?" She gestured to the machine.

"No, you're alright. A good old Newcastle company, you know, Greggs," he said, putting the box down on the kitchen table.

"I did not know that. That's where you're from, right?" They were still standing a little awkwardly in the middle of the kitchen, and Miranda found herself strangely unsure of what to do. He was here to do a job, but she was enjoying this conversation too much to get started.

"Aye, not far. I'm from Northumberland. The bit between Newcastle and Scotland."

"I've never been that far north. I've not been to many places outside of London, to be honest."

"It's the best place on earth, the North East." His face lit up with one of the warmest smiles she'd ever seen from him. "You should go someday."

"Would you show me around?"

"Aye, of course."

His words seemed to hang in the air for a moment. Maybe he was doing what she was doing, imagining that scenario, but he was probably being much more sensible than her and realising that it was a pretty unlikely one.

"Anyway," Miranda said, as brightly as she could manage. "We should get started. The doughnuts will have to wait. Grease and sugar and this dress … well, you'll see. I thought maybe the garden?"

He looked out the window thoughtfully, and she saw the transition she'd come to recognise already, the slip into artist mode. "Yeah, sounds good. The light's nice this morning."

"Excellent. Follow me."

15

MIRANDA'S garden was as tasteful as the kitchen and the other rooms they'd walked through to get here. Michael particularly loved the white-walled corner that looked like a Mediterranean courtyard, all palm trees and expensive floor tiles. That could work, depending, of course, on what kind of feel she wanted this shoot to have. He turned around to ask, and his mouth went completely dry.

"Wow."

The word flew out before he could stop it, and he wanted to punch himself for being so unprofessional. He wasn't here to salivate over her. But god help him, he would defy anyone to have any other reaction.

Her blonde waves had been straightened and slicked back from her face, which was made up far more dramatically than he'd ever seen it, he realised now the bright sunshine was highlighting it in all its glory. The first time she'd been the epitome of youthful, fresh innocence. Last time she'd been cool, calm strength. Today, she exuded glamour and fire. Her cheekbones seemed sharper, and the slick gloss on her lips was possibly the sexiest thing Michael had ever seen. But that was until he let his eyes fall to the dress that had been hidden by her thick white robe. Vibrant turquoise satin flowed like liquid over her gentle curves. The neckline plunged almost to her bellybutton, and above the thigh-high slit in the skirt he couldn't see any evidence whatsoever of underwear. He told himself that it was his photographer's eye that noted that there were, however, definite signs of nipple. It would make the pictures sexier, and that was clearly what she was going for, so he'd make sure to capture that if he could. That was all he needed to think about.

She twirled for him. "That's the reaction I was hoping for."

"You look ..." Nope. Still no proper words were coming to mind. "I take it we're going for a sexier vibe today?" he managed to say while somehow sounding vaguely like someone who did this for a living.

"Much sexier," she said, and the twinkle in her eye made him think that she knew exactly how havoc-wreakingly hot she looked. "I did not come to play."

She certainly did not. She would have half the world in love with her the second she posted these pictures, even if he did nothing but point the camera in her direction. But he could do better than that.

"Then let's get to it. I'm thinking this corner?"

"Great," she said, giving him that megawatt smile he was becoming familiar with but didn't think he'd ever get used to. "I think this is my favourite part of this garden."

"It's gorgeous. You don't mind showing it in public?"

She waved a hand. "No, it's fine. I've posted photos from here before. We're not all Devon Grant, you know."

Michael laughed. "He's actually chilled out a lot since he married Cleo. Last time I saw them, he took his sunglasses off in public for a whole twelve seconds."

"Wow. Love really does do strange things to people."

Maybe he was imagining it, but he thought she looked a little wistful at that. But it was gone as soon as it had come. She stood in the middle of the courtyard, awaiting his instructions.

"Let's start here for now. I may need some extra light when the sun moves, but let's see how we go. Just ... move how you want." He knew from the last two shoots that he didn't need to direct her movements or poses much, except when he had a specific idea he wanted to try or tweak he wanted to make. She knew exactly what to do with her body. He watched as her eyelids dropped a little and her lips moved into a subtle pout, and she looked at him over her shoulder as if she were reading the deepest, dirtiest corners of his mind. Holy crap, she was dynamite. He snapped a couple of pictures, adjusted the exposure, took a couple more.

"Hey," she said, barely disturbing that pout. "Did you manage to find those extra pictures for Hugh?"

"Oh, yeah. Maybe bend that left knee a bit? Yeah, I did. Sent them last night. Not sure about all of them, but I found a few old ones from my degree that I forgot about, then put in a couple more of my mam, and one more of you. Then I was still two short, so I asked the guy who runs the shop near my flat if I could take a couple of him. He was a bit confused, but he said yes.

Tilt your chin up? He has really nice eyes. You can tell they've seen a lot."

She stretched her arms over her head and arched her back, tipping her face towards the sky. "I hope Hugh decides to help you. It could be just what you need. Is this too much, do you think?"

"Hmm, maybe." He pressed the shutter anyway, because her back looked like poetry at that angle.

The luxurious daybed was also too much – the sexuality she was projecting became almost comically overdone the second she got anything close to horizontal. Sitting on the stone bench lost all the drama of the dress. No, standing was better, but he wanted more shape.

"Hey, let's try those steps," he said, changing his lens. In the very corner was a small area where whitewashed concrete planters and some steps leading nowhere in particular created a few different levels. He wasn't sure what the point of that was, but it looked good, and he supposed people with this level of wealth didn't have to have points to things. He'd avoided it before in favour of the sunnier open area, but this was worth a try.

She worked her magic, striking pose after effortless pose, using the steps to show those spectacular legs at new angles.

"Miranda, could you move your left leg? Your dress is doing something a little weird."

"Like this?"

"Yeah, but ..." The dress was flowing like water again,

but now there was a tiny annoying shadow falling over her foot. "Maybe slightly less?"

"Better?"

No. The shadow was still there, just a fraction, not enough to warrant dragging out the reflector but enough to bother him. And her dress was starting to wrinkle again.

"Erm, can I just ..." He came closer and gestured to her ankle.

"Sure." She smiled. "Manipulate away."

He knelt at her feet. Taking a deep breath for reasons he didn't really understand, he clasped a hand around her ankle. Her sun-warmed skin might have been the smoothest thing he'd ever touched in his life. His heartbeat seemed to speed up a notch, and he told himself to get a fucking grip. This was not the first time he'd ever been near an ankle, for crying out loud.

He shifted her foot the tiny fraction he needed, and then ordered his reluctant hands to let her go. But he made the mistake of looking up first. Her gaze met his, and he didn't know if he was imagining it or if it was a trick of the sunlight framing her face, but he thought her blue-green eyes looked a little surprised, in a way he couldn't quite identify.

Then his phone rang, the moment shattered, and he lost his sodding balance.

Instinctively, he grasped the nearest solid object. Which happened to be Miranda Janes's silk-draped thigh.

"Shit," he said, scrambling to his feet and just

managing to avoid falling on his arse. "Sorry. I should have turned that off. Sorry, I'll turn it off."

She laughed gently. "Don't be silly. Take it, it's fine."

He pulled his phone from his pocket and pressed the green button, too flustered by what had just happened to even glance at the screen. "Hello?"

"Michael, Hugh Humberstone-Ridley."

"Hugh, hi." Every muscle in his body coiled itself into a tense knot. Miranda held up crossed fingers. "Did you get my pictures?"

"I did. I wasn't sure after our meeting that you'd do it, but you did. And I'm impressed."

"You are?" But what did that mean? What was Hugh ringing to tell him?

"I am. Listen, Michael, you have no experience and no contacts ..."

There it was. Michael braced himself for the inevitable.

"But you have talent. And I've got a feeling about you. So I want to mentor you, no charge. You've got a lot of potential, and I'd hate to see it go to waste. I think I can help you find the opportunities you need."

He closed his eyes and tipped his face towards the sky, feeling the sun on his skin. Fuck yes.

"... have lunch, talk about what we can do. I'll email you." Hugh was still talking, apparently unaware that he'd hit Michael in the face with a sledgehammer made of relief and gratitude.

"Well?" Miranda mouthed at him, breaking him out of his trance.

"That's great, Hugh," he managed. "Thank you. Thank you so much."

"The pleasure's mine. Speak soon."

He hung up. Michael just stood there, phone still to his ear.

"Michael?"

"He wants to mentor me," he said, relishing the feel of the words in his mouth. He knew that, logically, this was nothing to get too excited about. Hugh was just some guy who knew some stuff. But after so much time getting nowhere, it felt like everything.

With a shriek, Miranda threw her arms around him, and his own closed around her back without thought. "That's incredible! I'm so happy for you."

"Thank you." He shook his head, trying to clear the daze. "I just hope he'll be able to help guide me in the right direction. I don't have a clue what I'm doing."

She stepped back and grinned at him. "No one does. We all make it up as we go along at first. But if I can help you in any way, I will."

It didn't seem like empty words. The way she was looking at him, with genuine happiness, told him she meant it.

"You've already done so much. I'm not sure how I'll ever repay you."

"Oh, I'm sure I'll think of something eventually," she said easily, but he thought he saw a brief flash of ... he didn't know what in her eyes.

He cleared his throat. "Anyway. We should ..." He held up his camera and pointed it in the direction of the steps.

Miranda frowned. "We can take a break, you know. Let the good news sink in."

He shook his head. "It's fine. We're on your time, and I think I was just about to get it, if I can get your foot back where I had it."

"You're a dedicated man, Michael Hedley. You're going to make a wonderful artist."

He let a huge grin spread over his face. An artist. One with a mentor, someone to help him navigate the world that had seemed so impenetrable. The happiness stayed with him as Miranda resumed her position on the steps, as they eliminated every wrinkle and shadow, and he got the shot.

16

"SO, I guess I'll get going," Miranda heard Michael say as she frowned at her phone.

"Yes, about that ..." She turned her screen so that Michael could see the message.

> FRANK: Don't leave the house. Street swarming with press. See Becky Nolan's Instagram. Monitoring the cameras from my phone.

Michael wrinkled his nose in confusion. "Is Becky Nolan that TV presenter?"

"That's her. She lives next door." Miranda opened Instagram and clicked on Becky's story. "Oh dear."

"What's up?"

"She and Aaron broke up again." Becky's husband was Tottenham Hotspur's star ... something or other. Miranda had never gotten to grips with soccer. "Only this time she moved out, took the baby, and told the whole world that he's been sleeping with a model who befriended Becky in order to get into his pants."

Michael rubbed a hand over the back of his neck. "Wow. That sounds messy as hell."

"Exactly. So now there'll be a swarm of photographers outside their house waiting to see if he'll emerge.

I thought I heard some noise before but I didn't think anything of it."

"And if I leave, there's every chance a bored pap will spot me and they'll get more than they came for, or they'll think they have." He gave a wry bark of laughter. "I know how that works."

She inclined her head towards him. "Of course." She almost forgot, sometimes, how she came to be aware of his talent in the first place. "Do you have anywhere you need to be today?"

"Nah," he said with a smile. "I was maybe going to go the gym, but otherwise I was just going to get to work on these." He shrugged the shoulder his camera bag was slung over.

Phew. He didn't seem to be taking this too badly. Miranda was well accustomed to this kind of thing, but the people in her life weren't always so willing to roll with it. Although she supposed he understood this circus better than most. How strange for him to be on the other side of the fence. Almost literally, although it was in fact a nice sturdy brick wall with electronically controlled gates.

"Well, I have some gym equipment in the basement if you'd like to work out, and possibly even a pair of shorts that would fit you, somewhere." She glanced over at the kitchen table. "Or ... we could celebrate your mentorship with some champagne and those doughnuts instead."

"Hmm." He looked thoughtful, but she could see a twinkle in his eye, a playfulness she'd never seen before. Was it the offer, or the prospect of sugar? "I mean, it's not a big deal, not something worth celebrating really. But I can never resist a Greggs."

"Progress is always worth celebrating." She walked over to the fridge and pulled out a bottle of Veuve Clicquot. "Yes, I have one chilling just because." She shrugged. "I am nothing if not a cliché. Glasses are behind you."

Michael put down his stuff and took two glasses from the cupboard. Miranda popped the cork and poured the champagne. She picked up her glass and held it aloft. "To you, and this exciting opportunity. May it be the first of many steps towards a glittering art career."

He smiled awkwardly and picked up his glass. "Thanks." He clinked it to hers. "It's a bit weird getting my head around even this. I'm not used to celebrating." He winced. "Sorry. That sounds so self-pitying."

"Don't apologise." Her heart was going out to him. He sounded so unsure of himself. "I think–" Her phone buzzed. She read Frank's message and sighed. "OK. Apparently Aaron is due at training this afternoon, at which point those guys will probably leave, but not for a few hours. So ... you can either wait them out, or we can try to sneak you out. Or you could just take your chances." She shrugged. "I'm way past caring what anyone writes about me, but it could bring a lot of attention your way."

A careful look clouded his face, as if he were cautiously weighing up all the options. "I don't really care about the press either, but it doesn't seem worth the potential trouble if I don't have anywhere to be." He gave her a hesitant smile. "As long as you don't mind me hanging out here. I wouldn't want to be in your way."

She smiled back, disproportionately pleased that he wanted to stay. "Not at all. It's nice to have the company. We can watch a movie or something. Although I should change into something more suitable." And put some underwear on. Forgetting about what she was or wasn't wearing was an occupational hazard, but Miranda was suddenly acutely aware that she was wearing only one layer of very beautiful but extremely thin fabric. "I'll go do that," she said hurriedly, then pointed to the champagne and doughnuts. "Why don't you take all this into the living room, through there."

Calm yourself down, she told herself as she went upstairs. There was no reason at all she should feel this happy that he was effectively trapped in her house, but there was a lightness in her chest that she couldn't control. She was desperately curious about this man. He had a lot of passion, yet something was also holding him back. He seemed to take life seriously, yet he showed her glimpses of a great sense of humour. He was interesting, she decided, and she liked getting to know interesting people. It had nothing to do with her teensy little crush on him.

As if to prove this to herself, she cleansed her face until every last scrap of makeup was gone and didn't even bother reapplying mascara to her pale lashes. She stepped out of the turquoise dress and pulled on baggy sweatpants and a T-shirt. No one ever saw her like this, except her family.

When she got back downstairs, Michael was standing in front of her bookshelves. He didn't seem to have any kind of reaction at all to her appearance; he just nodded towards the shelves and said, "Quite the eclectic collection."

She laughed. "Oh, I know. I enjoy reading all that bold, innovative Proper Literature, you know? But I guess I'm also just a sucker for a love story." Her sister always said that it was Miranda's addiction to romance novels that gave her unrealistic expectations of love. And Jen said this without a trace of irony, despite having been in a prime example of a blissfully perfect relationship since she was a teenager.

Michael let out a small, sardonic huff, but he didn't say anything. Miranda gestured to the sofa. "Shall we?"

They sat down. Miranda picked up her doughnut and took a small bite of sticky, sugary goodness. "Ohhhh, these are the best. This kind of stuff is why I have to have a gym in my house."

He smiled. His smiles really were very cute. His eyes showed that they were real, but his mouth rarely extended into a full grin, as if his face were keeping something in reserve. "I would never have had you down as a doughnut fan."

"Lots of people have me down as one thing or another." She suppressed the spike of irritation the thought always provoked and took a sip of champagne instead. "But I am woman. I contain multitudes, and I sometimes contain extremely unhealthy foodstuffs. But enough about that." She walked over to the cabinet that housed her Blu-rays. "What are you in the mood for?"

His eyes widened. "That is a lot of films."

"It is, isn't it? I go overboard buying them sometimes. And I don't know why, because I have Netflix and all those things too. I feel like a relic of a bygone age every time I buy an actual disc." She turned and scanned the shelves. "I guess that when I love something, I want it to be truly mine."

Oh god. Why had she said that? It sounded disturbingly intimate, and now there was a weird awkward vibe in the air. Her mind scrambled for a joke to make of it, but then Michael said, softly, "Yeah. I can understand that," and the thoughts all screeched to a halt. She felt him move closer, until all of a sudden he was at her shoulder.

"How about this?" He reached past her, then stepped back, and as he held up her copy of *The Banshees of Inisherin*, it was as if a rush of cool air filled the space he'd been in and slapped her in the face. She had to get a hold of herself.

She pulled a smile onto her lips. "Excellent choice."

17

MICHAEL made a huge effort to concentrate on the film, because he'd never got around to watching it before, and it was really bloody good. But in the many gentle, quiet moments, his eyes kept trying to stray towards Miranda. She looked so different in joggers and no makeup, but no less beautiful. It was weird, sprawling here on her amazingly comfortable couch, drinking fancy champagne with her, and at the same time it wasn't. He hadn't felt this relaxed anywhere in a long time.

The end credits rolled, and Miranda raised her arms and stretched. Her T-shirt lifted just the tiniest bit, showing a hint of her flat stomach, and he felt unnervingly distracted by that. He'd spent the entire morning trying to showcase the acres of perfect skin she'd been displaying, yet this tiny sliver of it had his thoughts wandering places they shouldn't be allowed to go. It must have been the champagne. The doughnut clearly hadn't been enough to stop it going to his head.

"Are you hungry?" Miranda asked, as if reading his mind. "I could make us some lunch ... late lunch? I don't know. Time seems to have no meaning today."

He knew what she meant. It was as if today existed outside all the normal laws of space-time.

"Lunch or whatever it is would be good, thanks." He followed her to the kitchen.

She started pulling things from the fridge – salad leaves, grilled chicken, vegetables, cheese. "I'm not very good at cooking, but I am exceptionally talented at chopping things and assembling them on a plate. Hope that's OK."

"Sounds great," he said, smiling.

"If I had the ingredients, though, I might be demanding you make those mashed potatoes you told me about."

"Wow. You remembered that? Maybe next time."

"I'll hold you to that." She was slicing a tomato and not looking at him, but there was something in her face, a hint of a promise, maybe ...

He cleared his throat. "Anything I can do to help?"

"Sure." She waved her knife at a pepper. "Slice that for me?"

They prepared the food in an easy silence, then ate at the kitchen table as Michael filled her in on the details of his meeting with Hugh and she told him about her agent's latest conversation with AJ. He was happy the photo campaign seemed to be working, but it struck him how different their attitudes were to their respective triumphs. Miranda was all resolve and determined confidence; he was still trying to resist the urge to ring Hugh back and tell him this was a terrible mistake. He couldn't be part of Hugh's fancy art world, could he? If not for Cleo and Devon, Michael would be on the other side of Miranda's garden wall right now, waiting for some dipshit footballer to get into a Range Rover.

"What's wrong?"

Michael realised he'd fallen silent. Miranda's ocean-coloured eyes held the purest look of concern he'd ever seen. His hands itched for his camera.

"Sorry, yeah, no. I'm fine."

"Don't believe you."

He smiled weakly. He must have lapsed into what Cleo called his resting misery face.

"Do you want to talk about it?" Miranda asked, pushing away her empty plate. "You don't have to. I'm a very nosey person; it's one of my flaws. But I know what it's like to be far away from the people you normally talk to."

He put the last bite of chicken into his mouth and chewed it for far too long. "I'm not sure I'd know where to start," he said eventually.

She tilted her head. "At the beginning?"

"Well, I was born in Northumberland ..." He gave her half a smile. "Doubt that was what you meant."

She shrugged, and his heart did some weird kind of skip as he realised he did want to talk to her. He wasn't totally sure what about, or why she would want to listen him banging on about his woes, but he did want to, very much.

"Well ..." Miranda checked her phone, and her brow furrowed. "We potentially have a lot of time. Aaron has not left for his training session." She looked up at him. "You sure you don't want me to have Frank get you out in the car?"

He should go home, work on the photos. He could slouch down in the car; chances were no one would see him or recognise him, even the guys he knew. They'd probably already started getting bored and leaving. Staying was overcautious.

"I'll stay," he said, and her face broke into a smile that could light up an amphitheatre.

"In that case," she said, standing and heading for the fridge. "Let's open another bottle."

* * *

"Wait, wait. Let me get this right." Miranda leaned closer from her side of the sofa, eyes wide. "You have a half-brother you've never met, who messages you on Facebook, but neither of you speak to your dad, who is also on Facebook but has never tried to get in touch?"

"Yup." Michael nodded. This had long stopped being painful or even weird for him. "My brother's name is Jack. He seems like a nice enough lad. I'll probably try to meet up with him some day. My dad lives in Hull, apparently, with his fourth wife. He kept in touch with Jack for a few years, which is more than he did with me – I was a baby when he left, and my mam literally never heard from him again. Heard from the bailiffs, mind. And some guy named Big Mick who was not impressed that he'd disappeared. And a woman called Sonia who he was sleeping with behind my mam's back."

Miranda's mouth was hanging open by this point, which Michael found extremely amusing. He couldn't believe he was telling this woman – this gorgeous, rich celebrity with a picture-perfect life – his sordid backstory, but oh well. The champagne must have loosened his tongue. But she seemed interested. Or maybe she was just entertained. He couldn't imagine she came across many people with such a fucked-up family.

"Oh my," she said. "That sounds ..."

"Like something off *Eastenders*, I know. Certainly caused a lot of gossip in a small town. Which obviously my well-to-do grandmother loved. She should have been there for her daughter, but she was so horrified that it only made her more determined to be a complete ..." He gulped down the last of his champagne to avoid finishing his sentence, but it couldn't wash away the familiar bitterness that had flooded his mouth. "Sorry," he said. "This is why I normally avoid the subject of my grandmother."

"Ah yes," Miranda said, taking his empty glass from him, which he now realised he had been gripping a little too hard. "I've heard that avoiding subjects that have a profound effect on you is a healthy habit." Her tone was light, but her face was gently sympathetic in a way that didn't irritate him the way the concern of others often did.

"Why?" he said, more sharply than he'd intended. "Why would you want to listen to me rant about my mess of a family any more than I already have?"

"Because." Her blue-green eyes looked directly into his. "I think of you as a friend, Michael, and I care about the things that hurt my friends." She shrugged.

"But you don't have to talk about anything you don't want to. We can change the subject."

And maybe it was the champagne, or maybe it was that this had been a monumentally weird day, or maybe it was just that he hadn't ever talked about this with anyone who wasn't part of it themselves, but he found himself saying, "No." He told her everything – about how his grandmother had turned his back on him and his mam when they had nothing, how he'd grown up watching his mother sacrifice everything for him, how his grandmother had bought their house for them and never missed a chance to remind them of what they owed her. About the years of condescension and sneering and telling him how he'd never amount to anything. About how the only thing he'd ever achieved was ruining his mother's life.

He told her about Cleo and how Margaret had decided that marrying her would keep him on the straight and narrow instead of drinking cider in bus stops and scrawling graffiti on fences. Never mind that he'd already seen that he was never getting out of that town and that life if he carried on like that. He told her about the years of lies and how shit it had made him feel every single time, but that he'd done it for his mam because he'd do anything for his mam, just like he'd chased down celebrities in the street to make money to help chip away at the debt his wanker father had left her in.

He told her that his mam had somehow reconciled with Margaret, and that there was a thick cream envelope sitting in his desk drawer that he still hadn't opened because he didn't know what was in there, and he couldn't talk to anyone about it, not even Cleo, because he didn't know if it would only make him angrier at all of them. Or if it might take away some of the anger, and he didn't know what was scarier because he sometimes thought that his anger was the only thing holding him together.

And then he realised he was holding precisely fuck all together, because he'd been kind of shouting and now Miranda's hand was on his arm, and ... shit.

He dropped his head into his hands. "Sorry. I'm so sorry, Miranda. I didn't mean to–"

"Hey." She squeezed his arm gently. "You don't have to be sorry, not at all. It's OK. It's more than OK. You needed to get that out, I can tell."

He let out a long exhale and heard how much it shook. "I did, I guess. But I'm still sorry." He turned to face her. "I don't normally lose it like that. God, what you must think of me."

She shifted on the sofa until her body was angled towards his. "I think ..." she said softly, and then she looked up, and her eyes met his, and he wanted more than almost anything to ask her to finish that sentence, to find out what she thought of him, but the only thing he wanted more was to stay in this silence, looking into eyes that were the colour of an ocean, bright as falling stars.

And then he didn't know who was moving his arms, because it sure as hell wasn't him, they were wrapping themselves around her waist entirely independently of him, and her hands were sliding up to his shoulders, and her lips were gently parting, and his head was leaning close, so close he felt her breath on his skin, and then his lips touched hers in the barest whisper of a kiss and ...

Whoa. Fuck. Oh no.

He leapt away from her as sense and reason belatedly gave him a much-deserved kick in the balls. This was a client. His only client. They'd been drinking all afternoon. And he'd just made an absolute fucking tit of himself by letting his emotions burble out of his mouth at a rate of knots.

"Sorry," he said for what felt like the millionth time today. "God, I'm sorry. I shouldn't have done that." He got to his feet; he needed to put some distance between them before he made an even bigger fool of himself. For fuck's sake, hadn't she just said they were friends? So why the hell had he decided to try to kiss her? Miranda fucking Janes? What was wrong with him? "I'm so sorry. I'll go, get out of your way."

"Hey, it's OK. You don't have to go." She sounded as kind and friendly as always, if a touch confused, but he couldn't look at her to see her reaction.

"No, I should ... it's late, and I ..." He looked around for his stuff, spotted his bag over by the door. "It'll be safe by now – the light's crap, and they'll have gone off in search of the evening crowd. So I'll ..." He needed to get out of here while he could still pretend he had a scrap of dignity.

"Michael–"

"I'll get to work on the photos first thing in the morning and send you some as soon as I can. I know you need them quick. Thank you for today. It's been really nice, and I'm sorry I spoiled it like a total arsehole."

"You didn't, honestly."

He risked a look at her, still avoiding meeting her gaze, but he couldn't quite read her expression. She didn't look like she wanted to kill him, so he let himself relax a tiny fraction. She was probably used to men losing their senses around her.

He mustered up a quick smile. He didn't want to make things any more awkward than he already had. "Thanks," he said, stuffing his feet into his shoes.

"I can get Frank to take you home."

"That's OK." He forced himself to laugh. "I think I could definitely do with some fresh air. I'll send you these shots tomorrow." He resisted the urge to apologise again.

"OK," she said softly.

Out on the street, Michael saw he'd been right – the gaggle of photographers had given up. He kept his head down and walked quickly anyway, just in case, and he let the evening air fill his lungs and penetrate the last of the champagne fog. Jesus Christ, he was an idiot. He couldn't say he regretted sharing everything he had with Miranda, if he was honest. It had felt like a relief, and he was grateful to her for that. But he should have kept control of his attraction to her. He'd been doing so well. He'd just have to make sure not to let his guard down again.

18

MIRANDA looked at the photos on her computer screen. He'd done it again. Sheer perfection. Exactly the strong, sexy vibe she'd been trying to capture. She looked at her favourite, and she was pretty sure she knew when it had been taken. On the steps, one of the first shots he'd gotten when they'd gone back to work after Hugh's call. When her skin still burned from the feel of his hand around her thigh.

Just like her lips still tingled now, sixteen hours and twenty-eight minutes later, with his almost-kiss. The disappointment when he sprang away from her as if he'd been electrocuted had been like nothing she'd ever felt before, but she understood. She flicked from the photos to his email.

> I'm sorry again for last night. I'll totally understand if you don't want to work with me anymore, but I promise it will never happen again.

Maybe she was deluding herself, but Miranda was choosing to interpret this as disappointment in himself for crossing some professional boundary. It wasn't because he wasn't attracted to her. Right? She'd told herself from the beginning that he wouldn't be interested in her, that she wasn't his type. And maybe she wasn't.

But there was something there between them, she was sure of it. Every now and then, she could see that careful, detached facade slip, and in those moments, the way he looked at her sent a thrill down her spine. And yesterday ... Yes, there'd been champagne, and yes, his emotions were running high, but when his arms had tightened around her and his mouth had been right there next to hers, she'd been absolutely sure that he wanted her just as much as she wanted him.

There was no point in trying to avoid it any longer. She'd promised her sister and herself that she wouldn't fall head over heels this time, and she wouldn't. But damn it, she had to have this man. Whatever he would give her. She knew that in the short term, as long as he was working for her, that would be nothing.

It was time to get moving. She was done waiting on everyone else.

She picked up her phone. "Aisling," she said when her assistant answered. "I'm going to LA. As soon as possible. Can you get right on that?"

"Of course," Aisling replied, unflappable as ever. "Do you need me with you?"

"You can come if you're free and you want to. But I'll be fine if you'd rather stay here." Rose, her endlessly wonderful LA housekeeper, would be able to take care of anything Miranda couldn't do herself or Aisling couldn't do from England.

"I'll stay, if that's OK. I'll go and book you a flight right now."

"Thanks, sweetheart."

On to the next thing on her mental list. She opened Michael's link on her phone, found the picture and posted it to Instagram with a line from Courtney's new single: "Stars shine bright in the afternoon sun". Almost instantly, the flame emojis began to roll in. Miranda would normally take some time liking and replying, but not today. She appreciated the support as much as ever, but she was a woman on a mission.

She tapped out a text.

> MIRANDA: Nora, I'm coming to LA. Can we set up something with AJ? I have nothing on my schedule. I will jump through as many hoops as he wants.

Keeping her diary clear would mean she wouldn't be able to squeeze in a trip to Seattle as she usually did, but her dad's birthday was only a few weeks away. She'd see them all then.

> NORA: I'll do my best. When will you be here?

At that moment, an email came through from Aisling with her flight details.

> MIRANDA: Sunday morning. Thinking I'll stay for a week but I can stay longer if need be.
>
> NORA: Got it. Leave it with me.

She sent a quick message to Cleo and Courtney asking if they were in LA next week, then hit reply on Michael's email.

Of course I still want to work with you. But not for at least another week – I'm going to LA. Time to go after what I want.

* * *

"Oh, it's so good to see you!" Miranda threw her arms around Cleo and squeezed her tight. "Both of you," she said, hugging Courtney too. She couldn't believe how much she'd missed them. Miranda had plenty of friends all over the world, but for some reason, the bond she'd formed with these two women felt special. She'd barely known Courtney before Cleo's wedding, and they'd only managed to meet up a few times in person since then, but through the magic of cell phones they'd established a firm friendship. Miranda felt as though she could tell them anything.

Almost anything. She had no intention of telling Cleo that she had a crush on her best-friend-slash-ex-husband.

She looked around Cleo and Devon's impressive home. It was decorated in a typically sleek, stark LA way, and Miranda would have bet that Devon had lived with it as a glamorous but sterile box from the moment he bought the place. But touches of Cleo were everywhere – brightly coloured vases and throws, pictures of smiling friends and family in cute frames, a phenomenal number of pillows littering the couches. It was full of her friend's energy, and Miranda loved it.

Cleo brought snacks and drinks out from the kitchen, and the three of them settled in the living room to catch up.

“So is the album done, Courtney?” Miranda said, reaching for a slice of melon. It smelled like heaven. She loved England, but the fruit could not compare to California’s.

“Pretty much.” Courtney opened a bag of potato chips. “I have to go back to Nashville next week to finish up some stuff with the producer there, but everything I wanted to record here in LA is sounding good, I think. I don’t know. I feel like I’ve been out of the game so long I don’t even know what I’m doing anymore.”

“That’s bollocks,” interjected Cleo. “This woman’s a genius, and don’t let her tell you otherwise.”

“You’ve heard it?” Miranda said as Courtney rolled her eyes, looking a little embarrassed by the praise. “The single is amazing, so I can totally believe that the whole album is going to be awesome too.”

“I’ve only heard a few little bits, but it’s bloody fantastic.” Cleo raised her glass of orange juice towards Courtney. “If it doesn’t win a Grammy, I’ll eat my own hair.”

“Why would you eat your hair?” Courtney asked.

“I don’t know. It was the first thing that came to mind. Not that it matters, because you’re going to win a Grammy, and I won’t have to do it.”

Miranda giggled. “I have no doubt about it. I saw Henry the other week and he looked so proud of you. It was the cutest thing.”

“Yeah, he said he’d seen you.” Courtney studied the fruit platter intently. “Was he OK?”

Miranda’s brow furrowed. “How do you mean?”

"Oh, nothing," Courtney said with a little shake of her head. "He's so busy, that's all. I always worry he's working too hard."

"He looked good," Miranda replied. She hoped everything was OK. Courtney just nodded.

"Speaking of looking good ..." Cleo broke the ever so slight tension that seemed to have fallen. "How hot are your new Insta photos? That one from the other day in the blue dress? Jesus Christ, woman, I almost choked on my granola."

Miranda grinned. "They're fabulous, aren't they? God, that sounds so vain. But honestly, I love them. Michael's so talented. I–"

"Wait." Cleo held up a chip. "Michael took those?"

"Yes." Miranda was confused. He was still saying he didn't want to be credited, but surely Cleo knew? Miranda had told her, hadn't she? Maybe she hadn't. They'd all been quiet on the group chat lately. But Michael must have?

"My Michael?"

"Yeah. We've been working together for a couple weeks. Didn't he tell you?"

"No, he did not," Cleo replied, and Miranda wanted to sweep her up in a hug when she saw the troubled look on Cleo's pretty face. "We haven't spoken all that much recently, though. He's kind of pissed off at me, I think."

"About his grandmother?" Oh no. Should she not have said that?

"He told you about that?" Cleo's eyebrows were practically in her hairline.

"Yes," Miranda said cautiously. "We had a press situation the other day so he was stuck at my house for a while." At least she wouldn't have to explain any further to Cleo and Courtney. They both knew what that was like. "We talked about some stuff." *And he sort of kissed me and now the crush I have on him is raging out of control.* Which of course she didn't say.

"Oh." Cleo sighed. "Well, it's good he's talking to someone. Is he really mad at me?"

Miranda bit her lip. "I don't think so. He loves you a lot, and he definitely misses you. That much is clear. So even if he is mad now, I think he'll get over it. I kinda get the impression this whole thing with his grandmother and his mom is just raking up some things, you know?"

"Yeah, I know." Cleo fell silent, and Miranda did too. Why hadn't Michael told Cleo? Was it because he wasn't speaking to her? Or was there some other reason that he didn't want to admit to working with Miranda?

Courtney leaned forward. "Tell me about this audition you're in town for, Miranda," she said, obviously eager to steer the conversation in a more comfortable direction, and Miranda was happy to let her.

"I don't have one. Yet," she said, turning her mind back to the thing she was here to do. "But I will get one. AJ has to give me a chance. I'm perfect for this part, and the photos were my way of showing him that he doesn't have to cast some model. My agent is working on him, and I came out here so he'd see I was willing to chase after this, but I need a firmer plan of action."

Courtney tapped a purple-painted fingernail against her chin. "Hmm. Let me send a few messages." She took out her phone and started typing.

Miranda took the opportunity to lean closer to Cleo. "You OK, sweetie? I'm sorry if my hanging out with Michael has caused problems."

"Oh, don't be daft, babe." All this time in LA had done nothing to dent Cleo's adorable northern accent. So like Michael's. "This shit was always going to resurface one day, and I'm just glad he has someone he can talk to. He doesn't do that easily, you know. You guys must be getting on really well."

Miranda thanked the heavens for the talent and training that allowed her to maintain a perfectly neutral expression. "He's a great guy."

"He's the best." Cleo met her eyes. "Look after him for me."

"I will," Miranda said softly, feeling unaccountably emotional. She squeezed Cleo's hand.

"OK," Courtney announced. "Do you ladies have plans for tonight? Jet lag gonna kick your ass, Miranda?"

"I'm flying out to see Devon first thing tomorrow morning, so I need an early night," Cleo said.

"I slept on the plane," said Miranda. "And I'm free."

"Excellent." Courtney flashed her a dazzling smile. "We're going to a party."

* * *

The party was in full swing. Music was playing, drinks were flowing, and Courtney looked deathly pale.

"Oh, shit." The knuckles on the hand curled around her beer bottle were white.

"What is it, darling?" Miranda asked. "Are you … Oh."

"Yeah."

Mya Hudson was here. Courtney's ex-girlfriend, with whom she'd had a somewhat … tumultuous relationship.

Courtney took a huge swig of her beer. "I haven't seen her in, like, years. And that was … well …"

Apparently that was all Miranda was getting in the way of information, but she didn't mind. She knew there was an awful lot of history there. She hadn't been friends with Courtney at the time, and of course she knew that the tabloids wrote whatever they felt like, but she also knew that some of the information that had escaped about their relationship was true.

"Sweetie, do you want to leave? We can–"

"Oh hell no." Courtney shook her head adamantly. "I'm not letting my car-crash romantic history get in the way of you meeting AJ. Yasmin said he'd be here. You go look for him, and I'll just get some air."

Miranda gave her a dubious look. Courtney was an absolute angel for bringing her to this party, but there was no way she could let her friend down now.

"I'll be fine, honestly." Courtney kissed Miranda on the cheek and headed for the patio, where a spectacular infinity pool overlooked an even more spectacular view of Hollywood.

"Are you stalking me, Miss Janes?" a wry voice said behind Miranda.

This was it. She took a deep breath, pulled on her brightest smile, and turned around.

"AJ Hollinger, we meet at last." She kissed the air next to his cheek. "And I'd say that stalking is a strong word for it."

He raised an eyebrow. He was better-looking in the flesh than she'd realised, strongly built with scruffy stubble and twinkling blue eyes. In a sea of people dressed to impress, he was wearing a pointedly unremarkable T-shirt and jeans. "Oh? What would you call showing up at a party I just happen to be at?"

"I'd call it taking an opportunity." Miranda refused to let him intimidate her with his I'm-such-a-cool-tough-guy thing. Men always underestimated just how much fortitude a woman who regularly stood around with her ankles supported by nothing more than a dagger-like heel and a few leather laces could have. "A friend of mine is friends with Yasmin, our hostess. Rumour has it you're dating her cousin. We thought we'd come along and enjoy the party, and if you were here, perhaps I'd get to persuade you to give me an audition for *Ocean* in person instead of through Nora."

He looked amused. "You don't fuck around, sweetheart, do you?"

"I do not. I don't like wasting time." She took a sip of her champagne.

He watched her for a moment. "I'm not, by the way."

"Not what?"

"Dating Amira. We're just friends. I've dated too many models and it never ends well."

She tilted her chin up. "Perhaps you need to consider looking beyond models."

AJ laughed. "Touché." He raised his glass towards her. "I take it that's what the whole Instagram thing is about?"

There was no point in being coy about it now. "Of course it is. I know how people see me, so I assumed you saw me that way too. Always the wholesome girl next door. I wanted the world, and specifically the person directing a movie of my favourite novel, to see something different."

"They were ... eye-catching, for sure," he said, somewhat grudgingly. "But look, Miranda, I gotta be honest with you. I have a vision for this movie, and I still don't know if you fit that."

"AJ, come on. You want dramatic dark hair, put a wig on me. You want elfin angles, contour the hell out of my face. But this novel is a classic in waiting. This movie will have Damia fans going to see it in droves. You have to do her justice. And for that you need an actor. I'm sure Elia is a wonderful person, and lord knows she is a beauty. But does she have the experience I do? Can she command the army that will bring down the Shadow King? Can she look the love of her life in the eye then shoot him through the heart? I would give everything that I have to this role. Please, just give me a chance. If you still don't think I can do it after I audition, then

I'll be disappointed, but I'll understand. I just want to show you what I can do."

AJ ran his eyes over her from head to toe, not in a creepy way – and spending time in this town and this industry meant Miranda knew the difference all too well – but in a contemplative, assessing way that made her heart thud with the prospect that he was actually considering what she'd said.

"How long are you in town?" he said eventually.

"As long as it takes."

He chuckled. "Does all of Hollywood know you have balls like this?"

She shrugged. "More of it than you might think."

"OK. I'm having lunch with Seb tomorrow. Between you and me, the deal is all but done." Seb Akao, widely – and accurately, it seemed – tipped to play the male lead. "Join us." He handed her a card. "Contact my assistant for the details."

Miranda's fingers closed over the card as a victorious thrill ran up her spine. "I'd be delighted." She inclined her head towards him. "I'll let you get back to the party, and I should go find my friend. I'll see you tomorrow."

She walked off in search of Courtney. She stopped a couple of times along the way to exchange pleasantries with people she knew, but for once her mind was elsewhere. She'd done it. Wedged that door open just a little more. And she wasn't stopping until she was all the way through it.

19

THERE was something about fancy places like this, where the menu was fashionably undescriptive and the cutlery weighed a ton, that made Michael feel as if he might suddenly forget how to do basic things like chew with his mouth closed or drink water without spilling it all over himself. But Hugh had insisted on meeting here, his treat, so here they were.

"Obviously we're going to work on raising your profile, on networking, on finding those opportunities, but that's only part of it," Hugh was saying, waving his fork in the air. "We need to think about you as an artist, too. It's important to figure out what it is that makes you uniquely you."

Michael nodded and took a sip of his water – thankfully not spilling it – to avoid having to reply. Uniquely him?

"Versatility is important, in some respects," Hugh continued, "and your talent is undeniable, otherwise I wouldn't have agreed to do this. But you can't sell just "talent" to a gallery. They're looking for a vision, a voice. A *statement*. I'm here to help you with that, but it's something that's got to come mostly from your heart. So who are you, Michael Hedley, and what do you want your art to say?"

Who was he? Well, that was a fucking question, wasn't it? He'd been called so many things over the years – a mistake, a disappointment, a vulture – that he didn't know how to think of himself on his own terms anymore. He knew what he wanted to do – show the world the things he saw in people's faces, the strengths and vulnerabilities they didn't know were there – but he didn't know if that was the same as what he wanted to say. He wasn't used to the idea that anybody might want to listen.

Hugh seemed to realise he wasn't getting a sensible answer out of him anytime soon and kept going. The man could talk for England. "I'm sure you'll know that most galleries are fully programmed for the rest of the year at least, so that means we need to be thinking ahead about where might be a good fit for you. I know a few places that are always open to portraiture, but they'll only be interested in work with that strong statement. That's something you won't have had to be concerned with for some time, but it's time to get your head back in that game, if this is what you truly want."

"It is," Michael said automatically. His mind was already racing with questions and worries, but he didn't want Hugh to think he was an idiot. "It's just ... that pivot, you know? From my pictures being all about the subject, to them being more about me. It's a difficult thing to wrap my head around." He forced a smile onto his face. "But I'll figure it out."

"I'm sure you will." Hugh picked up his wine and peered keenly at him. "It's your time, Michael. Time to be more than just some guy hanging around waiting for reality TV stars to fall out of a bar."

Michael knew that Hugh meant well, but that didn't take the sting out of his words. Would this shame ever leave him? Would the world ever let it?

Truth be told, snapping reality TV stars as they left a bar had often been one of the more enjoyable parts of his former life. They'd tended to love the attention, and he'd captured some genuinely joyful moments full of friendship and laughter, the pure exuberance of youth. But he doubted he'd ever be able to explain that to someone like Hugh.

It didn't matter. Hugh was on to the next topic already. "Tell me about your support network. It can be a strange life, that of an artist. Most people will never understand what it's like to commit to creativity and all the ups and downs that brings. It can help, to have people around you that at least care."

"My mother–"

"That's the older woman, in the picture you sent?"

Michael smiled, because it was impossible for him not to smile when he thought about his mam. "That's her. She's always happy to pose for me. Always supportive. She's convinced I'm one step away from having my work hung in the National Portrait Gallery or something."

"Yes, mothers can get like that sometimes. Although mine is still convinced that there's still time for me to pack all this in and use my estate management degree," Hugh said dryly.

"I just want to give her something to boast about for once. She's had precious little chance of that for most of my life." He veered away from that thought before he could let his brain play over it for too long. "And my best friend ..." He fiddled with the roll on his bread plate. Some best friend he was. He was still avoiding talking to Cleo, and he could pretend it was because he was busy all he liked, but he wasn't convincing himself and he sure as shite wouldn't be convincing her. "She's the one who made me promise to do this." Where would he be without her unshakeable belief that some day he would be worth something? Still standing around on pavements, probably, if he'd even got near a career in photography at all. But he couldn't help it – whenever he thought of her, he thought of their last conversation, and the fact that she'd kept things from him, and ...

"It's good that you have them in your corner," Hugh said, breaking into Michael's thoughts. His gaze wandered wistfully into the middle distance. "Anyway, what we—" His phone started ringing. "Do excuse me. This is a collector, one I must talk to but who never answers his bloody phone."

Hugh walked away from the table, leaving Michael alone with the last sip of water left in his glass. He wasn't sure what to do with himself now. He didn't even dare look around the restaurant, because some tiresome part of him was convinced that everyone would be staring at him, wondering who let the oik in. It was bollocks, he knew it was. He wasn't that important, and he looked perfectly presentable anyway, even if he was dressed in

H&M's finest rather than Givenchy. But this sort of place gave him the jitters.

Ah, sod it. He pulled out his phone. Probably not the done thing, but he couldn't just sit here feeling like his skin was about to crawl outside of its own accord. He tried to look as though he was working on Very Important Things, but in truth he was flicking through Instagram. He'd started following a load of new artists lately, hoping that their work would inspire him. Some of it did spark some new ideas, but mostly it just made him wonder if he could ever be that good. He flicked away from his main feed and decided to let Instagram show him whatever it was in the mood to deliver ... oh. He must have looked at one too many pictures of Miranda this week, because the algorithm was giving him pages and pages of her. Some old photo shoots, some movie promo shots, and some recent paparazzi pics of her in LA. He clicked on one because ... because professional interest? Curiosity about what his friend was up to? Who was he kidding? He clicked because he'd take pretty much any opportunity to look at her.

But the picture wasn't just of Miranda. She was stepping out of a restaurant or something, with a tall, handsome man hot on her heels. His jet-black hair and sharp features made a striking contrast to her soft, golden beauty, and Michael suddenly felt as if he'd been punched in the chest with a block of ice.

Don't be so fucking ridiculous, he told himself, forcing himself to look more closely at the picture. The man was Seb Akao, the guy most likely – according to the movie-news articles Michael couldn't stop searching out – to play Faran, the male lead in *An Ocean of Fallen Stars*. And as he scrutinised the picture further, he could see that another person was about to emerge from the door, and that someone looked about the right height and frame to be AJ Hollinger. Michael was almost certainly looking at a triumph for Miranda – she'd somehow swung a meeting with not just the director she was looking to impress, but her potential co-star. He felt a wave of pride for her. But why wasn't the ice-punch feeling receding? For fuck's sake, was he jealous? At the mere sight of her in what was probably a totally platonic situation with a man? OK, he was an unfeasibly good-looking man, but there was no sign of anything going on between Miranda and Seb. And even if there was, why should it bother him? They were just friends, for many reasons, not least because she was about as far out of his league as Arsenal were out of Blyth Spartans'.

He looked at the picture again, taking in the little smile on her face. Who was he kidding? He'd had a thing for her long before he knew her, and getting to know her had only made it worse, no matter how hard he'd worked to keep those feelings locked down for the sake of professionalism. He missed her, he realised. She'd been gone less than a week, and he missed her. And he was irrationally jealous of the guy who'd been fortunate enough to spend some time with her. This was more than a case of physical attraction to a beautiful woman. He had it bad.

Before he could delve too deeply into the implications of this, Hugh returned.

"Sorry, Michael. No rest for the wicked."

Michael smiled weakly.

"Are you alright there?" Hugh said, studying his face. "You look ... perturbed."

"I'm fine," said Michael, giving his head a much needed wobble. "I was just thinking. About what you said. About my work making a statement."

Total lie, of course. He wasn't thinking about the pictures he could take, but the ones he shouldn't. He couldn't work with Miranda again, surely. He couldn't risk making more of a fool of himself than he already had. Besides, it looked as though it wouldn't be necessary. He'd be willing to bet everything he had that Miranda would be confirmed as Damia within a week. If Michael could see how perfect Seb and Miranda looked together, AJ Hollinger would see it too. So she wouldn't need him and their shoots anymore. He could give his full attention to his art, like he was supposed to be doing, and she'd go off like the star she was born to be. It was for the best. Really. It was.

20

MIRANDA sipped her freshly squeezed orange juice and gazed out of the window at the clouds below. The executives at the other end of Henry and Courtney's jet weren't paying the slightest bit of attention to her, which was nice.

This week was working out beautifully. Just as Miranda was finished in LA, Courtney had texted to say that Henry had called some kind of huge meeting that required his top people to fly out to the UK as quickly as humanly possible. Miranda had been only too happy to hitch a very stylish ride.

She smiled. It had worked. All of it. Nothing was official yet, of course, and she was sure Nora's hands would be kept pretty full with all the negotiations that had yet to happen, but that part was *hers*. She knew it in her bones. The lunch with Seb had been fantastic – he was a delight, and they'd gotten along instantly, laughing and joking as if they'd been friends for years. AJ had spoken little, but she'd caught him watching them both appraisingly, and she was unsurprised when, at the end of the afternoon, he'd invited her to test with Seb.

Miranda had thrown everything she had at that test. The second she'd stepped into the room, she'd done everything in her power to be Damia, to leave them all in no doubt that she was who they wanted. And as she'd left, AJ had said, "You continue to surprise me, Ms Janes. I think the world would bow to you."

That was when she knew she had it. "*There is no world, Damia, that would not bow to you should you demand it.*"

She murmured the next line from the book: "'And there is no world I would not burn to keep you with me.'"

"Did you say something, Ms Janes? Is there something you need?"

Oops. She hadn't noticed the passing cabin attendant.

"No, thank you. I'm fine." She grinned at the young man. She was way too happy to be embarrassed about being caught talking to herself.

Everything was falling into place. Now it was time to go back to London and ... what? Await news from Nora, she supposed. Sit down with Aisling and make sure her schedule was as clear as it needed to be.

She put down her glass. There was another thing she wanted, almost as badly as she'd wanted this part. Time to make that happen too.

* * *

Miranda had been home for barely ten minutes when she picked her up phone and called Michael. There was no time like the present, after all.

"Hi," he said, and the warmth in his voice felt as though it spilled out of the phone and settled somewhere in her chest. "How was LA?"

"Amazing," she replied. "I am ninety-nine percent sure that part is mine." The heat in her chest mingled with the sparks set off by saying it out loud, until it felt like the Fourth of July beneath her breastbone. "And I couldn't have done it without you."

He laughed. "Of course you could have. But I'm glad to have helped."

"Cleo says hi, by the way."

Michael made a non-committal noise.

"Why didn't you tell her we were working together?" This had been bothering Miranda for days. Michael and Cleo told each other everything – it had been a problem when Cleo had started seeing Devon. Was this thing with his grandmother really coming between them?

Michael sighed. "I don't know. We haven't talked lately. It's ... complicated. Or maybe it's just me being an arsehole. Who knows?"

"You're not an asshole, Michael. But you should talk to her. She cares about you as much as she ever did. You know that, right?"

"Yeah, I know. I will."

"Promise?"

Michael chuckled. "Yes, I promise."

"Good." She knew this was none of her business. Cleo and Michael's friendship went back two decades and ran deep, and she'd been on the scene five minutes.

But she couldn't stand to see these two people she'd come to care about being unhappy.

"So," Michael said, clearly looking to change the subject, "tell me more about LA. You met Seb Akao, by the looks of it? I saw a picture on Instagram."

His tone was casual, almost deliberately so, but there was a strange kind of evenness to his words. She'd seen some pictures of her and Seb too, laughing and joking as they left the restaurant. They looked great together. Was that what he'd seen? Was it possible that he was jealous?

That was wishful thinking. For all she knew, he was a Seb Akao superfan and trying to be cool about it.

"Yes, AJ took us both out to lunch, and when he saw how well we got along, he asked me to do a screen test with him, which went really well. I think we've got some good chemistry. Not chemistry chemistry," she rushed to add. For all she kind of liked the idea that Michael might feel a bit of jealousy over her, she didn't actually want him to get the wrong idea. "Screen chemistry. It's a little hard to explain."

"No, I get it. I've seen movies before, remember? I'm really happy for you. You and Seb will make a perfect Damia and Faran." He sounded genuine. Miranda wished she'd video-called him instead. She wanted to see his face, see if his brow was relaxed and easy or if it had that little wrinkle that appeared whenever he was struggling with something.

"Thank you. I hope so." She squared her shoulders. To business. "Anyway, I called to ask you something."

"Fire away."

"Do you have a passport and any plans for the weekend?"

"Yes, and no, nothing important. Why?"

She smiled. "What do you say to one last photo shoot?"

There was a brief pause before he answered, and Miranda wondered if it was because the idea of it being the last time they would spend together did the same thing to him as it did to her.

"Of course," he replied, and she thought he sounded a little sad. He didn't need to worry. She had no intention of walking out of his life, unless he wanted her to. And if he did ... well, she wasn't going to think about that right now. "Where did you have in mind?"

She let her smile spread into a full-on grin. "One of my favourite places in the world. Paris."

The city of love. She knew it was a cliché, and she knew there was a lot about Paris that wasn't romantic in the slightest. But she couldn't help it – she was a sucker for a cliché. And if it all went wrong, at least she could console herself with croissants.

"Paris," Michael repeated slowly, his northern accent wrapping itself around the two syllables. "I'd love to."

21

MIRANDA made a gorgeous brunette, Michael decided. She made a gorgeous anything, but the straight bobbed wig she was wearing under her baseball cap seemed to make her turquoise eyes shine even brighter than usual. She sipped her complimentary coffee as the Kent countryside flew past the windows of the Eurostar.

"Have you ever been to Paris?" she asked him over the rim of her cup.

"Once," he said. "With Cleo." Bittersweet memories assaulted him. "Right at the end of our marriage. We stayed in this absolute craphole in Montmartre owned by a terrifying guy called Charles. It was so awful that we walked for hours and hours round the whole city, trying to stay out as long as possible while also not spending any money."

Miranda smiled wistfully. "Sounds ... well, not nice, exactly. But like a good way to take in the sights. I managed that for about two hours once, then a photographer found me and started following me everywhere, and it sort of ruined the mood. I try not to let that happen, but the European press can be a bit much at times."

He winced. This was the kind of shit he'd never let himself think about back then. "Sorry."

"Why?" She shrugged. "It wasn't you. You don't have to apologise on behalf of your former profession for the rest of your life, you know."

"I know." Although he didn't know if he'd ever get over the guilt he felt at the misery he must have caused people like her.

"Anyway," she said, giving him that diamond-bright smile of hers, "this trip won't be like that, I promise. No terrifying men named Charles. Aisling booked us into my favourite hotel. Wait until you see the views."

"And it won't mean the end of my marriage this time either," he said, almost without thinking. Why had he dragged up the past like that? There was something about Miranda that seemed to pull his thoughts out of his soul in a way he found extremely unnerving.

She raised an eyebrow. "That must have been one terrible hotel."

"Oh, it was." He shuddered at the memory of the huge brown patch that had covered most of the ceiling. "But it wasn't the hotel. It was a make-or-break holiday kind of thing. And we broke. Or were already broken, and the trip made us admit that."

"Been there, done that. Although not with a marriage, obviously. And certainly not where I kept hold of a friendship afterward."

"Yeah." The memory of getting off the train at St Pancras and slinging his arm around his best friend flew into his mind. The relief they'd felt when they realised they could stop trying to force something back to life that was long gone. He smiled. They were so lucky, he and Cleo. How many people got to shift their relationship from friends to lovers and back to friends again so easily? And here he was, jeopardising it with his stupid issues. He should stop being an arse and call her.

But that was something to worry about later. "So, do you have a plan for the shoot? I know Operation Damia is over, but what are you thinking for this set?"

"Oh, I don't know," Miranda said airily. "The suite I've booked at the hotel is stunning. I'm sure it will inspire you in some way. Like you said, I don't need to focus on anything in particular this time so let's just ..." She met his eyes. "See what happens."

Her eyes stayed on his. There wasn't a hint of flirtation in her voice or on her face. Her expression was calm, neutral. But the sense of possibility held in her words hit him like the train that had just plunged into the darkness of the Channel Tunnel.

He was the first to look away, but he still couldn't seem to find a reply. Words had floated away from him, ceased to be any kind of viable option.

It didn't matter. She took charge of the situation like she always did. "I can't wait for you to try the food at the restaurant in the hotel. It is to die for. I mean, they don't serve caramel doughnuts, which is obviously a travesty, but they have this lamb cooked in pine needles, which sounds weird but is out of this world."

Food. Right. He could talk about food. "Sounds good. Last time, I remember being absolutely bloody starving on the Champs-Élysées and not being able to afford anything but McDonald's. I was pretty excited that you could get beer there, though."

"You can get beer in McDonald's in France?" Miranda looked as astounded by the information as he'd been as a twenty-year-old with a typical British twenty-year-old's attitude to booze. "Although I don't know why I'm so surprised. I haven't been in a McDonald's since I was nineteen."

"You're not missing much," Michael said, taking a bite out of his croissant.

"Oh, I'm sure." She wrinkled her nose. "Don't worry, I wasn't about to go all 'poor little rich girl, complaining that she doesn't get to go to McDonald's'. I'm perfectly aware that my life is nothing to whine about." She settled back in her seat.

Michael took in her expression of contentment. "You really like your life, don't you? In a way that people don't always manage. Like, obviously it's full of great things because of what you do, but I know that doesn't make problems disappear. I know Devon finds a lot of the celebrity lifestyle pretty stifling, but you just ... don't."

She smiled. "Of course I don't. If I did, I would stop doing it."

"Just like that?"

"Just like that." She turned those captivating eyes on him again. "I don't believe in putting up with stuff that you don't have to. There are enough people in the world who are unhappy because of circumstances they can't control. I'm not about to add to the amount of misery in the world if I can help it. If I can choose happiness, I will."

It was an alien way of thinking to him. He'd grown up as one of those people she was talking about, trapped in the poverty his father and grandmother had plunged his mother into. He'd never imagined he would be in a position to choose anything, let alone happiness. And now ... was he there? Things were looking up for him, that was for sure. He had been enjoying life lately, despite the still overwhelming self-doubt and uncertainty, hadn't he? Could he simply start trying to let go of some of the misery he'd carried around with him his whole damn life?

God, it was far too early in the morning for these kinds of thoughts. He shoved them away and let his back relax into the contours of the business class seat. Choose happiness. That might be a tall order for a miserable arsehole like him. But spending time with Miranda always seemed like an adventure. He could abandon himself to that for the weekend, at least.

* * *

Michael was dreaming. He must have been. Paris stretched out below his feet. The rooms behind him were fit for a king. And the most beautiful woman in the world had just come out onto the balcony, dressed in a thick white robe.

"I can't decide what to wear." She tilted her head. "Come help me?"

He followed her through the outrageously luxurious sitting room into her bedroom. The suite she'd booked them into made his flat look like a postage stamp. A very shabby postage stamp.

Three dresses were laid out on her bed – a flowered cotton sundress, a gold silk evening gown, and a short black thing with complicated-looking straps. She would look spectacular in any one of them. But as Michael opened his mouth to say so, an idea came to him and he found himself saying, "How do you feel about a full-on cliché?"

Her lips curved slowly into a smile. "Very good indeed. What are you thinking?"

"Wait here."

Heart pounding, he quickly walked to his own room and pulled his best shirt from his case. He'd bought it for Cleo's wedding – a basic white shirt, but one of the nicest things he'd ever owned. What was he doing? Why had he said this? He was supposed to be an artist, yet here he was suggesting the most hackneyed, least innovative shot in the history of the world.

He hadn't been able to help himself. The thought of her wearing his clothes had chucked itself into his head and out of his mouth before he could question the wisdom of it. And he was practically sprinting back to her room now before he could tell himself to come up with a better, less creepy idea.

The sensible part of his brain wrested back control as he held out the shirt to her. "Sorry," it made him say. "This is daft. It's totally corny. One of the dresses would probably be better. The flowery one would be good for a sweet and innocent vibe, or that gold one is stunning and would look good against–"

"Stop." She held up one hand. "I love it."

She did? "You do?"

"Totally!" She beamed at him. "It'll be like my very own perfume ad. Man's shirt, cup of coffee, Paris balcony ... I absolutely want to do that. I don't care if it's corny. I'm corny. Let's do it."

Her enthusiasm washed away his doubts. He'd made her smile, and he thought it might be the greatest achievement of his life. "OK. I'll go and set it up."

* * *

"So you've never done a perfume ad? How is that possible?" Michael asked as he took shot after perfect shot. Those ads were exactly what this looked like – the air seemed to have that grey haze to it that in London looked grimy but here looked strangely seductive. And seductive didn't even come close to describing how she looked with that crisp white shirt – his shirt – grazing her smooth thighs as she leaned against the balcony railing. He was asking inane questions about her modelling opportunities because if he let his thoughts stray any further towards her legs he'd forget everything he knew about composition and depth of field and essential functions like standing and breathing.

"Just hasn't worked out, for one reason or another," she said, smirking at him from behind the huge coffee cup room service had sent up. "It's on my list, though."

"I'll expect it within the year, then," he said, and as she laughed in response she tipped her head back at an exquisite angle that Michael hoped he'd caught.

But then she focused her gaze squarely on him. "How does the shirt look? Should I undo another button?"

He swallowed. Lord no. "It's good how you have it."

"It's a really nice shirt. Thank you for loaning it to me." She turned around, leaned on the railing and looked back over her shoulder at him. "How's this?"

Michael had been telling himself since the moment he set eyes on her that he was a terrible person, a terrible photographer, for not being able to stay detached in this situation. But as his shirt rode a centimetre closer towards the curve of her arse, now pointing unignorably in his direction, and she levelled him with a stare that held enough heat to incinerate the whole of Paris, there was an unmistakeable note of challenge in her voice. Was it possible that she was *trying* to fluster him? She was certainly bloody succeeding.

He realised he hadn't answered her. "Yeah. Sorry. You look great." He pressed the shutter. "If you—"

"Enough." She pushed herself away from the railing and walked towards him. "Do you have some good shots?"

He nodded, because apparently one syllable was beyond his capabilities. Of course he had good shots.

She placed her hands over his and gently lowered the camera. "Then I think we're done here."

22

MICHAEL was staring at her with an expression somewhere between confusion and panic. Miranda bit back a giggle and just smiled.

"Don't look so worried. I meant that we can stop working now. You're officially off the clock."

"Oh." His handsome face relaxed. As much as it ever did, anyway. "OK. I'll start packing up, then." She watched for a few moments as he put his camera away, took down the tripod he hadn't ended up using. Strange little nervous butterflies seemed to be fluttering about behind her navel. Was she nervous? Why was she nervous? She'd known what she was doing when she invited him here, known all along that now was the time to grab the bull by the horns.

But now it came down to it, she hadn't expected to feel this way. For the first time in her life she could see the appeal of playing it safe. Because what if she was wrong? What if she'd misjudged this whole thing and she lost him as a friend? Now that they weren't going to be working together, if she screwed this up ... she might never see him again.

The thought was unbearable.

"So," he said, because somehow he'd managed to completely finish putting away his stuff while she'd been having her uncharacteristic little episode. He didn't seem able to look at her properly. His gaze hovered somewhere around the collar of the shirt she was still wearing. Maybe he felt it, the energy that was thrumming around her body, and it was making him nervous too. "What now?"

She reached for her phone and pulled up her emails. "I'm sending you your e-ticket for the train home."

Finally, he met her eyes. His were wide, dumbfounded. "You want me to leave?" The tension was back in his jaw, but Miranda couldn't figure out what that meant. She wanted desperately to believe that it was disappointment.

"Not at all," she said, taking a step closer. "I just want you to know that you can."

He said nothing, but she thought she saw understanding settle in his hazel eyes.

She took a deep breath and another step. "I would very much like you to stay."

In the eternity of silence that followed, Miranda wondered if she'd ever felt this vulnerable, wearing nothing but his shirt, waiting for nothing but his answer.

Then he gave her a delicious half-smile that made her heart stutter in her chest. "Then I'll stay."

23

"ARE you sure you don't mind being down here?" Miranda asked him after they'd been seated in a quiet corner of the hotel's elegant residents-only dining room.

"I'm fine with it if you are," Michael replied, and he meant it. She was the famous one, after all, the one who would be pestered by fans. Although it seemed unlikely. The room oozed exclusivity. The other diners looked rich and beautiful and glamorous in their own right. They were in a high-backed booth, and the lighting was low enough that getting a decent-quality picture of them would be difficult, especially as he was taking care to position himself at an angle that would make it even more so. Not that it mattered – most members of the public would just be excited to see Miranda and not care about some nondescript companion.

"Good." Her smile was radiant. "Room service gets very boring after a while."

"I bet." As if he knew. It had never been worth paying an extra fiver to get a mediocre burger delivered to a Premier Inn room.

He couldn't think of anything else to say, and he hated it. He and Miranda had never had a problem with conversation. But that moment between them earlier had put something weird in the air. The implications of what she'd said had been clear – she was ending the professional relationship between them. Removing an obstacle to … something more. It was hard to interpret her words as anything other than an invitation. But he was still having trouble believing it. It had been difficult enough to convince himself that Miranda Janes would genuinely want to be his friend. To think that she might actually be attracted to him …

Michael had never, not for a single second, let himself imagine that she might want him as much as he wanted her. He'd never even let himself fully admit how much he did want her. He'd needed to stay professional, so he had, and now she'd ripped that shield away from him and he didn't have a fucking clue what he was supposed to do now.

"Michael." Her soft voice interrupted his chaotic muddle of thoughts. She was looking at him, her eyes sparkling with amusement. "Don't think. You think too much. Look at your menu. Drink your wine. You're having dinner at one of the best restaurants in Europe, not facing a firing squad."

"Did I look that worried?"

"Sweetheart, you always look worried." Thankfully she didn't ask him what he was worried about. "But there's no need tonight. We're just here, having a nice time. That's all."

It wasn't all. Of course it wasn't. But for fuck's sake, could he not let himself *be*, just for a second? Could he not accept the moment for what it was without getting in his own head about it?

He fixed his eyes on her beautiful face and let her smile melt his anxieties away to nothing. Or nearly nothing. He picked up his glass of the wine that probably cost as much as his council tax and raised it towards her.

"To fallen stars."

She lifted her glass and clinked it against his. "And rising ones."

He tamped down the voice that was trying to whisper *she didn't mean you, dickhead* into his brain. Both of them had their dreams within their grasp. When she was off shooting her multimillion-dollar movie and he finally had a show in a gallery, he'd look back and remember this night, these weeks, and smile.

The thought cut into him, a sweet-sharp shard of pain. It was over. He'd always known his time with her wouldn't last forever, but now the photo shoots were done, she had no more need of him. Whatever promise may or may not have been in her asking him to stay, life would pull them out of each other's orbits before long. Tonight might be all there was.

A waiter came to take their order, and Michael realised he hadn't paid the slightest bit of attention to the fancy menu, so he waited for Miranda to order and asked for the same. He didn't care what he ate. He suddenly didn't care about anything but savouring being here, with her.

"You're looking at me funny," Miranda said teasingly.

"Are you mad that I ordered the thing you wanted? I had an ex who was so weird about that."

"What? Who would be weird about that?"

"He was weird about a great many things. He thought it was a wasted opportunity not to try as many items from the menu as possible. But then he'd get pissed if I ordered first and 'took' the things he wanted." She shrugged. "I don't know where I find these prizes, really I don't."

He wanted to reach out and smooth away the tiny wrinkle of sadness that seemed to have appeared on her brow, but he settled for taking a deep breath and saying, "You look beautiful tonight, by the way." It was stupid, because she always looked beautiful and she knew that, but he figured it was probably always nice to hear. And it was true. Her blonde hair hung in waves over her shoulders, and her simple red satin slip dress shimmered over her willowy body. He was reminded of the blue dress, the way the silky fabric felt under his hand as he steadied himself on her that day in her garden. And he shouldn't have let that memory into his head, because it sent a rush of heat straight through him. He took a very inelegant gulp of water.

She smiled. "Why thank you. You look pretty good yourself."

He looked down at himself as if he'd somehow managed to forget what he dressed himself in a whole hour ago. He'd felt a bit of a twat packing his only good suit and best shirt for a work trip, but he'd suspected he'd be needing them, and he'd been right. He couldn't have shown up down here in the crappy T-shirt and jeans he'd had on all day. The shirt still held the faint scent of her, something slightly spicy, slightly sweet, wildly sexy. Another thought he shouldn't have let into his brain.

"Thanks," he said, realising he'd neglected to answer her for an uncomfortably long time. She lifted her wine glass to lips that matched her dress, apparently not about to rescue him from his conversational ineptitude. "So, tell me ..." What? What did he want her to tell him about? He was fucked if he knew – he was just trying to keep his thoughts in a restaurant-friendly place. "Tell me how you became an actor."

"It isn't a very exciting story. I did it the way most people do anything – I found something I loved and I worked hard at it until I found an opportunity."

"You make it sound so simple."

"Sometimes things are simple. That doesn't mean they're easy."

Their food chose that moment to arrive. A beautiful dish of rare beef garnished with curls of various brightly coloured things was placed in front of him. Michael wanted to take a photograph of it, but he also didn't want to be that person in a place like this, so he settled for committing the sight to memory and picking up his fork.

"God, this is good," Miranda said after her first mouthful. "Why did I move to London when the food in Paris is like this? Anyway, I'm not saying there wasn't an awful lot of luck involved, or that everything went smoothly. I started acting when I was a kid, in school plays, you know, and I fell in love with it. My parents didn't think it was a viable career, but I paid for extra acting lessons myself and eventually they realised I was serious about it."

"Yeah, my mam told me about that."

Her eyes lit up. "She did? Oh, your mom is so cute, honestly. I had a blast talking to her."

"I'll tell her that. It'll make her day." He grinned at the idea that this Hollywood superstar thought his mam was "cute".

"So I took these lessons in Seattle, and that was it. Any thought that I could do something else with my life vanished. I applied to Tisch and Julliard but didn't get in, so I went to UCLA instead, but I dropped out when I got a part in this little indie movie. Then there was another indie movie, and a bigger indie movie, and some tiny parts in huge movies, and then along came *Iris Jackson*. So, yeah. If I wanted to be pretentious about it, I guess I could say that I've always been an actor. It just took some time before anyone would pay me to do it, and even longer before anyone would pay me well."

Michael was about eighty percent absorbed in what she was saying, and only twenty percent thinking about the way the soft light kept catching on her golden hair. She grabbed hold of that last fifth of him when she said, "Kind of like you."

"Me?"

"Yes, you. You've always been a photographer. You're just still figuring out the best way to make it your life in a way that makes you happy."

It blew his mind that she could think they were similar, but he found he couldn't argue with her. The way she believed in him and his art, it meant something to him in a way he couldn't articulate. She made him feel, somehow, like nothing was out of reach.

* * *

"That was the most amazing meal I've ever had," Michael said, leaning back in his chair, resisting the urge to pat his belly like some jovial grandad after Christmas dinner.

"I told you." Miranda gave him a direct, assessing look. "Hey, how brave are you feeling?"

After two glasses of superb wine, three courses of unbelievably good food, and a whole day in her company? He could have taken on the world. "What do you have in mind?"

"A walk. I know, not something that normally requires bravery, right? But there's always the chance I'll be spotted. *We'll* be spotted."

"If it doesn't bother you, it doesn't bother me. And I know how to avoid it, to an extent."

Her smile was brighter than all the stars in the sky. "Great. I'll just go get my wig."

"I'll meet you outside." He'd take the opportunity to check for photographers. He hadn't noticed anyone so much as pointing a phone in her direction here in the dining room, but in the lobby and on the street, it might be a different story.

Ten minutes later, Michael was standing on the hotel steps, as satisfied as he could be that there were no paps in sight. News of her stay must not have slipped out yet. And then she was next to him, a cream jacket over her dress, the sleek brown hair of her wig falling over one side of her face. Michael moved to her other side, where his body would block it from view.

"Oh, shoot," she said, her gorgeous face falling. "I should have asked if you needed your coat."

"I'm from Northumberland, pet. I never need my coat." Besides, although the night air did hold the slightest unseasonable chill, he felt at least ten degrees warmer when she threaded her arm through his.

"Then let's go."

They started walking. Michael steered them off the main thoroughfare and down some quiet side streets. Less picturesque, perhaps, but also more chance of noticing if anyone was following them.

Miranda chuckled. "I feel like I'm back in *Into the Dark*. Even Frank doesn't whisk me around like I'm in an action movie."

"Sorry." He winced. "Am I going over the top? It's just I know what they're like. What I was like, sometimes."

"Hey, I'm kidding." She squeezed his arm. "I kind of like you taking care of me like this."

He swallowed. The way her voice caressed those words sent his head into a spin. He took a deep breath, which didn't help in the slightest because the breeze only carried her perfume into his nostrils, and suddenly all his senses were full of her.

"I, er, yeah. I think we're in the clear." It was obvious no one was following them, which meant they could relax a little. The odd member of the public might recognise her despite the high-quality wig, but if that happened, it would take time before any hordes descended. He took a right turn, down a street he guessed would take them towards the river. "Sorry. When you said you wanted a walk, you probably didn't mean down empty residential streets with nothing to see."

"I don't mind," she said with a little shrug. "I just wanted to be outside. Besides there's more to a city than the tourist spots. The places where people live are as much a part of Paris as the tower and everything."

"You're right," he said. "What's a city without its people? Maybe that's why I do what I do, or what I want to do, because I like finding the people at the heart of things."

"I love the way you see people." Was it his imagination, or did she lean a little bit closer to him? "That's why I came to you. Every picture you've ever taken of me, even the ones before I knew you, they showed me something in myself I'd never seen before, but that felt familiar all the same." She laughed. "Does that make any sense?"

"Yeah, it makes ..." His feet stopped walking as his eyes left Miranda's face and took in their surroundings. They were by the river, near the edge of the Trocadéro Gardens, on a corner he knew.

"What is it?" Miranda asked, putting her free hand on his arm.

He let out a huff of a laugh. "Wow. This is the place I realised my marriage was over."

"It is?"

"Yup. That night I told you about." The memory overlaid itself on the present; he could almost see it. "We'd spent all day together, having the best time. We had fun like we hadn't had in ages. And we were wandering all over the city, avoiding the hotel, and we were here. For some reason, we both stopped at the same moment. I looked down at Cleo, and she looked back at me, and she just gave me this massive hug, and we both knew. Whatever we once had, it was gone."

"Oh," Miranda said softly. "That must have been very strange."

"Yeah," he murmured. Strange, and yet not. He remembered what it had felt like, that night. They'd been standing on this very spot, with the kind of warm buzz you got after a couple of beers and a whole load of crisp night air. The Eiffel Tower had loomed in the background; the Seine had glittered with the reflections of the streetlights. "It should have been the most romantic moment of my life, but ..."

At some point in the last minute or so, his and Miranda's bodies had somehow stopped being side by side, and now she was almost facing him, her arm still tucked into his. She was so close. Too close.

"But?"

"I didn't want to kiss her." He'd looked down at Cleo, lovely Cleo, his actual wife, and had no desire to kiss her. He hadn't felt even the tiniest urge to bend his head, to cup her face, to let her breath play over his lips, to pull her to him until his mouth captured hers, to tangle his fingers into her hair and let them stay there as his tongue …

"Michael," Miranda murmured.

Oh shit. He realised he was staring right into eyes that weren't brown but the colour of an ocean, and that her breaths were coming as fast as his, and that he had in fact bent his head a fraction, and that he was standing on the edge of a precipice … and that a young woman a few feet away was staring at them curiously.

No, not at them. At Miranda. Crap.

He slung his arm around her shoulders and pulled her in towards his chest. "I think someone's seen you," he said, and his voice sounded ragged to his own ears. "This way."

His arm still around her, he turned them back towards the residential streets. She lowered her chin and kept her face to his chest, and he wanted to relish the feel of her against his body but there was no time. It was only a member of the public, and maybe she hadn't even recognised Miranda – maybe she'd just been amused by the spectacle of a guy who was so clearly punching above his weight – but if she had and then posted on social media about it, they could have paps on them in minutes.

They hurried through the warren of apartment buildings, and Michael was impressed that Miranda was keeping up the pace in those shoes. The streets were deserted, and after a few minutes he was sure they were alone. No one had followed them. It was fine. He could see several hundred yards in both directions, and there was not a soul in sight.

He stopped and let his arm fall from her shoulders. "OK. I think we're OK." He needed a minute to catch his breath. But then his eyes met hers and he found he couldn't, because it wasn't the speed of the walk that had stolen it. The tension that had crackled between them a few minutes ago hadn't been broken, only suspended, and now it grabbed him by the throat and wouldn't let go.

"Michael." It was the same soft murmur she'd spoken in back by the river, and there was something low and urgent in it that made any last vestiges of control or sense that he might have had evaporate into the night. He took her hand, and for the briefest second he just let himself feel the softness of it, feel how right it felt in his.

Then he pulled her into the shadows of the nearest alleyway. *Don't think. You think too much.* With her words from earlier echoing in his ears, he took her beautiful face in his hands and let his mouth find hers the way it had wanted to do for weeks. Her lips were as soft as he'd imagined they'd be but her kiss was anything but. It was searching and fierce and not nearly enough. She pulled him closer and he went willingly, pressing her back against the cold wall of the alley.

Christ, this was intoxicating. She was intoxicating, taking him over until he no longer knew which way was up. Her lips parted for him, and when he flicked his tongue over them, the low, soft moan in her throat made him forget where they were and why doing this was probably a spectacularly bad idea. But now he was here, tasting wine and chocolate on her tongue, he didn't know if he'd ever be able to stop. She slipped her hand under his jacket until it splayed over his ribcage, her touch scorching him through his shirt, a heat that could burn him to ashes for all he cared.

As the kiss grew into something wild, he could have laughed at the fact that he'd wondered if she could ever possibly want him. Her answer was in the hand in his hair, tugging him closer, in the curve of her body as it arched into his, in the gasp that told him she felt him rock-hard against her. He was more turned on than he'd ever been in his life. He'd never fucked anyone in the street – the thought had never even crossed his mind, and it wasn't as if he was about to start now – but every fibre of his being was screaming for it.

Jesus, they had to stop before they did something extremely unwise, but he couldn't seem to tear his lips away from her. Finally, with a force of will he didn't know he had, he managed it, resting his forehead against hers. The air between them filled with shaking breaths and naked desire.

Miranda closed her eyes, opened them again, and in a low, uneven voice said, "Let's go."

24

MIRANDA kept her eyes on the map on her phone as they walked at blistering speed back to the hotel. She wasn't sure it was necessary – Michael seemed to have an impeccable sense of direction – but she needed to focus on something that wasn't him. If she looked at him, if she saw the same kind of need in his hazel eyes that was pulsing through her right now, she'd probably melt into the sidewalk. Or do something else on the sidewalk that people who were as famous as she was absolutely should not.

Things between them had gotten pretty wild in her fantasies, but her imagination could never have conjured up the way he'd kissed her, with such searing intensity that she'd felt it with every inch of her body. She'd wanted him for a long time, but the pounding, overwhelming desire she'd felt, was still feeling as they hurried through the city, was like nothing she'd ever dreamed.

Why weren't they at the hotel yet? Damn it, she needed to be alone with him, and part of her worried that he'd pull back from her again, that he'd retreat and the moment would be lost. But that part of her wasn't the parts that had had his lips on her, his hands. Those parts could not imagine that either of them could walk away from the fire that had been lit in the shadows of some alleyway. He was walking by her side, not touching her, but close enough that their arms brushed with every step, and even through his jacket and hers she imagined she could feel the heat of his body, and it was sending her pulse through the roof.

Finally, finally, the opulent facade of the hotel came into view. His gait sped up a little and he stopped looking straight ahead and looked around them instead, clearly searching for photographers. Miranda was glad – she didn't usually care who saw her or what they made up, but she felt sure that her desire must be written all over her face. She shook her wig until it fell over one cheek again, then lifted her phone and pressed it to the other. She lowered her head as she followed Michael up the hotel's front steps. Her heels clicked over marble as he kept up his relentless pace and made a beeline for the elevators.

When the elevator doors shut behind them, she turned to face him, but he stayed staring resolutely in front of him. He almost looked like he was mad at her. Oh god, was he mad at her?

"Michael, are–"

"Don't. Not here," he said through gritted teeth, his voice as tight as a guitar string about to snap.

Her gaze travelled from his jaw to his hands. His knuckles were so white that she could practically see the last thread of his control clenched in his fist. For one brief moment she let herself imagine him letting go of it, imagined him pushing her against the mirrored wall of the elevator the way he'd done the wall in the alleyway. Then she imagined the headlines when the security footage leaked, and settled for wrapping her arms around herself to keep from reaching out to him.

This was the longest elevator ride in the history of elevator rides. Why did penthouse suites have to be so damn high up? After three hundred hours, during which the air seemed to grow thick enough to slice, the doors finally opened on their floor. Miranda strode into the lobby, pulling her keycard out of her purse as she went. The lock buzzed and lit up red. Her trembling hands tried again, but Michael was right there behind her, and the warmth of his body made it impossible to focus. She let herself lean against his chest for a second. His hand rested gently on her hip and she felt him take a deep breath, like he was breathing her in, and lord, she had to get this door open right this minute, had to do something about this deep, sweet ache inside her.

The lock beeped and let them into the room, the beautiful, luxurious living room of the suite that could have been a swamp shack for all she cared – it had four walls and a door that locked and that was all she needed right now. The second the door slammed shut behind them, Michael backed her against it. She raised her face for his kiss, but it didn't come. Instead, he curled his hand lightly around the base of her throat and lowered his head until his lips grazed her jaw. She gasped, a bolt of electricity coursing through her veins as his mouth moved over her skin, not touching, or maybe touching, she couldn't even tell, and it was maddening and beautiful and so, so hot that her knees threatened to buckle beneath her.

"You want me," he said, moving his lips to the other side of her jaw. It was a question as well as a statement, but it held no trace of the uncertainty she'd seen in him so many times before.

"Yes."

He slid his hand upwards and ran his thumb over her lip. "Are you sure?"

He caught her in his stare, and the sheer force of it almost made her forget to answer. He'd been lighting her up with his mouth and his touch, but the way he looked at her did something to her deep inside, something she couldn't explain but made her feel like she might never be the same again.

"Yes," she whispered.

He pulled her to him and kissed her, hard. She moaned into his mouth as his arm tightened around her waist, crushing her body to his as if he couldn't ever get her close enough. She knew the feeling; there was an intolerable amount of clothes between them. She pushed his jacket off his shoulders and slid her palms over his firm chest. His hands moved up into her hair and ... wait, that wasn't her actual hair. Damn it. She didn't want to break the mood, but she needed this, all of this, to be real.

She moved away. "Sorry," she said, trying to catch her breath. "I want to ..." She gestured to the wig.

"Oh." He looked a little dazed, then gave her a smile that could have almost been sweet, were it not for the blazing lust in his eyes. "Sure." He stepped away from her, and she missed his body the second he did.

God, she had to get a hold of herself. It had been a while since she'd been with a guy, but not so long that a few kisses should have turned her into this absolute wreck of a woman. She walked over to a console table below a gilded mirror, threw her coat over a chair and started to unclip her wig. In the reflection, she saw him sit down on a gold brocade chaise longue and start taking off his shoes. She felt his eyes on her the whole time, and it was almost the same feeling she had when he was photographing her, that feeling of being seen in a way she never had been before. Except this was about a thousand times hotter. She reached for the next clip.

"Slow down."

She looked over her shoulder at him. He settled back on the chaise, his gaze never wavering.

"Take your time," he said, his voice lower than she'd ever heard it. "We're in no rush, are we? And every move you make, Miranda ... god, it's poetry."

Maybe she should have been surprised by his dark, confident intensity, but she wasn't. Or maybe she was too turned on to care. Even though she was burning for him to touch her again, she slowed her movements to a teasing, languorous pace. She let her fingers trail over her neck and shoulders as she took out the grips holding the dark wig in place. Through the mirror, she watched him watch her remove the wig and let her blonde waves tumble free. Their eyes met in the reflection and she was frozen for a second, trapped in his gaze. Nobody had ever looked at her with such unguarded hunger. It was as if all the desire she'd suspected was there, simmering behind his professional mask, had bubbled over at once and now there was no holding it back.

Heart pounding, she turned and crossed the room towards him. She was wound up so tight that each step was almost painful. She stopped at the end of the chaise and put her gold-sandaled foot up on it.

"Would you mind?" she murmured.

He leaned closer. "Not at all." He wrapped one hand around her calf, and she had to hold back a moan at the mere feel of his skin on hers. Dear lord, how much of this would she be able to take? Michael's sandy curls did that unbearably gorgeous flopping-forward thing as he bent over the delicate buckle holding the leather straps of her shoe in place. The customary shiver of relief that came with the undoing of complicated shoes only added another note of pleasure to the ones already surging in her bloodstream. She changed feet and let him unfasten the other shoe, but then he didn't let go of her calf right away; he leaned in and grazed a feather of a kiss over the small indentation the buckle had made on her skin. She closed her eyes as tiny lightning bolts skittered through her.

Taking a deep breath, she placed her foot back on the floor and then moved until she was standing over him, one foot either side of the chaise longue. His hands slid up her thighs to rest on her hips, and for a second the two of them just stayed there, looking at each other, breathing hard. Then his hands tightened on the fabric of her dress, and she lowered herself into his lap and brought her lips to his. This kiss was every bit as spine-tingling as the previous ones, but this time as she caught his lower lip between her teeth and heard him moan, she could also feel him hard beneath her, could feel the heat of his skin through his shirt and her dress, and it still wasn't enough. She brought frantic hands to the front of his shirt and fumbled with the buttons, giving up on kissing him in favour of exposing the body she had been dying to unwrap for weeks.

And oh man, what a body it was. He inhaled sharply as she stroked his well-defined pecs. Miranda's usual artsy, skinny type didn't always work out as often as Michael clearly did. He pulled the shirt off his strong arms and threw it onto the floor, then robbed her of the chance to admire him any further by catching her in another fierce kiss. With one hand he pushed her skirt up her thigh, leaving a trail of sparks in his wake, while the other slipped one delicate strap from her shoulder. His mouth moved to where the strap had just been, and he placed gentle kisses on her sensitive skin as his fingers traced over her breasts. She gasped as he circled the silky fabric over her tight nipple, and the reflexive grind of her hips made him groan into her shoulder, so she did it again, not reflexively this time but one hundred percent on purpose, shuddering as she felt the hard ridge of him beneath her almost certainly soaked panties.

His fingers curled into her thigh, biting deliciously into the flesh. "Jesus Christ, Miranda," he hissed. "You ... I ..."

But he seemed to think better of trying to find words and opted instead to drag her dress up over her head and fling it aside with a disregard for the luxurious fabric that would have horrified the designer but Miranda was more than alright with. Then he flattened his palm against her back and pressed her body forward so he could close his mouth over her nipple, and all thoughts of absolutely anything were obliterated by molten shocks of pleasure. His hands, his lips, his tongue were all that existed. With a small groan, he released her nipple, and if she'd wanted a second to take a breath, he wasn't giving it to her; he moved to her other breast and sucked until she was practically incoherent with lust.

When he slid his hand between them and stroked her gently over her thong, she thought she might lose her mind. The assault of sensation was almost overwhelming. She pulled his lips back to hers and kissed him again, her tongue desperately exploring his mouth as he lifted her body and slid his finger beneath her panties.

"Michael. Oh god. I–" His finger slipped through her wetness and inside her, and she couldn't stop it, she felt herself clench around him and then his thumb was on her clit and she was burying her head in his shoulder as the wave of tension she'd been riding broke around her. He held her tightly as she trembled from the unexpected force of her orgasm. Sweet Jesus, she had never come so fast before.

"You OK there, sweetheart?" he asked, stroking her hair.

"Yes. God, yes." She kissed him wildly, unable to steady her breathing and not even wanting to. "I am ..." What was she? Both satisfied and needing more, blissed out and wound up.

"I've never seen anything more beautiful in my life," he murmured, and although his eyes were still full of that searing heat, she thought she saw something like awe in them too. He kissed her, slow and deep, then pulled away from her lips and said, "Do you have a condom?"

"Yes. Stay here." She dashed to her bedroom and to her nightstand, wanting to kick herself for telling him to stay there. Why had she done that? If he'd followed her, he could have been inside her right now, and that thought banished the last scrap of post-orgasmic satiety and brought back her need full force.

He was still on the chaise longue where she'd left him, and despite her impatience, she gave herself a moment to take in the sight of him. He had no idea how hot he was, what he did to her. But then he said, "Come here," with the kind of smirk that told her that on some level he at least had an inkling.

"I will if you take off your pants," she said, although she was moving towards him anyway because she couldn't not. He stood and did as she asked. She pressed her lips together, hypnotised by the muscles in his arms. Those muscles weren't even particularly doing anything, but she wanted to lick them anyway. *Later*, she promised herself. "Those too." She nodded at his underwear. He cocked an eyebrow and she realised she was still wearing hers, although "wearing" didn't feel totally right, because they were still pushed slightly to one side and clinging damply to her. She peeled them off, never taking her eyes off him.

Naked before her, he took a step closer. His hands closed around her ass and he yanked her to him, pressing her tight against his body. She moaned. He was so hard, so thick.

He ran his tongue up over the side of her neck and said hoarsely, "I have never, ever, wanted someone like this. I don't know what you're doing to me."

She wanted to reply that she felt the same, that she didn't know either, but her knowledge of language was hovering out of reach, blocked by a thick cloud of lust. So she lay back on the chaise longue and pulled him down with her. He took the foil packet from her hand, and though he worked quickly she was sure she lay there for an age, wanting him, waiting for him, needing him to stop this ache between her legs. Finally he crawled over her, his body hovering above hers.

"I need you," she said, but he just smiled slowly.

"Is that right?" He grasped his cock and leaned closer but not close enough. Damn him.

"Are you going to make me beg?" She squirmed closer to him, close enough that he nudged at her entrance, and she smiled in triumph as his breath hitched and he closed his eyes.

"Not tonight," he said, and she wondered if that was a promise of another night when he would, but she had no more time to think about that as he pushed inside her, and oh god *finally*. "Fuck, Miranda, you feel incredible." He dropped a line of kisses along her collar bone.

Incredible ... it didn't even come close, and she didn't understand. This was only sex. She'd done it before. So why did this feel so damn perfect, like he was made for her?

You said you wouldn't fall in love with him.

Shut up.

He silenced her irritating inner voices with a twist of his hips that drove him deeper inside her, making her breath catch in her throat and her eyes roll back in her head. He was watching her, of course he was watching, in that way he did that told her he missed nothing when it came to her. He did it again, and again, at that exact same sweet, perfect angle, and the breath ripped itself from her throat and came out of her mouth in a startlingly loud moan. A devastatingly sexy little smile appeared on his lips as he kept moving and a swirl of silver tension gathered at the base of her spine. She wrapped her legs around his back to keep him right where he was, but she wasn't sure she needed to, because he seemed content to stay there, oh hell yes, right there ...

This time when she came, it seemed to start from some place deep inside her she never knew existed, and it grabbed hold of her and held her tight until her body was shaking and she was letting out cries she didn't recognise. Through the fog of her climax she heard him mutter, "Oh fuck, Miranda", then he shuddered and groaned and dropped his head to her shoulder.

And as she lay in his arms, limp and exhausted and trying to get her heart to calm the hell down, she vowed that she would not let this be it. Once wasn't enough. She'd been foolish to ever think it could have been.

25

MICHAEL was the kind of guy who started his day with instant coffee, a quick shower and a bowl of Crunchy Nut Cornflakes. He was not the kind of guy who started it in a Parisian bed that could comfortably sleep seven, with one hand holding a glass of vintage Krug and the other on the naked arse of a sensationally beautiful actress he'd spent the night with. Yet here he was.

Said sensational woman was trailing her manicured fingernails over his chest in a way that was making his dick stir back to life again, which should surely be a physical impossibility after last night. He hadn't been able to get enough of her. The insatiable hunger had surprised him, but he guessed it was his subconscious telling him to take full advantage of this once-in-a-lifetime opportunity. Miranda had seemed more than happy to oblige.

"Do you know," she drawled, circling his nipple with her finger, "you are incredibly cute when you're overthinking?"

He put his champagne down and pulled her on top of him. "I am not."

She tilted her head. "Not cute, or not overthinking?"

Hand in her hair, he tugged her in for a kiss. "Neither." He was only doing a regular amount of thinking, thank you very much. "Do we have to get out of here anytime soon? I have no idea what time it is." They had fallen asleep ... at some point, and then woken up at some further unknown point, limbs tangled together, and Miranda had ordered a ridiculous champagne breakfast, and at no point had checking the time seemed remotely important.

"Me either. I don't think it's afternoon yet. I paid for late check-out, though."

"You did?" He raised his eyebrows, then felt like a right idiot. Of course she did. She probably did it all the time. People that rich and beautiful didn't need to be rushed.

She brushed his hair off his forehead so tenderly that it gave him a weird, swirling feeling behind his ribs. "Of course. I very much hoped we'd need it."

Oh. Oh. So all those times he'd convinced himself that her flirting was nothing, that he'd been imagining the hints, that she hadn't been seducing him, he was, in fact, being an absolute plank. He never realised he was so bad with women. Or was it just with ones he thought were so completely out of his league? But she really was, wasn't she? She might have been willing to enjoy him as a weekend's distraction, but ...

"So cute," she murmured, running her tongue over his neck and flicking his earlobe with it.

He couldn't argue this time. She had him bang to rights, on the overthinking part, at least. He rolled her over and caught her lips in a ferocious kiss. "Cute?" he said, letting her feel him harden against her.

"Adorable," she said around a gasp.

He reached for the drawer of the bedside table. "We'll see about that."

* * *

Michael wandered around the bedroom he hadn't even slept in. It was every bit as beautiful as Miranda's, and he found it touching that she'd splashed out on this gorgeous two-bed suite even though it appeared she'd had every intention of not needing it. The view was spectacular. He grabbed his camera and took a couple of quick shots.

"Hey." Miranda appeared in the doorway. "I found these under the chaise," she said, holding out his boxers. He suppressed the image of her ordering him to take them off, because they were supposed to be leaving in a minute and he really could not get horny again today. He took a step towards her, but maybe he hadn't quite succeeded in stopping his eyes from darkening at the memory.

"Uh-uh, don't give me that look," she said faux-sternly, before chucking his pants at his head.

Her laughter was like pure golden joy turned into sound, and her smile ... He lifted his camera, because that was a memory he couldn't bear to let fade.

"Michael! What are you ..." She stuck her tongue out at him, so he took a picture of her doing that, too. "Oh god, you're going to sell these, aren't you? They'll be all over the internet by this evening." She was still laughing, thank goodness, but he lowered the camera anyway and looked right at her.

"Hey," he said. "You know I wouldn't do that, right?" He'd taken it in his stride when he found out that Devon had accused him of that kind of behaviour, because who could have blamed him, but things were different now. And he hated, hated, the idea that Miranda could think that badly of him for even a single second.

"Of course I do," she said, so airily that he felt like a twat for even asking. She'd clearly been joking, and he hadn't needed to get sensitive about it.

"Sorry," he said. "Just checking."

She shook her head. "No, I'm sorry. I shouldn't have even joked about it. I trust you." Her eyes sparkled. "Besides, if you wanted to sell something to the press, 'My Parisian Night of Passion with Miranda Janes' would be worth way more than some make-up-free goofy-face picture. And before you ask, I know you won't do that either."

She had that right. The idea of the world knowing anything about last night made him feel sick. Those were his memories, to keep with him and cheer him up when he was a lonely old man.

"The car's here," Miranda said, looking up from her phone. She pulled her blue baseball cap over her blonde ponytail. "You ready?"

Michael put his camera back in its case and picked up his bag. Ready? To leave this suite behind and go back to reality? Hell no. "Sure," he said. "Let's go."

* * *

Ah well. Michael blinked in the bright sunlight as they emerged from the tunnel. *Hello, England.* One more step closer to the end of the weekend. He wished it didn't have to come. He'd have been quite happy to stay here on this train, especially as Miranda had fallen asleep with her head on his shoulder. He'd looked around the carriage, but it was half empty and none of the other passengers seemed to have recognised her, so he let her stay where she was, although he resisted, with great bloody difficulty, the urge to put his arm around her. He couldn't even breathe in the scent of her hair like some weirdo, because she was still somehow wearing her cap. It didn't make for the most comfortable seating position, to be perfectly honest, but he didn't care. He could have stayed there forever.

So of course his phone rang. Miranda jolted awake.

"Hugh, hi," he answered, instantly missing the warm weight of her head against him.

"Hi, Michael. Good weekend?"

"Aye, not bad," Michael replied, because he was British and that was the only permissible response to that question, even if it did make a mockery of the word "understatement".

"Excellent. Listen, I'm calling because I heard about a new gallery that's having an opening-night party on Tuesday. I don't think the gallery itself is going to be anything much to shout about, but there'll be lots of the right people there, so I've got us invites."

"Oh. OK." Michael wasn't sure what to make of Hugh's tone. He sounded decidedly unenthusiastic about the gallery. Wasn't any gallery better than none, which was how many were currently interested in him? But Hugh was the expert. If he thought it was nothing but a good networking opportunity, who was Michael to argue? Ugh. Networking, though.

"I'm bringing Aidan, by the way," Hugh said. "Tuesday's normally date night. Hope you don't mind. You have a plus one too, so feel free to bring someone."

He could feel Miranda's eyes on him. She was right next to him, so she'd be able to hear every word of this conversation. Should he invite her? That was a daft idea, right? Totally inappropriate.

The train passed under a bridge, cutting Hugh off as he was rattling off the details of the party. Michael would have to text him later.

"A gallery opening, huh?" Miranda said casually. "Sounds like a cool opportunity. You're going to go, right?"

"I ... yeah. I guess. This is the way the art world works, Hugh says, schmoozing at parties and all that. I suppose I've got to get used to that sooner or later."

"I am excellent at schmoozing at parties, you know. You want me to come with you?"

He just stared at her for a moment. She was offering to come with him? Why? Like a date? Or because she knew he was beyond shit at this kind of thing and was taking pity on him? What did that offer mean?

Fuck's sake. Look at him, what-does-this-mean-ing all over the place. Did he have no chill?

She grinned at him, bringing his runaway train of thoughts to a grinding halt. "Michael, look. I'm sure you won't be surprised to learn that I don't believe in tiptoeing around stuff."

"Very not surprised."

"So, here it is." She lowered her voice, even though there was no one near them. "Last night was amazing. Truly, one of the best of my life. But what happens now is up to you. We can leave it all in Paris, one wild and wonderful weekend that we'll always remember, and we can go on being friends, if that's what you want. Or …" She turned her body so she could look straight at him, and his eyes found hers as if drawn by magnets. "Or we could see what this – you and me – could be. My offer to come to the party with you stands either way."

He was tempted to say they should be friends. To walk away while it was still a perfect, unsullied memory, to keep it frozen behind glass like a photograph only they could see. He didn't need the complication of dating a movie star. But then he thought about never kissing her again, or holding her again, or making love to her again, and again, and again … who the fuck was he kidding?

"OK," he said, taking her hand in his. "Let's see."

26

MIRANDA'S house felt too quiet. She was vibrating with energy and there was nowhere for it to go. She'd unpacked all her things. She'd caught up on the parts of her skincare regimen she'd neglected this weekend. She'd even gone downstairs and worked out, but still she couldn't settle down.

Paris had been better than she'd ever dared to dream. Her skin tingled just thinking about it. And even better, he hadn't taken the out she'd offered him. He was hers for a little while longer.

She'd seen that he was tempted to run away. Hell, a part of her wondered if it would be better to quit while they were ahead. But she couldn't let go, not yet. The way he'd made love to her was a revelation. In so many ways, he was unsure of himself. He was a man trying to figure out where his life was going to go, and she could see how much that scared him. But in bed, he became the man he was behind the camera. Intensely focused, controlled, confident in his ability to direct her body. She felt a pang of regret at not having invited him to come home with her, but she supposed that sleep was kind of important. And besides, she'd see him on Tuesday. That was only two days away.

Her phone buzzed with a message, and she gave

her heart a firm talking-to for beating slightly faster at the thought it could be from him. *For crying out loud, Miranda, you saw him two hours ago.*

It wasn't from him anyway.

> NORA: I'm expecting a formal offer tomorrow. I know you really want this, so I'm not gonna play total hardball, but I have to put some effort in. We've got reps to protect.
>
> MIRANDA: I wouldn't expect anything less.
>
> MIRANDA: As long as I don't get less than Seb, I'm happy.
>
> NORA: We're going for more. You're the lead, not him.

Miranda chewed on her lip. Nora was right. AJ had sent her a script, and it looked as though it was staying pretty faithful to the book, especially in terms of Damia's prominence as the protagonist. And although she wanted this part so much she could cry, would have done it for a dime if she had to, this was important. She wasn't going to let anyone undervalue her and her work.

> MIRANDA: You're right. I trust you to come away with the goods.

She put her phone down and felt a strange daze come over her. Could it really be? This time tomorrow, could she officially be Damia? Could all her dreams be coming true?

She had to talk to someone. Of course her first

thought was Michael, but she should give him some space. She did the time-difference math and worked out that it was lunchtime in Seattle. Maybe Jen would be around.

"Aunty Rand! Aunty Rand!" Izzy's excitable face filled the screen. Like, totally filled the screen. Miranda could practically see up her niece's nose. "Daddy let us help wash the car! Tommy got super wet."

"That's great, sweetie. Is it all nice and clean now?"

"Yup. Daddy said we did a super good job and that we are the best helpers ever."

"I'm sure you are, baby." Miranda smiled. "Where's your mom? Does she know you have her phone?"

Izzy nodded. "Uh-huh. I'm not allowed to touch her phone anymore unless she says so, because of that time I dropped it in the toilet. She's making our lunch. We're having grilled cheese sandwiches and potato chips and vegetables because Mommy says we have to eat vegetables—"

"OK, Izzy, your lunch is ready." Jen took the phone from her daughter. "Hey, Rand. Bryan! Come eat lunch with the kids while I talk to Miranda! One minute ..." There was some shuffling and a volley of instructions and a shout of "Hi, Miranda!" from her brother-in-law. Miranda's heart warmed, as it always did when she saw the cosy domestic chaos of her sister's life, but the ripple of jealousy that often accompanied the sensation didn't come today.

"So, to what do I owe the pleasure?" Jen asked as she settled into one of the living room chairs.

"Do I need a reason to speak to my favourite sister?"

"Of course not. You just don't normally call at this time, especially without warning. Is everything OK?" A tiny furrow of concern appeared on Jen's brow.

"Everything is more than OK," Miranda reassured her, and she couldn't stop a huge grin spreading over her face. "Everything is fantastic."

"Oh my god, you slept with him, didn't you? The photographer guy." Jen smiled victoriously. "I knew you wouldn't last long."

"Excuse me," Miranda said in mock outrage. "Why did your mind go straight there? Maybe I've had some major professional triumph or something."

"Have you?"

"Yes, actually, although I probably shouldn't say anything yet. But ..." Ah, screw it. She couldn't keep all this bottled up. "But also yes."

Jen cackled with laughter. "I can read you like a book, Randa. So? How was it?"

"Oh god, Jen, it was amazing. He's amazing. We went to Paris for the weekend, and we had the best time."

"Well, you – or he – held out longer than I thought you would. I owe Bryan ten dollars now."

"Jen! You bet on my sex life?"

Jen waved a dismissive hand. "You know I have no other sources of entertainment in my sad little life, babe. So, what now? Just a one-time thing, or have you fallen head over heels again?"

"Um ..." Miranda thought about it. "Somewhere in between, I guess? I'm seeing him again, but I'm gonna try not to get ahead of myself this time. I've been down that road way too many times. There's definitely something there between us, so we're going to see what happens." Even as she said the words, she wondered how true they were – could she really keep a level head this time? Not get far too invested in something that would probably go the same way it always did?

Her sister seemed to be thinking the same thing. "Just be careful, OK? I know it's been a while since you were last in a relationship, but I don't want to see you get hurt again. Or end up having to hurt someone else. Just let things ... be. Go with the flow. Don't try to become the flow."

Miranda rolled her eyes. "Yes, Guru Jen."

Jen looked as though she would say more, but she changed the subject. "Anyway, I can't believe we get to see you soon. Only a few weeks! I ordered the cake, and balloons, and I had that photo of the four of us framed, you know, the one from Palm Springs. I can't wait for this, Rand. Honestly, you have no idea. Getting away from it all ..."

"Yeah, it's going to be so good to spend time with everyone." Her mind conjured an image of the idyllic cabin near the falls, all isolated luxury, and she imagined curling up on the sofa with her family, a glass of wine, and ...

"No, stop. I can see what your mind is doing and you absolutely cannot invite him, Miranda." Jen's voice shattered the fantasy.

"I wouldn't! This is family time." Jeez, she needed to get a grip on her brain.

"That's not why you can't invite him, you dork. 'The more the merrier' might as well be the family motto, and you know Mom and Dad would be thrilled to meet anyone you're dating. It's because it's too damn soon. You'll terrify the poor guy."

Miranda nodded. See, this was why she needed her big sister to talk some sense into her. "You're right. I'm sorry. I was doing it again, and I promise I will make a real effort to stop and play it a bit cooler for once."

"OK. Good." Jen looked unconvinced.

27

"KILL me now," Hugh muttered, downing the remainder of his bright pink cocktail. "I'm terribly sorry, Michael. I wouldn't have suggested we come if I'd known it would be like *this*." He waved his hand around.

Michael had to confess that he wasn't totally certain what *this* meant. Sure, it wasn't exactly what he'd expected. The other few gallery openings he'd ever been to had had a much more exclusive, hipster vibe. Whereas this one ...

"A neon sign Instagram wall. I mean. Are we at a Pretty Little Thing party?" Hugh said.

"Oh hush." Aidan, Hugh's partner, smacked him lightly on the shoulder. "It's ... refreshing. Your breeding is showing, darling."

Michael suppressed a snort. Despite being the poshest person in the world, Hugh did normally take pains not to come across as a snob, for which Michael was extremely grateful. Tonight must finally have broken him. Waiters circulated with lurid cocktails instead of champagne, and the décor said "influencer nightclub" more than "serious art gallery". The room was full of arty types, as expected, but there was also a heavy sprinkling of models and minor celebs. Michael supposed that might mean Miranda would blend in a bit more once she arrived. Why hadn't she arrived yet? She was still coming, right? His heart rate kicked up a notch, but he couldn't work out if it was out of fear that she would bail or sheer excitement at the thought of seeing her again. He'd done nothing for the past two days but relive every second of the weekend, and he'd better not start doing it again now in front of all these people he needed to impress.

He cleared his throat of the tickle in it and his brain of unhelpful thoughts. "So, Hugh, do I need some kind of networking strategy or something? I don't know if you realised, but I'm very, very bad at this."

Hugh chuckled. "Stick with me. There are some useful people here. I want to introduce you to—"

"How about starting with me?" a smooth voice asked. Hugh, Aidan and Michael turned to see a handsome but slightly oily-looking man standing beside them. "Although that would necessitate me introducing myself to you all first. Brad Conway. Thanks for coming." He smiled widely. "I hope you're all having a good time?"

Ah. The gallery owner. Time for Michael to practise being a professional.

"Hugh Humberstone-Ridley," Hugh said with his usual impeccable manners. "This is my fiancé, Aidan Donnelly, and this is Michael Hedley. He's an exceptionally talented photographer."

"Pleased to meet you all. I know your name, of course, Hugh. And yours, Michael."

"Mine?" Christ. *Smooth, Hedley. Really smooth.*

Brad – honestly, what kind of a name for an art gallery owner was Brad? – gave him a wink. "Of course. Photography is my passion, it's most of what we'll do here, so I make sure to keep an eye out for new talent, from all different directions."

Realisation dawned. "You follow me on Instagram. You're TheConMan. I almost blocked you, name like that."

Brad let out a comical sigh. "I know. It's a long story. Anyway, it's fantastic to meet you. I have to go work the room, but I'll come and find you later for a chat."

Hugh made a vague murmur of goodbye that wasn't the friendliest sound Michael had ever heard.

"Oh, by the way," Brad said as he was turning to leave. "I suspect you might already know this, but we'll have some pretty famous faces here tonight. I know they say all publicity is good publicity, but I think everyone would appreciate some discretion with regard to photos and that kind of thing. Sure you understand. Catch you later." And he was off, swooping onto the next group.

"Now, now," Aidan said, staring pointedly at Hugh. "There's no need to bristle. Other people are allowed to speak about etiquette, you know. It's not solely reserved for the landed gentry." He turned to Michael. "Honestly, he's not normally this pissy."

"Aidan," Hugh snapped. He took a deep breath and kissed his fiancé on the cheek. "I need to talk to Michael. Would you please go and find me some wine? Please?"

Aidan rolled his eyes. "Sure. Please be in a better

mood when I get back." He went off in the direction of the bar.

"Sorry," Hugh said. "This is why I try not to bring him to these things."

"It's fine." Michael decided not to tell Hugh that Aidan was hilarious and that he was enjoying this little sneak peek into his mentor's personal life. "Are you OK, though? You seem kind of fed up."

"I'm just not sure it was worthwhile, our coming here. This isn't the kind of place you're going to waste your time on."

"It's not?"

Hugh scoffed. "Of course not. Look around. Brad's clearly just some guy who has more money than sense or taste. We'll find some people to introduce you to, but really. He seems more concerned about his celebrity guests than anything else." The disdain in Hugh's voice was clear.

"Yeah," Michael said, shifting uncomfortably from foot to foot. "About that ..."

Hugh raised an elegant eyebrow.

"I think one of those celebrity guests might be, well, mine."

The eyebrow rose even higher.

"Erm, Miranda Janes is my plus one."

"Oh," Hugh said. "I know she was at the event when we first met, but I'd rather assumed you were there as a friend of Henry's. Are you seeing her?"

How to answer that one? He had barely even asked himself that question. "Maybe?"

"Hmm."

"What?"

Hugh looked around, as if for hidden microphones or something, before saying, "It could be … a distraction, that's all. I'm not denying that publicity can be a good thing, if managed well, but trying to launch a career as an artist at the same time as having a relationship with a movie star …" He shook his head and rolled his shoulders back, and when he spoke again it was in the more relaxed tone Michael knew. "It's just not something I've ever attempted to guide an artist through before, is all I'm saying."

Oh god. Did Hugh think he was making a huge mistake? Was he making a huge mistake? Was this going to blow his career up before it even started? Could his brain please just stop doing this for one fucking second?

And then a familiar scent hit him and all his questions fell away.

"Hey, you," she said.

"Hey."

He turned and took her in. She was breathtaking in a simple navy dress, her hair in a loose plait. She looked outrageously beautiful because she was outrageously beautiful, but she'd obviously gone for a deliberately low-key look, and the thought that she'd done that because she was simply there to support him was touching in a way he couldn't begin to process. He leaned in and gave her a chaste kiss on her flawless cheek, perfectly platonic, but he didn't miss the way her eyes fluttered closed as he did so.

She and Hugh exchanged pleasantries, but Michael wasn't paying attention. Would he get to take her home tonight? They hadn't discussed that. And by home he probably meant hers – he couldn't imagine her in his tiny, unimpressive flat. She belonged in luxury.

He dragged his mind back into the room. "When did you get here? Did you have any trouble?"

"Just now," she replied. "I had Aisling get in touch with the owner about sneaking in the back, which he was only too happy to help with. He seems like a very nice guy. Have you met him yet?"

That explained the "famous face" comment. "Yeah, we met him just before," Michael said. "He's not what I expected."

"Well, people surprise you." Her lips curved into a smile.

"You can say that again," Hugh muttered. Michael had almost forgotten he was there. "I'll leave you to it and go and see where that man of mine has gone. I'll come and find you later, connect you with some people, OK?"

And then they were alone. But not alone. In a crowded room, although he noted that she was attracting relatively little attention. A few glances, of course, but it seemed that people were actually honouring Brad's request. Or perhaps, despite Hugh's disdain, no one in this crowd wanted to be the first person uncool enough to make a fuss.

"You look beautiful," he said, because she did.

"This old thing?" She grinned, then lowered her voice. "I prefer your shirt."

If his hand had been around her waist, his grip would have tightened on it, but he had to settle for making a fist. "You're a menace, Janes."

"So they tell me."

God, he wanted to kiss her. But somehow he didn't think the disinterest of the crowd would last through that.

She laughed. "Sorry. I'll behave. How's the party going?"

He let out a breath. "OK, I guess. Kind of weird, though. Hugh's in a bad mood. I don't think he's very impressed with this place, or Brad. I guess he doesn't think it's serious enough or something?"

"And what do you think?" she asked, her gaze piercing.

"I don't know. He's probably right, right? I don't know anything about this. It's been so long since I was even remotely connected to this world, and even then, back at uni, I never knew how to navigate it. It's not exactly crawling with people like me."

"Good, kind, immensely talented people?"

"You know what I mean."

She smirked at him. "I do. I'm choosing to ignore it. They're all just people, Michael, and you navigate this world the same as you navigate any other – by knowing where you're going."

He could fall in love with her when she talked like this, when her confidence lit her up from within and she made it so easy to believe that anything was possible.

Whoa. Where had that thought come from? He was

not the falling-in-love type. He'd done it precisely once, and it had taken him years. And falling for a movie star was undoubtedly an even less wise move than falling for his best friend had been. *Stop being a dickhead,* he ordered himself.

"And where am I going?" he asked, trying to keep his voice lighter than his thoughts.

"We're going to find Brad," she said decisively. "I need to thank him for helping me slip in unnoticed."

They found him in the main gallery space, standing by a small display of photographs of a busy city and chatting to a woman. He saw them coming and beckoned them over.

"Michael, hey. And Miranda, good to meet you." He exchanged air kisses with Miranda.

"Brad, delighted to meet you," she said, in what Michael now recognised as her full-on charm-the-pants-off-people mode. "Thank you so much for helping me sneak in here. It's always nice not to have to run the press gauntlet."

"No problem." Brad turned to the dark-haired woman he'd been talking to. "Michael, Miranda, this is Kimiko." They each shook her hand. "She's exhibiting here in a few months, and we're very excited about that. Our theme for this season is 'Inside/Out', and she takes these incredible shots of apartment blocks in Tokyo." He gestured at the wall. "See?"

Michael leaned closer to the pictures. "These are wonderful," he said. They truly were – the startling details she'd captured were breathtaking.

"Thank you," she said with a smile.

"Michael's a photographer too," Brad told her. "Although not exhibiting anywhere yet, that I'm aware of?"

"That's right," Michael said, trying not to feel self-conscious about it. How did this guy know so much about him? "Still pretty new to the scene."

"What kind of work do you do?" Kimiko asked.

"Portraiture," he said. He stopped himself from saying more, that he was still trying to figure things out, because he was pretty sure that confessing to a gallery owner, even one his mentor had misgivings about, that he still had no sodding clue what he was doing wasn't really how networking worked.

"Michael has taken the most wonderful pictures of me lately," Miranda interjected. "We've been working together for a while and I'm not sure how I'm going to let anyone else photograph me ever again!"

Brad laughed, but Michael thought he saw the tiniest frown wrinkle Kimiko's forehead.

"So, is that what you do, then? Fashiony, celebrity sort of stuff?" she asked, her voice almost too neutral.

Michael felt a surge of discomfort in his stomach. "I've done celebrity photography in the past, yes," he said, declining to mention the part where he did it standing outside in the rain while getting elbowed in the balls by someone else fighting for the same shot. "And I really enjoyed working with Miranda on her project. But that's not necessarily what my art is focused on, no." *Please don't ask me what my art is focused on.*

But she didn't. She seemed to have lost all interest in the conversation. "I see. Well, it was very nice to meet you, Michael. You too, Miranda. Please excuse me – my drink needs refilling. I'll see you later, Brad." She walked off without a backwards glance, leaving Michael feeling like he'd said completely the wrong thing, although he didn't entirely know what.

But Brad didn't seem as put off as Kimiko had. He was looking curiously at Michael. "You know, you're an interesting one."

"I am?"

Brad nodded slowly. "Very much so. Not many people take your career path."

Michael's mouth went dry. "You know about the ..."

"You were a paparazzo, yes. I have a strange habit of doing an internet deep dive whenever I see a picture that interests me. Which happens often – don't ask me how I ever get any work done. And Devon Grant's wedding photos interested me greatly. I think the world got to know him a lot better through those few shots he released than it had in all the previous years of his career."

"Wow. Thanks." That wasn't the first time he'd heard something like that – the few people who knew Devon well had all expressed similar sentiments in the past. But the intensity with which Brad said it had Michael wondering if Hugh had rushed to judge him too soon.

"That's exactly how I feel about Michael's work," Miranda said, beaming at him. "That's why I hired him. He sees me so well, the real person on the inside, not what the rest of the world sees. The outside versus the inside, you might say." And, to Michael's astonishment, she winked at Brad.

Brad burst out laughing. "Subtle."

Miranda shrugged, not the least bit embarrassed, unlike Michael. He was kind of wishing the ground would swallow him up.

"Our season is full, I'm afraid," Brad continued. "But don't worry, Michael. I'll be keeping an eye on what you do next."

28

MIRANDA watched Brad's retreating back. He seemed like a good guy. Terrible hair, but one couldn't have everything. The important thing he had was an art gallery, and now he also had Michael on his radar. This was shaping up to be a great night already.

"Hey," she said to Michael. "Why don't you show me around the rest of these photographs? You can tell me whether they're any good and I'll pretend to understand." She smiled at him, and he returned it, but it didn't reach his beautiful eyes.

"Sure," he muttered, avoiding her gaze.

"What's wrong?"

"Nothing." He walked them closer to a collection of black-and-white portraits hanging from the ceiling on wires. "These are good."

She waited for him to say more, but he didn't. OK. Something had clearly pissed him off. Was it her? It must have been.

"Michael?"

"What?"

"Please tell me what's wrong. Did I do something?"

He looked around them and sighed. "Look, not here, OK?"

God, she had pissed him off. She should throw on

a smile, leave him to it and talk about it later. But she couldn't. She couldn't bear him being unhappy with her. She never wanted him to even be unhappy in her presence. She wanted only good things for him.

"Come with me," she said, walking across the room and towards the corridor that led to the back-of-house area she'd come in through. She figured it would be quiet back there, and it was; there was no one in sight. "OK. What did I do?"

Michael looked at the ground. "It's ... Never mind. It's just me being a dick."

"Hey." She put her fingers under his chin and tipped up his face. "No. If I did something to piss you off, I want to know about it. Not everything is your fault, Michael."

He let out a long breath. "Ah, fuck. It's ... It was just ... I don't know. What you did back there, talking about my work and hinting that Brad should book me. It kind of bothered me, I suppose." He still wasn't looking at her. His head was tilting down again, and that damn curl dropped over his forehead in that damn way that made it hard to focus on his words.

"I don't understand. I thought you were here to network. I know you don't like promoting yourself, so I was only trying to help."

"I know," he said, finally looking at her and, after a quick glance down the hall, putting his hands on her arms. "I know," he repeated more softly. "This isn't my comfort zone, you're right, and I know that I need pushing out of it." He shrugged, and she saw a world of confusion and apprehension swirling in his eyes. "But the art world, it's strange. I'm still trying to figure out how it all works, but I don't think it's like Hollywood. Some people are just so ... snobby, I guess. I mean, did you see Kimiko's face when she said the word 'celebrity'?"

The woman's face hadn't done anything, in Miranda's opinion, but she'd been in England long enough to know that one could start a war with a nose wrinkle if the circumstances were right.

Michael ran a hand through his hair. "I think ... I don't know. I guess I just don't know what the best approach is yet, and I need to figure that out. For myself."

"Ah." She smiled ruefully at him. "And I came in like a brash arrogant American and steamrollered all over everything and embarrassed you."

"No," he said quickly.

"Relax. I'm kidding, kind of. I know you don't think that of me. But I'm not entirely wrong, am I?"

His shoulders slumped. "Not entirely. I got embarrassed, yeah. But that's my hang-up, and something I need to get over. You were trying to help, and it's true I'll never get anywhere if I'm too afraid to put myself out there. Just ..." He scanned the area again and then put his arms around her. "This isn't something you can do for me, and it isn't something that comes easily. I'm not like you."

"I know," she said, relishing the feel of his body next to hers. "I'm sorry. I know I can be kinda pushy."

"I'm glad you are," he said, his voice lowering a notch. "We wouldn't have had Paris if you weren't."

The mention of the city was all it took to send a flood of memories crashing over her, and with them all the desire she had for this man. Paris had done nothing to lessen it; she wanted him even more now than she had before. Damn, why did they have to be in such a public place?

Michael must have been thinking the same thing. He took her hand and led her further down the corridor. The entrance to the back-of-house area was just ahead, but it would probably be locked. But Michael tried a door to their left she hadn't seen before, and a shiver of anticipation ran down her spine when it opened to reveal a huge empty storeroom. He pulled her inside, and her eyes scanned the space, checking for cameras. She didn't see any, but then the room was plunged into darkness.

"I found the light switch," Michael murmured into her ear. "Better safe than sorry, right?"

And then before she could answer, he yanked her to him and kissed her. Her hands flattened on his shoulders as he crushed her lips to his, hard and bruising, and she was glad she'd gone for a neutral lip and simple hair tonight, because he was kissing her with no regard to either. She slid one hand around the back of his neck and pulled him closer. Her lips parted for his tongue as her back hit the wall and the full length of his body pressed against hers, the way it had that night in Paris. That hadn't been a one-off, then, a passion born of the romantic setting and his memories and their pent-up desire. The fire between them was real, and the flames licked at her now as he groaned into her mouth and ran his hand over her hip and up to her breast.

She arched into his touch, and then it was gone, the bastard. His body was still pressed to hers, but now he was only grazing one teasing finger down her bare arm.

"What would you let me do to you," he murmured, "here in the dark?"

He sounded almost casual, but she could feel him hard against her, and the sensation made her want to lose control, to let him take it from her, and to hell with where they were and who might find them.

"Anything," she said, a confession, a reckless challenge, a desperate plea.

Then his body left hers, and she missed the pressure of it until she felt him drag her panties down to her knees. He left them there, and something about the slight restriction made her feel deliciously wanton. She pulled up her skirt, baring herself to him. She was rewarded with his tongue along her thigh, its upward trail branding her with its heat, until she could feel his breath on her clit.

"Anything?" he murmured, his voice reverberating through her. "You know, I think you would."

And then oh, Jesus, his tongue was on her and his hands were gripping her ass and she bit her lip to hold in the noises she wanted so badly to make. With every circle his gorgeous, talented tongue made around her clit, she felt her legs start to shake. It was too much and at the same time she needed more, she needed …

"Michael …" she gasped. "I …"

"You need something, sweetheart?" he said against her. He moved one hand around to the front of her thigh, tantalisingly close but still far too far.

"I need …" Why did he think she could form words right now, let alone whole sentences?

He chuckled. He was doing this on purpose. "I was always taught that if you want something, you should ask nicely." He resumed licking her clit, his fingers stroking maddeningly at the very top of her thigh.

"Damn it, Michael. I want your fingers inside me. Please."

"Of course." He eased one finger inside her, and she moaned at the feel of it. Something fluttered at the base of her spine as he put his mouth back on her and moved his finger slowly, gently. "Like this? Or …" He thrust another finger inside her, harder this time, the gentleness gone, and she gasped and felt herself tighten around him. His tongue flicked back and forth over her clit in a relentless rhythm as he worked her with his fingers, and the quake in her legs took over her whole body. Miranda stuffed her knuckles into her mouth as the orgasm tore through her, white-hot electricity that flared behind her eyes in the pitch-black room.

As she came back down to earth, she had to push his head away from her oversensitive clit. "Jesus *Christ*."

Pulling her panties back up, he stood and took her still-shaking body in his arms. He kissed her sweetly and she kissed him back, tasting herself on his lips as he cradled her close, stroking her back. Goddammit, how on earth was she supposed to not fall in love with him when he made her come like that then held her like she was something delicate and rare? Couldn't he at least demand a blowjob or something? Although Miranda knew that if he did, she'd drop to her knees without a second thought.

"You know," Michael said. His voice was relaxed, but there was a slight rasp to it that sent a rush of heat to her core. "I really hate networking. You want to get out of here?"

He should be here. This kind of thing was important to his career. They should tidy themselves up, go find Hugh, talk to people. He needed to make connections, be seen at the right places.

"I'll call Frank."

29

MIRANDA lifted her head off Michael's chest and propped herself up to look at him. Her eyes were sparkling, and her hair was a just-fucked mess. He'd never seen anything so beautiful.

"OK, so," she said. "Don't take this the wrong way, but how did you get so good at that? I mean, you've never mentioned any other girlfriend than Cleo, and you don't strike me as the playboy type. But boy, do you have *skills*."

"Just naturally talented, baby," he said, with the creepiest leer he could manage. She hit him in the chest. "No. You're right, I'm not the playboy type, and I haven't had many girlfriends, but I've probably been around more than you think." He shrugged.

"Go on."

He raised an eyebrow. "Really? You want to talk about this?"

"Yes," she said matter-of-factly. "It's only fair. You know everything about my love life, I assume, because the whole world does. But I know nothing about yours. Tell me everything. I'm nosey."

She had a point, he supposed. The world knew about her every date, her every relationship, her every heartbreak. He had no idea how the press hadn't caught wind of the two of them yet. It was only a matter of time.

"OK." He blew out a breath in preparation for this strange dive down memory lane. "Obviously Cleo was my first, and we were sixteen. And then by the time we broke up, I was twenty and very aware I'd spent the whole of my late teens with one girl. I guess I felt I had to make up for lost time, so I basically shagged my way through the art department of the university."

"Oh my. I wasn't expecting that." She did indeed look kind of shocked, which Michael found amusing. This had happened before, though. No one ever expected him to have had a slutty student phase, not that that was anything to be ashamed of.

"Yeah, well. I did calm down eventually. Since uni, there haven't been nearly so many women. A few very short-term flings, a friends-with-benefits thing with this woman from my gym. And ..." Should he say this? It was already a deeply weird conversation. He might as well make it even weirder. "I suppose if you want to thank anyone for my 'skills', as you call them ..."

"Please, tell. I should send her a fruit basket or something."

"OK. You have to promise you will never tell Cleo this."

She crossed her finger over her heart. Well, her naked breast, to be precise, and Michael couldn't resist following suit and brushing her nipple with his thumb, eliciting a small gasp.

"Stop distracting me. I promise."

In for a penny ... "I slept with Priya a few times."

Miranda's hand flew to her mouth. "Cleo's roommate, Priya? From the wedding? Isn't she gay?"

He smiled. "Pansexual. With the attention span of an easily distracted goldfish. Anyway, they'd thrown a party one night, the kind that doesn't really stop, people just pass out in various corners. Cleo had a guy in her room, and someone was asleep on the sofa, so Priya said I could crash in her room. And we were tipsy and horny and bored, so we had sex. And then it happened again on a few more occasions."

Miranda still looked adorably surprised. "And what, she became your sex instructor or something? Because I can see why you didn't tell Cleo that."

Michael laughed. "No. That would have been weird. Although I suppose it was weird enough in its own way. Priya does not have any kind of filter, so the next morning we ended up having a hungover and bizarre conversation about ... how it went, I suppose? It was very surreal." He smiled at the memory. He had never had a post-shag performance review before, but he'd rolled with it, the way you just had to do when Priya started on something. "And I told her that I'd scared a lot of women off in the past by being too intense, in bed, I mean. And in life too, probably. She said to embrace it, and to sleep with women who already knew that about me and would be into it."

"Hmm." Miranda's blue-green eyes were fixed on him. "So if I'd propositioned you that first night we met, at the wedding before I knew you, you would have turned me down?"

He bent his head and kissed her, because he would never get tired of kissing her. "Are you kidding me? Of course I fucking wouldn't have." He'd been fascinated by Miranda for years, and that night at the wedding, he hadn't been able to take his eyes off her. "But I might have … held back."

She stroked his jaw. "Then I'm glad I waited," she said in a low murmur.

He was too. As much as he'd felt – still felt – that he was punching way above his weight, he'd somehow known from the second his lips first touched hers that she wanted what he had to give. When he was with her, there was no space to think about what he should or shouldn't do. All he knew was that he had to show her how much he wanted her, how much his body craved hers, how he would do anything to make her fall apart in his arms. He was addicted to finding and memorising the thousand little ways of making her breath hitch. Like when he trailed his fingers over her right hip like this …

But she caught his hand and brought his fingertips to her lips, kissing them gently. "How come you never told Cleo about Priya?" she asked. "Do you think she would have cared?"

He lay back and thought about it. "I'm not sure. She wouldn't have been jealous or anything. That's never been an issue for us. I reckon she would have thought it was a bit odd, because she and I were so close and she and Priya were so close. The two of us certainly thought it was odd, so I guess that's why we didn't say anything at first, and then the more time passed, the stranger it would have been to bring it up. I think it's probably the only thing I've never told her. Or at least it was, until recently ..."

A familiar lump came to his throat as he let himself think about Cleo. Their friendship was always going to change now that she was half a world away, but he shouldn't have let his anger and loneliness drive even more distance between them.

"She misses you too, you know," Miranda said softly. "She loves you as much as she always did. I can't stand to see both of you in pain when it's so unnecessary. Just pick up the phone and call her."

"I will," he said, because he finally understood that it really was as simple as that. He pulled Miranda on top of him. "Later."

* * *

The worst thing about the time difference was the waiting, Michael realised. He'd decided to get over himself and phone Cleo today, but her today wasn't the same as his today, so after leaving Miranda's house this morning, he'd been forced to wait until it was a sociable hour in LA. As soon as it was, he'd texted her, asking when she had time to chat.

He wasn't all that surprised when his phone rang at three thirty that afternoon. First thing in the morning for her. And it made him feel kind of shit, because it meant that she was jumping at the chance to speak to him, when he had been doing everything he could to avoid talking to her for weeks.

"Hi," he said as Cleo's face appeared on his screen. Her curly hair was all over the place, because she'd just woken up, but she never cared about anything like that, not with him. They'd been through far too much together for that.

"Hi," she replied, and for one awful second, they didn't seem to have anything to say to each other, for the first time in twenty years, and then he realised that there was only one thing to say.

"I'm sorry. I'm so sorry, Cleo. I've been avoiding you, and it was absolutely shit of me, and you didn't deserve it, and I'm sorry, and I'll never do it again."

She smiled. "Good. You should be sorry, you arsehole. But I get it."

He smiled back, but not easily. "You do? I'm not sure I do."

"Yeah, of course I do. I know how you feel about Margaret, and I knew that once you found out about her and your mam that you'd freak out, which was why I didn't tell you. I hated keeping that from you, so I'm sorry too, for that."

"No," he cut in. "You don't have anything to be sorry for. It wasn't your story to tell."

"Perhaps. But you know I hate keeping secrets from you."

"I know." He hated it too, which was why he knew that he'd be spilling his whole guts before this conversation was through. He was half amused and half nervous about her reaction.

"Have you read the letter yet?" Concern filled her chocolate-brown eyes.

He sighed. "No. I've talked to my mam and I feel … mostly OK about the whole thing, I suppose. I trust her to do the right thing for her, and it does feel different this time. I don't think she's being taken advantage of or anything, for once. But that's them. Me and her … I don't know. I still don't know if I'm interested in anything she has to say, and … wait. How did you know about that?"

"Your mam told me, of course. But she sent me one too."

"She did?"

"Yes." A note of hesitance entered Cleo's voice. "Do you want to know what mine said?"

Did he? He imagined that at least some of it was the same as his, and he had been very strenuously avoiding even thinking of the damn thing since his mam had given it to him. In the end, intense curiosity won out.

"OK. Hit me with it."

Cleo chuckled. "Sorry. I know you have complicated feelings about all this. But the way you're bracing yourself, you'd think it was for being run over by a train and not hearing the very polite words of an old woman."

He laughed despite himself, just grateful that the recent distance between them hadn't affected her ability to rip the piss out of him. "Yeah, yeah, I know. I've got issues, we know this. Tell me what she said."

"Well, it was all very restrained and refined, obviously. But more humble than I ever would have imagined in a million years."

Humble? Margaret didn't know the meaning of the bloody word.

"She said that she owed me an apology," Cleo continued. "That she understood why I lied to her all those years. She said– Oh, what was it? Hang on." Cleo's face disappeared from the screen as she leaned to one side, and Michael heard the sound of her rummaging through a drawer. When she reappeared, she was holding a piece of thick cream paper. "OK, she said, 'I would say that I forgive your dishonesty, but we both know that you neither want nor need my forgiveness, because I have come to understand that I am not the wronged party. I placed you in an impossible situation, and you did what you felt best. For many years I thought I was doing the same, but it is clear now that my actions were harmful to the people I should have treated with more care. I do not expect you to believe me, or, if you do, I would not be surprised if you think this letter nothing more than the words of a lonely old woman who is doing too little, too late. Perhaps there is much truth in that. Nevertheless, this apology is owed to you, and I offer it with no condition or expectation.'" Cleo looked up from the letter. "That was pretty much the gist."

Michael didn't say anything. He wasn't sure what he could say. The formal tone was unsurprising, but the content ... An unreserved apology. No manipulation. No condescension. No underlying hints of disappointment. Just the truth. Something that had been absent from their family dynamic for far too long.

But of course, he didn't need to say anything at all. Because this was Cleo, the person who knew him better than anyone else on the planet.

"I know, right? This whole stunned goldfish thing you've got going on was pretty much what I did for a full half hour when I first read it."

"Yeah," he said, finally pulling a word out of his arse. "I mean ... yeah."

"I don't know what yours says, but I imagine the sentiment is similar. I do believe she's seen the error of her ways, for what it's worth." Cleo gave a little shrug. "But that's easy for me to say. She's not my grandmother, and I live thousands of miles away."

Michael opened his mouth to protest that Cleo was family and always had been, but she jumped in before he could say a word.

"It's different for me, especially now. There's no denying that. It doesn't mean I love you and Liz any less."

She was right. It didn't. But something tore at a corner of his heart anyway. Life was moving on in wonderful ways, but that didn't mean there weren't parts of his old life that he missed.

"So, anyway," Cleo said brightly, because one of her unfailing talents, one of the many things that made her a brilliant interviewer, was knowing the precise moment a change of subject was needed. "What have you been doing with yourself while you've been avoiding me?"

"Well, I assume my mam's told you about Hugh. That's been pretty interesting."

She beamed a smile so big Michael was concerned her face might split. "I'm so happy for you, Michael, you have no idea. I knew it wouldn't take long for someone to recognise your talent. How did he find you, or you find him, or what?"

He couldn't believe he hadn't told her any of this. He'd limited their communication to basic texts for so long that she didn't know how the best opportunity he'd had so far had come about. Or who had brought it about. Ah, bollocks. The minute he got onto this subject, her reporter instincts would be sparked and she'd find out just how much he'd been keeping from her. *Here goes ...*

"It was through Miranda Janes, actually. She dragged me to this party Courtney's Henry was throwing, and I met Hugh there."

Cleo narrowed her eyes. "And that's another thing, I've seen all those photos of Miranda and she told me you took them! I'm not going to lie, mate, it hurt that I didn't know that."

He felt it in his chest, the pain that he'd caused her, and he wished that he could turn back time and not act like such a massive twat. "I'm so sorry, Cleo. She first messaged me the day after we had that conversation, and I was still kind of reeling from it, and then she asked me to be discreet about it, and then more time passed and I was still being a dickhead, so ..."

She waved her hand. "Hey, don't worry about it. It's

done, we're cool," she said, and Michael felt a rush of affection for her and her endless capacity for forgiveness, her ability to move on. She was the best. "The photos are stunning, Michael. I mean, I know she's a fucking goddess to begin with, but I don't think anyone else in the world could have captured what you did. You work well together."

It was a totally innocent comment, and there was nothing in Cleo's tone that suggested she thought they had anything other than a professional relationship. But he felt his face redden anyway.

"Yeah. So. About that ..."

"You shagged her!" Cleo's hand flew to her mouth. "Sorry. That was crass. I am sure one does not 'shag' Miranda Janes. But you totally did, didn't you? It's written all over your face."

He sighed. Him and his stupid face that she knew so bloody well. "Yes. Although you're right, I wouldn't have put it quite like that."

She gave him a shrewd look. "Then how would you put it?"

Good question. How to encapsulate how he felt about her, what they were like together, what they were doing ...

"Erm ... I don't know. She took me to Paris last weekend, and stuff happened. And now we are, in her words, seeing what this could be." He shrugged. "I don't really know what that means yet. She came to a gallery opening last night as my date, so ..."

Cleo squealed, and he was certain that she'd be

clapping her hands together like a small child if one of them wasn't holding her phone. "This is so exciting! You've fancied her for, like, ever. And she's the best, such an amazing person. Too sweet by far for your miserable arse, of course."

"Oh, I know," he said. A ridiculous soft smile spread over his face before he could stop it, and he braced himself for the inevitable piss-taking.

She didn't disappoint. "Oh my god, if you could see yourself!" she said gleefully.

He rolled his eyes, feigning annoyance but really just glad they were back to normal again. "I can see myself, Clee. We're on a video call and my face is right there on my screen."

"So you can see that you've totally got it bad for her?"

His smile faded as reality hit him in the face. Did he? Should he?

"Hey, what's the matter?" Cleo's glee was eclipsed by concern.

Where to start? He blew out a huge breath. "I mean, I don't know how I feel about any of this. Obviously, she's amazing. She's this force of fucking nature, and she decided she wanted me, and now ... she has me, I guess? Which I am not complaining about. There's something there between us, that's for sure. And when I'm with her ... I'll spare you the details."

She gave him a mock grimace. "Please do."

"But how long for, Cleo? We're seeing what this could be, but let's be real, what can it be? She'll be off filming ... something again soon." He stopped himself just in time from revealing the news about *An Ocean of Fallen Stars*, which wasn't yet official. "And I'll still be here, a struggling artist. She never sticks with one guy for too long, everyone knows that. And it's not even public knowledge yet, so what will happen when it gets out and we're under that scrutiny, and—"

"Michael," Cleo's calm voice cut in. "Calm your tits, will you? Take a breath."

He did as he was told, because he realised he had in fact turned into a blithering idiot.

"Listen," she continued. "I know how you feel. I really do. I have been there, exactly where you are, and I know it's confusing and terrifying."

He wanted to protest that it wasn't the same, but it was exactly the same, the only difference being that Cleo's situation had happened to her and not to him. But that felt like a big difference. At least to him.

"The only advice I can give you is to just go with the flow. Don't get all in your head about it."

"You have met me, right?"

She smiled. "Once or twice, yes. I know that's asking a lot. But try."

"I will," he said, and he meant it. Because whatever this was, this thing he was trying so hard not to over-analyse, he wanted to see if he could keep it, at least for a while.

30

THERE it was, in black and white.

Miranda Janes to play lead in An Ocean of Fallen Stars *adaptation.*

The headline she'd waited and worked for. The whole world knew that she, Miranda Janes, was Damia.

COURTNEY: You did it!

CLEO: Was there ever any doubt?

COURTNEY: You're going to blow everyone away. I can't wait to see you in it.

COURTNEY: Wait, are they doing the dragon horse things? Do you have to learn how to ride a dragon horse?

MIRANDA: Thank you, ladies.

MIRANDA: And I already know how to ride a horse horse.

MIRANDA: I don't think there are dragon horse riding classes.

Miranda smiled at her phone. She loved that her friends were so excited for her. They knew how much this meant to her.

COURTNEY: And you'll be opposite the very delicious Seb Akao *wiggles eyebrows*

Hmm. Should she tell them? This was a good opportunity. She knew that Cleo already knew, but she also knew that Cleo would never break Michael's confidence by bringing it up before Miranda did.

> MIRANDA: Well, delicious as he may be, my attention is elsewhere ...
>
> COURTNEY: ????????
>
> MIRANDA: I may or may not be somewhat involved with a certain photographer.

Courtney replied instantly with a string of emojis, not all of which made much sense, but never mind.

> CLEO: Eek! He told me yesterday and I am SO happy.
>
> MIRANDA: You're not mad that I had a secret crush on your ex-husband and never told you about it?
>
> Cleo: I'm mad that *he* never told me about it.
>
> CLEO: (not really)
>
> COURTNEY: I am mad that I am still in stupid Nashville and not in London to get all the tea.
>
> COURTNEY: You can tell me all the juicy stuff you don't want Cleo to hear ;)
>
> Cleo: *la la la not listening*

Miranda laughed, her heart full of joy. Today was the best day ever, and it was still only eight a.m. Which meant ...

MIRANDA: Court, you're still in Nashville? Isn't it the middle of the night over there?

COURTNEY: Yeah. Can't sleep.

MIRANDA: Everything OK sweetie?

COURTNEY: I'll be fine.

That didn't sound good. Was something up with Courtney? She started typing another message, but ...

COURTNEY: I should try to get some rest though.

CLEO: Yeah, me too. It's like midnight here.

CLEO: Have a great day, M xx

MIRANDA: Sweet dreams both of you xxxx

She put down her phone, still a little concerned for her friend. But then it buzzed again.

MICHAEL: On my way.

A huge smile broke out on Miranda's face. She had an awesome day planned. Just the two of them, spending time together. No photo shoots or work events – just fun. She couldn't wait.

* * *

"Hey, you," Michael said as soon as Miranda closed the door behind her. He pulled her into his arms and bent his head to hers for a kiss so sweet that she almost abandoned her resolve to spend some time with him doing fully clothed things. Wouldn't it be much nicer to stay here, like this, his arms around her waist and his lips on hers and ...

Well, yes, it probably would. But she was sure, so sure, that this thing between them was more than just sex, and she wanted to test that theory. She pulled reluctantly away.

"So, what do you think?" She turned to show off her appearance.

Michael nodded appraisingly. "Very good. Pretty unrecognisable."

"Only pretty?" She glanced in the mirror in the hallway. She was wearing the brunette wig again, plus a pair of black-rimmed glasses, heavy black eyeliner, and contouring that made her face look almost gaunt.

He reached out and took a lock of fake hair between his fingers. "To anyone else I'd say almost totally," he said, his voice soft. "But you can't fool me, pet. I look way too closely at you for that."

"You big creep," she said playfully, but she couldn't stop the heat from rising to her cheeks when she thought of the way he watched her when she undressed for him, when he touched her, when he made love to her.

Hey, Miranda. Daytime thoughts, please.

"Anyway," she said. "I thought we could go out today."

"Out?" His brow creased.

"If that's cool with you." Miranda was never one to curse her situation, but she allowed herself a brief second to wish they could just walk around without the risk of upending his life.

He seemed to think it over for a second, then he gave her the cutest little half-smile. "Yeah, cool. Let's go out. It'll be fine."

"Fabulous. It's such a gorgeous day. I thought we could go take a walk in Hyde Park, and then grab some lunch, maybe at Henry's hotel again, and the exhibition at the Tate Modern is supposed to be worth seeing, and then … what?" He was looking at her, the expression on his face half amused, half indecipherable.

"Nothing," he said, a little sheepishly. "You're just so beautiful when you get excited about stuff."

God, this man. He had to stop making her heart melt like that. She kissed him, quickly so she wouldn't get distracted again, and so she wouldn't do anything ill-advised like blurt out exactly how she was feeling. Her sister's instruction not to terrify him kept ringing in her ears.

"Let me grab my purse and I'm all set," she said with an insouciance she didn't feel, had never felt in his presence and maybe never would.

She led him to the car, and they sat back in its tinted-windowed comfort as Frank drove them across the city.

"So, you spoke to Cleo," she said, tracing circles on his palm with her finger.

"Yeah," he replied, and she loved the warmth that settled into his features. There was an ease about him today that she didn't realise had been missing, and she assumed that was because he'd repaired his friendship with Cleo. "We had a really good talk. I apologised for pushing her away, and she forgave me for being such a dick."

"You weren't a dick, Michael."

"Yes, I was. I couldn't handle what I was feeling, so I refused to face it, to face her." He squeezed her hand. "Thank you for encouraging me to call her."

She brought their hands to her lips and kissed his fingers. "You would have done it eventually."

"Yeah, I would have." He grinned. "She was very pleased to hear about *this*, by the way."

"I know. We messaged this morning." She couldn't stop herself, pictures started flashing through her mind: the four of them – her, Cleo, Michael and Devon – hanging out, in LA, in London, maybe they could take a vacation together sometime, maybe to Courtney and Henry's island, the six of them could spend time together ...

"Hey, we're here," Michael said, breaking into her reverie. He looked at her curiously. "You OK?"

"Yes. I was miles away." *And miles ahead of myself.* She recovered her usual bright smile. "Let's go walk."

* * *

Hyde Park was beautiful in the sunshine. And big. So big. How could there be so much space in the middle of such a dense city? Not that Miranda minded, not one bit. It meant that she could walk hand in hand with Michael without anyone coming anywhere near enough to recognise her.

Not that they were holding hands right now, because Michael had stopped to take a picture of a parakeet. She didn't want to break his concentration, so she just watched him follow the bright green bird with his camera lens. He seemed to be taking the task as seriously as he took, well, everything, but then he turned around with a smile that made her heart do some kind of strange skip in her chest.

"Fuck this," he said. "Birds are too hard. You've got to be unbelievably quick to do birds." He put his camera away and reached for her hand again, casually, as if he didn't even realise he was doing it.

"I thought you were quick," she said, intertwining her fingers with his and wondering why this felt as thrilling as when Bobby Hudson had held her hand on the sixth-grade field trip to the aquarium. "Wasn't that how you got that badass picture of me at the BAFTAs?"

He chuckled. "It was pretty badass. But that wasn't bird quick. Besides, I should confess that getting that shot was probably mostly luck. That's what the paparazzi game is all about, at the end of the day. Patience, and a shit-ton of luck."

For once, that shadow hadn't appeared on his face, the one that usually did when he mentioned his former career. Miranda decided to take advantage.

"I know there's a whole lot of negative stuff about the paparazzi, and I know you don't feel great that you did it, but you were certainly good at it, and there must have been something about it to make you stick with it so long." She swung his hand in hers, as if to remind him that it was a gorgeous day, they were somewhere beautiful, and this conversation didn't have to go down a dark path.

A sliver of the shadow flitted across his face, but mostly he looked thoughtful. "I guess ... I don't know. I sort of fell into it, as a way to make some quick money, which I really, really needed at the time. And then I discovered I was pretty good at it, even without crossing any of the lines I'd drawn for myself, and for someone who'd always been shit at most things, that felt ... refreshing. By the time the novelty wore off, I suppose I'd just got stuck. It had become what I did, who I was, so I kept doing it, even though the money got worse over the years and there were far better things I could have been doing."

He fell silent for a minute, but she didn't think he was done. It felt as though he were trying to confess something, almost.

"But yeah, if I'm honest, there were some things that were alright. Like, some people – the reality TV types, some of the footballers – did actually want you there. I built up some decent relationships with some of them – they'd drop me a message if they wanted me to be somewhere to get a good shot of them. I did as much of that as I could, so I didn't have to do the shadier stuff. And those guys, they knew their time in the limelight was short, so they just wanted to live their best lives and make the most of it all. They're shrewder businesspeople than you'd think, some of them."

He tipped his face to the sky, then looked at her,

one of those deep, intense looks he did so well. "I've never told anyone this, and it's kind of weird telling you, because you've been on the other side of it, and not always in a good way. But …"

"You can tell me anything, you know that." She squeezed his hand.

He squeezed hers back. "Yeah. Yeah, I do." He took a deep breath. "On the best days, when I got lucky and I got a great shot of someone who was perfectly happy to be out in the public eye … there was a kind of magic in it. Like, some moments, everything seemed to align, and I'd feel like I'd captured someone as they truly would want to be seen in that moment."

Did he realise that his face and voice had grown more animated as he talked? Did he know he was radiating a confidence that she didn't think she'd seen before? Was it weird that she was finding him ridiculously sexy while he was talking like this about a job that, at times, had been the bane of her existence?

"Like that picture of me," she said softly.

"Exactly." He nodded. "God, in that moment, you were … there aren't even words. But I got to capture it in a photo, and the world got to see it."

She smiled. "I'm glad you did."

He briefly scanned the area, then leaned in and dropped a soft kiss on her lips. "Me too."

31

AS Michael walked down Miranda's street, he couldn't help noticing how blue the sky was, how green the leaves of the trees were, how textured the road beneath his feet was.

It's not textured, you ridiculous tit. It's broken, like half of London is broken. This was inescapably true. But something seemed to have happened to Michael, and he was seeing things with an impossibly rose-tinted glow. He had an unnerving sense that he was about three minutes away from swinging around a lamp post and greeting a bird like some guy in an old movie.

Was this what a perfect day with Miranda did to him? And yesterday had been perfect. They'd walked around for hours, enjoying the freedom of London in the sunshine. They'd had afternoon tea in the hotel they'd done the first photo shoot in. They'd wandered hand in hand around the Tate Modern. They'd gone for a drink in a bar that was quiet enough and had enough darkened corners that no one would have spotted Miranda even without her disguise.

And then they'd gone back to her place and he'd spent hours of the night exploring new ways of making her gasp and moan. He was so busy remembering the way she'd shuddered as he'd kissed the back of her neck that the deep voice behind him made him jump out of his skin.

"Michael fucking Hedley."

Michael closed his eyes. He knew that voice. Maybe when he turned around, the owner of that voice wouldn't be standing in front of him.

No such luck.

"Baz," he said flatly. Of course it was fucking Baz. His former self-appointed mentor. The most ruthless pap in the city. The man responsible for exposing Cleo and Devon to the world.

Fuck this guy.

"Long time no see, Mike."

His name wasn't Mike. No one ever called him Mike. Except this prick.

"What do you want, Baz?" Maybe he shouldn't piss the guy off – he knew how capable Baz was of making someone's life a misery – but there seemed little point in niceties. Baz knew Michael didn't like him. He'd probably always known it, but for reasons best known to himself, Baz had tried to take Michael under his wing and teach him how to be a better pap. Better, of course, meaning the fucking worst.

"Is that any way to greet an old friend? Although looks like you're going up in the world, eh? Miranda Janes. Well, well, well."

There went Michael's last shred of foolish hope that Baz's being here was just a coincidence. He had no idea what kind of tip or instinct had led Baz here, and it didn't matter. He sighed. They were too far down the street for Baz to get a meaningful shot now, but he must have taken something already.

"What do you have, Baz?"

"Well, there's the thing, mate."

"I'm not your mate."

Baz ignored him. "You're a hard man to snap, Mike. But I suppose you know that. Learned from the best, after all, didn't you?"

Fuck's sake. This man was insufferable. "You taught me some useful things, aye. But let's not fanny about, yeah? What do you want?"

"I want something better than this, mate." Baz held out his camera so Michael could see the shot of a guy who could have been anybody leaving through Miranda's gate with his head lowered and his body hunched. Michael didn't bother biting back his smirk. This was a shit shot, worth nothing.

"Bad luck. Mate." Sod this. He didn't have to stand around here having this non-conversation. He started to walk away, but Baz called after him.

"Come on, Mike. For old time's sake. We can work something out, surely? It'll be worth your while."

Michael turned on his heel, almost quaking with rage. Who the fuck did Baz think he was talking to? Baz's gripe with him had always been that he wasn't willing to cross those lines, scrape the bottom of those moral barrels. Did the idiot seriously think he would sell Miranda out for a quick buck?

By the look in his eyes, he actually did. What a tosser. Just because Baz would have done it in a heartbeat, less than, he couldn't conceive that someone else might have a bit more of a fucking conscience.

"Fuck off, Baz." Michael turned and resumed walking.

"Don't say I never gave you the chance, Mike! You can't hide from me. You know it's only a matter of time." Baz's undeniable truths followed him down the quiet street.

* * *

The second he got back to his flat, he called Miranda. "We might have an issue."

"Oh?"

"Baz caught me leaving your place."

"Ah. That's the awful paparazzi guy, right?"

"Right. He didn't get a good shot of me, but it's just a matter of time before he or someone else does. Even without a photo, it'll get out. He's probably still tight with Arielle at *Buzz!*. It wouldn't surprise me if he's on the phone to her right now." Arielle Newton had been the other architect of Devon and Cleo's public outing. If she knew about them, it was as good as global public knowledge.

Miranda sighed. "The cat is well and truly out of the bag, then?"

"It will be by tomorrow. And then we'll both have people on our tail, trying to get a picture. You know how it works."

"As do you," she said. "I'm so sorry, Michael. I hate bringing all of this down on people."

"No need to apologise. It's not your fault, and it was always going to happen – we've just been lucky until now. Besides, it would be pretty hypocritical of me to complain, wouldn't it? The media circus has paid my rent for most of my life." He still got that slight distaste on his tongue when he thought about that, despite what he'd told her yesterday.

"Hey," she said softly. "There's no use in going over a past that can't be changed. What matters is what we do now."

He shook his head and got a hold of himself. "You're right. Any ideas?"

"Well, you're going to think this is my answer to everything ... but I think we should go to a party."

He laughed despite the tension in his stomach. "That does appear to be one of your go-to strategies, yes. But I see the logic. Get ahead of them, on our terms, right?"

"Exactly. And wearing something fabulous, of course."

"Of course." Not that he had anything "fabulous", but that couldn't be helped. He certainly didn't feel like going out shopping today. "It's a good idea. The first picture of a celebrity and their new ..." What was he? This wasn't the time for that discussion. "... interest is going to be valuable, and even more so if it's an exclusive. We appear in public in front of multiple photographers, and we vastly reduce the value of whatever Baz plans to hang around in bushes to get. With any luck, we might make it not worth his while."

"Sounds good. I'll call Aisling right away, see what

we can find. There'll be something worth going to in this city tonight."

"Tonight?" he said, sounding more taken aback than he'd wanted to.

"No time like the present. We can't be seen together before we do this, can we?" Her voice lowered a touch. "And I don't want to wait too long to be with you again."

Damn, he didn't either. They'd just spent twenty-four hours together, and yet he missed her already, missed her hand in his, her skin, her hair, her scent, her smile. It was new and alien to him, this feeling, and part of him wanted nothing more than to run away from it. But the rest of him only wanted her.

"Me either," he murmured, and for a moment they let the words and the longing hang in the air between them, until he wished he'd never left her bed this morning, because then not only would they not be having to deal with this, but he'd still be with her now, planting kisses on that spot on her neck that she loved, feeling her hands on his skin as she pulled him closer ...

"OK," she said, breaking the spell. "Stay inside and await further instructions. I'll find us something to do and let you know the plan. Oh, and text me your measurements. I can send my stylist to you if you want."

Michael didn't really want, because the thought was so weird. But he also didn't want Miranda to be splashed across the world's press with him looking like a scruff, and his one good suit hadn't been cleaned since it spent the night crumpled up on the floor of a hotel room.

"That'd be good, thanks. I'll talk to you later."

He hung up and let out a heavy exhale. Another party. He'd been to more fancy parties in the last few weeks than he had in the rest of his life put together. And by the end of this one – by five minutes into this one, most likely – the world would know that Miranda Janes was his ... his ... *his*.

The thought fucking terrified him.

But beneath that fear lurked something else, a sharp, hot stab of possessive satisfaction. Whatever this was, with her, whatever it would cost him, he did want to tell the world that this incredible, amazing, astounding woman had, for god knows what reason, chosen him.

And apparently, he discovered two hours later as a stylist named Blade fussed around him, he was going to be doing it in Tom Ford.

* * *

Michael waited, hand on the door handle, as the driver Miranda had sent for him listened intently to someone who was presumably Frank in his earbud.

"Three ... two ... one ... go."

Michael opened the door and glanced to his left to see Miranda emerging from the car next to his. Perfect timing. Shouts went up and cameras started flashing as they moved quickly towards each other. Jesus, he'd never realised how bright it was on this end of it. He slipped his arm around Miranda and rotated her towards a familiar face.

"This guy," he said into her ear, so she could hear it

over the clamour. "He's not nearly as much of a dick-head as some of the guys on the other side. Used to always share his crisps with me." He dropped a kiss on her cheek, making sure to splay his hand possessively over her hip, so that Steve and the others in the scrum knew exactly what they were getting a picture of.

"Guess you just made his day," she said, putting a hand on his lapel and throwing out a dazzling smile. "You look good enough to eat, by the way."

"God, please don't talk me to like that right now," he said through his plastered-on smile. They turned to face the other way, and he was pettily pleased to spot Baz there. He shifted his hold on Miranda into a slightly more chaste position, just to piss him off. They started to walk towards the door. "You look incredible too."

"Why thank you. You recognise it?" A tiny devilish smirk lit up her gorgeous face.

He did. It was the complicated-looking black dress she hadn't worn in Paris. On her sensational body, he could see how the delicate straps criss-crossed her smooth skin. They looked like they'd break apart at the first hint of roughness ...

He shook his head. *Focus!* They'd nearly made it inside. The job was almost done. The next guests had arrived, but he was sure he could still hear murmurs directed their way. The "Miranda Janes steps out with new beau" headlines were writing themselves as they spoke.

"Remind me what this thing is again?" he asked.

She leaned her head towards him, smiling prettily, which meant there must be another camera on them. "This is a fundraiser for Jessica Odutola's literacy foundation. You know, the author of that book that just had the BBC adaptation? Aisling is friends with her agent, and there were some last-minute cancellations, so they were able to fit us in with no trouble at all. It's perfect," she said, nodding gracefully to the doorman who pulled open the door and gestured for them to enter. "A few high-profile guests, ensuring there'd be press, but not so glitzy that it's a total frenzy."

It really was perfect. Was there nothing this woman couldn't arrange to her satisfaction?

The second they were away from the door, she turned to hug him. "Relax. We did it."

They'd done it. He moved his jaw around a bit, only now realising that he'd been clenching it. Now there was just the party to get through, although at least this one was a dinner. He'd be able to sit there like a lemon instead of standing around like a lemon.

When they stepped into the bar area, Michael was surprised to see a familiar face.

"Henry, you made it!" Miranda swooped down on Henry and kissed him on both cheeks.

"I did," he replied. He extended his hand to Michael. "Good to see you again." He turned to the attractive red-headed woman next to him. "Michael, Miranda, this is Eleanor, my global head of HR. I've kept her tied up in brain-meltingly stressful meetings all week, so when Miranda called and asked if I could come tonight,

I figured I could treat Eleanor to a fancy dinner to make up for what I've put her through." He gave them his usual friendly grin. "She's also the Deng Group's resident Geordie, so I thought you two exiles could bond over the lack of decent fish and chips down here or something."

Eleanor laughed. "It's something he's heard me mention once or twice. It's lovely to meet you both, even if I am a little starstruck by you, Miranda!"

Michael greeted her and then looked at Miranda, puzzled. Why had she asked Henry to come?

She seemed to read the question in his eyes. "I know how much you hate these things. I figured a friendly face, or two" – she nodded at Eleanor – "might ease the pain a little."

Something inside him melted like ice cream in the sun. He wrapped his arm around her waist, pulled her closer and dropped a kiss on her forehead. "Thank you," he said softly. To have someone care about his comfort like this, it was ... strange. Nice.

"So, Michael," Eleanor said, "shall we play the 'where are you from and how many of the same pubs did we used to go to' game?"

"Why aye, man," he said, and they launched into an enthusiastic chat about home that lasted until it was time to take their seats for dinner. Henry and Miranda were having a conversation of their own that seemed a little less jovial, but all he made out were the words "Courtney", "sad", and "nothing to worry about".

As the staff were clearing away the first course, he felt

his phone buzz in his pocket. He went to turn it off, but the message caught his eye.

> STEVE H: You're fucking Miranda Janes? You lucky, lucky bastard. How things change. Thanks for the shot.

A huff of laughter escaped him. He was glad Steve had been there. He really was several orders of magnitude better than Baz in the twattiness stakes.

"What's so funny?" Miranda asked quietly. He turned his screen to show her the message before turning off his phone and sliding it back into his ludicrously expensive pocket. She placed a hand on his thigh and leaned in closer. "Damn right you're lucky, Michael Hedley." There was mischief in her smile, and Michael wanted to kiss it away and turn it into something much less wholesome.

He settled for taking her hand in his and entwining their fingers. "Believe me, I know."

32

MIRANDA sat on her bed, flicking through the photographs of the event online. There was one of her laughing heartily about something with Jessica Odutola. Miranda and Michael. Henry and the loud man who owned that soccer team; she forgot his name. Miranda and Michael. The four of them – Miranda, Michael, Henry and Eleanor. Her finger hovered over that one for a second. She hoped Courtney wouldn't see that and get the wrong idea. It was rare for Henry to take another woman to an event, but she knew it was completely innocent. They were colleagues, and the woman had spoken of her husband and child with such pure affection that Miranda had felt a twinge of envy. But something was up with Courtney and Henry; she would have put money on it.

She shook her head. They'd be fine; they were rock solid. This was a stressful time for Courtney, and separation was always hard. Miranda could say that from experience.

She turned her attention to the news articles that had started cropping up overnight. A few referred to her new "mystery man", but many of them named him, which wasn't a surprise. Most of the guys who'd photographed them knew who he was, and word got around.

Cleo's website, with Michael's agreement, of course, was going to put something out later with a little more information about him, particularly the fact that he was an artist and had taken all those recent photos of Miranda. They were all in agreement that the less people had to go digging for stuff, the better.

The articles so far were positive, though, with several of them commenting on how happy she looked. Good. She was glad that was obvious. Miranda didn't know when she'd last been this happy. She wondered how long he'd be downstairs in the gym, and how much he'd mind if she went down there and disturbed him.

Maybe that wasn't a great idea. The man took his gym routine surprisingly seriously. She was beginning to suspect it was where he worked out a lot of his feelings, and she had no desire to mess with that. Especially considering the effect it had on his abs. And those arms ...

Her phone distracted her from her impure thoughts about Michael's biceps.

"Nora? Is something wrong? Isn't it, like, the middle of the night?"

"I've just been to New York. My body clock is so messed up," her agent said in her usual brisk tones. "Anyway, nothing's wrong. I just wanted to check you saw the schedule I sent you. He's sprung an extra week of rehearsals on there that I did not know about. It was a rehearsal-heavy schedule anyway – something about the fight choreographer – and now it's beyond intense. Check it over, let me know if I have to go back and kick some asses over it."

"Mm-hm. Yeah. Sure. Thanks, Nora." Miranda's mind raced as she hung up and scrolled to her email. She found Nora's message, and ...

Rehearsals for *An Ocean of Fallen Stars* would start in four weeks.

Four weeks, and then she'd have to leave London.

Leave him.

She stood up. Pacing around her bedroom, she tried to tell herself it wasn't a big deal. This was her life. It had been her life for a decade. And she'd been chasing this part the whole time she'd known Michael – it was the *reason* she knew Michael. So why was she acting like it was some huge surprise that she would actually have to go off and do it?

But she'd thought they'd have more time. She recalled what Aisling had told her: AJ worked fast. Decisions got made, then things moved at lightning speed. She should have been more prepared for this, and yet she wasn't.

She picked up her hairbrush, put it down. Walked over to the closet, opened the doors, then shut them again. Her limbs kept trying to find things to do to dispel some of the weird nervous energy she was brimming with, but her brain couldn't engage enough to figure out an actual useful activity.

She would miss him; that was the simplest part of it. She'd miss the way he held her, the way he kissed her, the way he made love to her. She'd miss the way his accent got deeper when he talked about home, until she could barely understand him sometimes and had to beg him to translate. She'd miss the way he found the beauty in everything and showed it to her too. She'd miss that curl of hair that fell over his forehead.

It wasn't just that, though. Missing people was an occupational hazard, and she'd been through this plenty of times before. Jake, Marcus, Ethan – it hadn't been the separation that had broken those relationships. Video calls were a wonderful invention, as were airplanes. But Miranda had never gone into the long-distance phase when things were still so new. What if they weren't solid enough yet? She thought they were, but what if he didn't? What if he decided it just wasn't worth the trouble? They'd never talked about the future, never even skirted around the edges of the subject. What if he just ... let go?

Miranda stopped in front of her mirror and stared her reflection right in the face. She couldn't let it happen. She wouldn't. She was falling in love with him – yes, she'd promised Jen she wouldn't, but she may as well have promised that the sun would stop shining. Falling in love was what Miranda did, and Michael had made it so damn easy. She wasn't giving him up now.

She had four weeks. That was plenty of time for him to fall in love with her too.

33

"WELL," Hugh said over steepled fingers. "This is ... a development."

"Yes," Michael said, his gaze shifting awkwardly around the bar. It was some combined gallery/social space Hugh had brought him to, to meet people and soak up the ambience or whatever. The surroundings were all exposed brickwork and daring art, but Hugh's tone was taking him right back to the headmaster's office at school and the time he'd been summoned there for sending an anonymous prank note to his English teacher telling him his car was on fire.

"This could change things for you, you know." From the disquieted look on Hugh's face, Michael wasn't sure he meant that as a good thing.

"It could?"

"Yes. It could open a lot of doors."

Michael's pulse quickened. This was ... good? He didn't particularly want this to be the way that his career finally got started, off the back of who he was sleeping with – who did? But on the other hand, he wasn't some idealistic kid anymore. He knew how the world worked.

"Magazines. Fashion. That kind of thing," Hugh continued. "You could be working steadily, for excellent money, in a heartbeat, now your name is associated with a major celebrity. And I'll put you in touch with some people who can help you make that happen, if that's what you want. But I rather thought you wanted to take a different path."

"I did. I do." He wanted to be an artist. That was the plan, wasn't it? He wanted to show his work in galleries. That was what he'd always wanted, what he'd promised Cleo he would do. He owed her that, and then some.

"I know. I understand. But it may be worth taking some time to think about this. There'll be a buzz around you in the media right now. There'll be opportunities that can provide security, a way of making your name outside the paparazzi stuff. The fine art world will still be there in a few years' time, and it might be easier then, when things might be ... different."

"When I'm not featured in the Sidebar of Shame, you mean?" Michael said bitterly.

Hugh inclined his head, his expression wryly apologetic.

What Hugh was saying made sense. He could build up a body of professional, more commercial work, and then perhaps the pivot into fine art might be easier. Right now, he was an ex-pap who was shagging a celebrity. That kind of person appeared on reality TV, not in art galleries.

It was the sensible option. It was the easy option.

Would Miranda take the easy option?

What would Miranda have done, if AJ had offered her a part in his next movie but not this one? If Nora had found her the lead in something else that would have netted her millions?

He didn't even need to ask himself those questions. She would have done exactly what she did do – followed her dream and fought for it. And she would tell him to do the same now.

"I still want a gallery show. Maybe that's a big ask right now, but the papers will get bored soon enough." And maybe Miranda would get bored of him too and the whole point would be moot, but that was too depressing a thought to linger on. "Please, Hugh. You said you believed in me as an artist. Was that true or not?"

Hugh sighed. "It was true. You know it was. I wouldn't be doing this otherwise." He straightened on his stool. "OK. We'll keep going down the gallery route. But do me a favour? Can you try to keep a low profile? As far as that's possible, of course. The sooner this whole furore dies down, the better."

"I'll do my best," he promised. "Trust me, the last thing I want to do is parade around for the press like I did the other night. It was a necessary evil."

"Good. Because we don't want people to think this is all you are." Hugh's tone was as impeccably polite as ever, but Michael couldn't unhear the barest tinge of something beneath it, something that felt a little like distaste. His insides wrapped themselves into a coil of unease, but then Hugh smiled, and Michael pushed it all aside.

Things were fine. They were great. His mentor still believed in him. They'd outwitted Baz. And Miranda was waiting for him.

34

MIRANDA Janes was peeling potatoes.

"When you said you were going to broaden my horizons, I didn't think you meant this. I can't remember the last time I peeled a potato."

"Listen, pet," Michael said, wrapping his arms around her waist from behind her and nuzzling her neck. "I have worn designer suits and sipped vintage champagne and made small talk with rich people with you. You can make mash with me."

She leaned into his touch and tried not to sigh contentedly. When he'd said he would come over today, she'd immediately started wondering how she could make it amazing. What could she do for him, to give him a day to remember, even if they had to stay in the house? She wanted every moment they spent together to be special.

But then he'd turned up with a bag full of groceries, because it seemed that what he wanted was to cook for her. Well, he'd said *with* her, but she was proving to be pretty useless with this peeler, and he seemed happy enough to do most of the work. He was possibly happier than she'd ever seen him, in fact, as he moved easily around her kitchen, stirring a pot full of chicken on the stove, chopping vegetables, watching in amusement as she took five minutes to peel each potato.

She loved that he was so comfortable here. It was clear that he'd rather be here than at any of the events she'd dragged him to, but the events had been worth it, hadn't they? Every single one had been necessary and beneficial. She was sure that in time he would look as at home on the red carpet as he did at her kitchen counter.

She imagined him on her arm at the premiere of *An Ocean of Fallen Stars*. Which she shouldn't have done, because of course it brought back to mind the thing she hadn't told him yet.

He was beside her before she realised, taking the half-peeled potato from her hand. "Hey, what's up?" he said.

"Nothing." She gave him a bright smile. "Just thinking how good this all smells. What is it again?"

"Chicken cacciatore. I did debate making a pie, but one, I wasn't sure if it'd be pushing this whole 'Hollywood diva meets common lad from a small town' thing a bit far, and two, I couldn't be arsed making pastry." He grinned at her. "Not sure if I'd horrify Italians by serving it with mash, but I don't care. I promised you mash, so you're getting it."

"Sounds good. I need to start carb-loading for all this training ..." No. She didn't want to think about that right now. "You like cooking for people, don't you?" she said instead, sitting down at the kitchen table and propping her chin on her hand. She might as well abandon any pretence that she was helping.

"Aye, I do. My mam's a feeder, and I guess I am too. I

used to cook for Cleo all the time, because she's a shite cook. The woman could burn water. I've had no one to do it for since she left."

"Well, now you have me," she said softly.

"Now I have you."

It was as if all the questions that came with that statement hung in the air of the kitchen. She could practically see them, taste them.

But before she could ask a single one, her phone rang.

The screen showed it was her sister, on a video call, but when she pressed the button, she was greeted with "Aunty Rand! Aunty Rand! Mommy says you have a boyfriend and that I could call you to ask you about him!"

"Oh for god's sake," Miranda heard in the background. Her sister rushed into view and took the phone from her daughter. "Sorry, Rand. Izzy, no, that is not what I said. I said that we could send Aunty Rand a message and ask if we could call her after school. And I didn't say anything about a boyfriend."

"Oh. Maybe that was Daddy. Sorry, Mommy. I thought you said we could call now, I really did." Izzy pushed her face back in front of the screen. "Sorry, Aunty Rand. Can we call you after school?"

"Why aren't you in school now?" she asked her niece.

"I have to go to the dentist. I ate a candy and my tooth went crack."

"Oh no, baby! Are you OK?"

"She's fine," Jen said, reappearing behind her

daughter. "I think it was about to come loose anyway, but Dad said to get it checked out just in case." She kissed Izzy on the head. "Honey, go get your shoes on. We have to leave soon and I want to talk to your aunt."

"OK! Bye!" Izzy scampered off.

"I'm sorry, Randa. I hope you weren't busy. It's, what, afternoon, evening, there? And I didn't tell her you had a boyfriend, by the way. Maybe Bryan said something, the ass. We saw the pictures, though. You looked so happy! And he's really cute. I can see why– Oh!"

Miranda had turned her phone to reveal Michael behind her at the counter, his back to the screen.

"Hey, Michael," she said. "Come here a minute."

He turned, wearing a smile that was an adorable mixture of awkward, sheepish and amused.

She tugged him down to perch on the edge of the chair next to her. "Michael, this is my sister, Jen. Jen, Michael."

Jen gave him a warm smile, recovering her composure. "Good to meet you, Michael. I've heard a *lot* about you."

Miranda tried to shoot a subtle glare at her sister. She hadn't talked about him that much, had she? OK, she probably had.

"Likewise," said Michael, but then lapsed into silence, apparently unsure what else to say.

"Anyway," Jen said hastily. "I better go. I'll let Izzy call you later and tell you about her tooth, if you're free. She's so excited about the falls it's unreal. We can't wait to see you. Talk to you later, bye!"

And then she was gone, and Miranda's heart was full. Her sister was the most important person in the world to her, and getting to introduce her to Michael, even just briefly, felt amazing.

"So that's Jen," Michael said, sitting properly on the chair and lifting her into his lap.

"That's Jen. It's always like that when we speak – the kids causing mayhem and her rushing around dealing with it all. But I love the chaos of it, and I know she does too. They're just this fantastic, gorgeous little family, so happy together. It's ..."

It's everything. It's all I ever wanted. It's what life is all about. Isn't it? Do you think that too?

Fortunately, she had the presence of mind not to say that to the man she'd been sleeping with for all of two weeks.

He didn't ask her to finish that thought. He just kissed her lightly, then said, "Come on. I'm going to show you how to use that peeler without looking like you're about to take all the skin off your hand."

35

MICHAEL had to remind himself to keep lifting his fork to his mouth, because he found himself lapsing into just watching Miranda eat. He'd been a bit apprehensive about cooking for her – what if the doughnut thing was her one guilty pleasure and other than that she was an exclusively fine dining kind of girl? But she was digging into her chicken and potatoes with an enthusiasm that warmed something deep inside him. She was a smart, fierce, independent woman who had an army of people to call on if she needed anything, but that phone call earlier had reminded him how far away she was from her family. How often did someone look after her just because they cared about her?

Christ on a bike. Was he casting himself in some kind of domestic protector role because he'd cooked her some chicken and she seemed to like it? What was his brain even doing?

She smiled up at him as she finished her last bite. "That was delicious. I don't know when someone last cooked for me like that." The smile turned devilish. "You may have to help me burn off some of these calories, though."

Oh yeah he would. "Of course. We'll get down the gym, do some burpees." He stood up, walked around to her side of the table and leaned over her shoulder for her plate. "Unless you had a better idea," he murmured.

She closed her eyes and arched her neck a little, so it would have been rude of him not to drop a soft kiss on her jaw. "You know I always have ideas," she said.

This was undeniably true. He'd never met anyone with more ideas and plans than Miranda. She wanted something, it was only a matter of time before she decided how she was going to get it. He'd always sort of known people like this existed, in some universe far away from him, but to see it in action – to be the object of those plans – baffled and exhilarated him in equal measure.

"It was nice to meet your sister before," he said as he took their empty plates to the sink. "And your niece is so cute."

"She is, isn't she? Dishwasher's just to your left."

"I can just wash these. There isn't much to do."

"But if you put them in the dishwasher, you'll have to bend down and I can check out your butt."

He laughed. "Fine. But I'll have you know I'm feeling kind of objectified right now."

"Only kind of? I'll have to try harder." She blew him a kiss across the kitchen. "I'm glad you got to see Jen. She's the best."

"You two are really close, aren't you?"

"Yeah." She smiled wistfully. "We always have been. She's always been there for me, no matter what. I don't know what I'd do without her."

"And Izzy is seven, right? And you have a nephew too?"

"Well remembered." She looked impressed. Didn't she realise that every little thing she said and did was unforgettable? "Tommy is five. He's a much more sensitive soul than Izzy. Much quieter. Which isn't hard, if I'm being honest."

"She certainly seemed to have a lot of energy. Does that run in your family?" He could see the little girl being a star one day, just like her aunt.

Miranda chuckled. "Kind of. Jen's got her forceful side too. But she's way more chilled than I am. Probably because she's been so nauseatingly happy for so long."

Her tone was bright, joking, but there was something in her expression that Michael couldn't quite decipher. It was too soft to be bitterness, too sharp to be wistfulness, too pure to be envy.

"Oh?" he said, because he wanted to dig deeper into whatever emotion was playing over her face, but he was terrible at having deep conversations with women he was involved with. Or at least he assumed he was. He didn't think he'd ever had one before, Cleo excepted.

"Yeah." She was quiet for a moment, and just when he'd decided she was done with that subject and he should find another one, she said, "She met her husband in college. They fell in love, like, instantly, and have been besotted with each other ever since. It all just seemed to fall into place for her, you know? They got married right out of college, and they both found jobs they liked, then they decided to have kids, and they had them. And sometimes I ..." She looked down at the table, lips pressed together.

Michael sat down on the chair next to her and pulled her to sit on his lap. "Sometimes what?" he said, wrapping his arms around her.

She shook her head. "It doesn't matter."

"Hey." He tipped her chin up so he could look her in the eye. "You can tell me anything, you know that, right? After everything I've told you, I'm hardly in a position to judge or anything."

"I ... No. I'm being silly." She flashed him a smile, jumped up from his lap, and headed for the fridge. "Drink? White? Or red?"

"White's fine," he said slowly. He'd been sure she was about to open up about something. Was she jealous of her sister's happiness? That was nothing to be ashamed of. God knew he was no stranger to envy. Maybe she wasn't ready to let him in to that side of her yet. Or maybe that wasn't how this worked, this thing between them.

There was one thing, at least, that always seemed to work. He walked over to her and took a long, cool drink from the glass she offered him. He reached behind her to place his glass on the counter, before sliding his arm around her waist and letting his lips find hers in a soft, searching kiss. The things he wanted to say – that he cared, that he was here for her, that he wanted to know the ugly parts of her heart as well the bright ones – seemed forever out of reach, so he tried to let his kiss say them for him.

But god, why did she have to feel so good in his arms? It was really fucking difficult trying to convey complicated emotions when her hair felt like silk and her tongue tasted like wine and her body was melting against his like that. He was about to pull back, to ask her again if she wanted to talk, but she grabbed the waistband of his jeans and yanked him closer to her, and all he could do was groan into her mouth. The tenderness of his kiss was obliterated by the intensity of hers. She held him as if she couldn't get close enough, and if that was the way she wanted it, Michael was happy to oblige.

He lifted her up and stepped forward until she was perched on the granite worktop. She wrapped her legs around his waist, still kissing him fiercely, still tangling her fingers in his hair so ferociously that he could feel a tugging at his scalp, a delicious almost-pain that made him forget any thoughts of gentleness. He splayed one hand over her backside and pulled her closer, pressing her against where his dick was straining at his jeans. Her gasp only made him want more, made him press closer still, until it hurt, until it felt almost like he was fucking her through all the layers of fabric still between them.

Too many layers. Far too many. He tore his lips from hers so he could concentrate on getting rid of some, but as his hands moved to her waistband, she stopped him.

"Upstairs."

Reluctantly, he stepped away from the counter to let her hop down. But he hadn't stepped back very far, so she hopped right back into his arms, and was it his fault if he just had to kiss her again? Upstairs was miles away, and his body strenuously objected to the idea of being separated from hers for that long.

"I said," she whispered between kisses, "upstairs, Hedley. Now." She squeezed his arse, hard, and stepped out of his embrace, one hand on the top button of her denim shirt. He followed her to the stairs, removing his T-shirt as he went, while she unfastened her buttons, letting the shirt slide off one smooth shoulder as she did so. He had no idea how she was managing to do that so artfully, but it was so fucking sexy that he didn't care.

The shirt hit the floor halfway up the stairs, and Michael couldn't help himself – he came up behind her and ran his hands up over her ribcage to cup her breasts in that tiny lace bralette. Jesus, her tits were perfection. He pulled one cup down and rolled her nipple between his fingers, lust raging in his veins as she arched into his touch. His other hand found its impatient way into her leggings, and oh holy fuck. He hadn't thought he could get any more turned on, but when his palm found a scrap of fabric clinging to her sweet, wet heat, it took every ounce of self-control he had not to fuck her right here in the middle of the stairs. He settled for roughly shoving down her leggings and helping her step out of them, and he unbuttoned his jeans and let them drop to the floor as her bedroom door was finally within reach. God, he needed to be inside her, needed to make sure she felt this electric need that had him in its grasp.

But she had other ideas. As soon as he stepped over the threshold of her room, she put her hand on his chest, and he let her push him onto his back on her bed. She normally let him take control, maybe preferred it, but not tonight, it seemed. Michael didn't care. All he wanted was her lips back on his, her body on top of him.

For one moment he had them, but then she shifted down the bed, leaving kisses over his torso as she went, and pulled off his boxers. When her hand closed over his dick, the heat that shot through his body threatened to undo him. He'd do well to last ten seconds in her hand, let alone her ... Jesus. Her lips curved into a seductive smirk, then parted as she lowered her head. He gripped at her million-thread-count sheets as her tongue flicked out and lapped up the drop of pre-cum at his aching tip, and if he thought that was the sexiest thing he had ever seen, it was nothing compared to when her mouth stretched around him and she sucked him hard, her gaze never leaving his. He had to fight hard to keep his hips on the bed and his brain inside his skull.

"Fuck, Miranda," he choked out as her lips moved up and down his shaft. "Do you ... shit ... do you have any idea how fucking good this feels? How beautiful you look right now?"

She moaned, deep in her throat, and the sound reverberated through every inch of him. He was lost in his arousal, drunk on the sensation of her warm, wet mouth. He wanted to tell her exactly how good she looked, how fucking magnificent she was, but he was beyond speech, beyond anything but surrendering to the pleasure she was giving him.

God, he couldn't take much more of this. As if she'd heard that thought, she stopped. She swirled her tongue around his head one more time, drawing a hiss out of him, then crawled back up the bed, her body hovering over his. He grabbed the back of her head and pulled her in for a searing kiss. His other hand reached between her legs. Fuck, she was wet. He started to move his fingers through that slickness, determined to take her as high as she'd just taken him, but she shifted to one side, reaching into her bedside drawer. She dropped a condom packet onto his chest and left him to try to concentrate on getting the bastard thing open while she wrapped a soft hand around his dick and began to stroke him up and down. What was she trying to do, kill him?

"Miranda, I want to touch you. Let me—"

"No." She took hold of his wrist and guided his hand downwards, and together they rolled the condom over his painfully hard dick. A blazing, intense look was in her eyes as she kissed him softly and repeated, "No."

She grabbed him and sank down the entire length of him, and Michael wondered if this was what dying and going to heaven felt like. Then she rolled her hips, and he was in the grip of a sensation hot enough to send him straight to hell. She rode him mercilessly, never letting him set the pace, never letting him catch his breath. There was something wild and desperate in her tonight, something he'd never seen before, and part of him wanted to stop and ask if she was OK, but he was ruled right now by the part of him that was lodged deep inside her.

He choked on his gasps and she ground her hips against him, taking him deeper still, and he needed to come so badly, but he'd be damned if he did before he made her come around him first. He tilted his hips until he found it, the angle that ripped a low, urgent sound from the back of her throat. The clench of her walls around him made his balls tighten, and the need to make her fall apart became urgent, desperate. He pressed the heel of his hand against her clit, and satisfaction registered somewhere in the back of his lust-fogged brain as he felt her start to shake. She fucked him almost frantically as he kept his hand on her and knew she was close ... almost ...

"Fuck yes," he hissed as his climax hit him like a tidal wave, at the same moment as she tightened around him and let out a sharp cry. She collapsed over him as pleasure released him from its grip and he came reluctantly back down to earth.

She moved off him and curled into his side, laying her head on his chest. It was as if all that strange fire had burned out and now she was oddly vulnerable again. He wrapped his arm around her.

"Babe," he said, the endearment feeling unfamiliar on his lips, "what's wrong?"

When she spoke, it was into his chest, as if she was trying to stop the words coming out. "I have to leave."

36

MIRANDA kept her head on Michael's chest as she spoke, as if the beat of his heart, still rapid but starting to calm, could steady her. "I got the schedule for *Ocean*. AJ wants three weeks of rehearsals, then straight into shooting. I have to be in LA in just under four weeks, and then I'll be gone for months."

It's too soon, she wanted him to say. *I'll come visit you. I don't want to lose you.*

What he actually said was "Oh."

This was the moment to have The Conversation. They should talk sensibly and honestly about what this was, and whether it had a future. Miranda had been having versions of The Conversation ever since she'd been in this business, and she'd never shied away from it before. It was important, to have clarity.

But too many of them had ended in a goodbye, and although she was used to those too, she didn't know if she'd be able to bear it this time. Not from him.

He still said nothing. Maybe he knew what should happen but was avoiding it too.

"But before that, I have to go home for my dad's birthday." The words were out before she could stop them. "We're staying in this gorgeous cabin by these beautiful falls. It's going to be amazing." *What are you doing, Rand?* shrieked a voice in her head that sounded remarkably like her sister's. She ignored it and finally propped herself up on her elbow to look at him. "Come with me?"

There was an unsettled look in his hazel eyes. "Come with you? To your dad's birthday?"

"Yes," she said, trying to sound nonchalant. "My family loves extra people. And the views are incredible, you'll get some really cool photos."

She sighed inwardly. He looked, as Jen had predicted, absolutely terrified. She leaned up and kissed him. "It was just an idea. I thought it might be fun. But you don't have to."

He kissed her back. "I'll think about it, OK?"

It wasn't a no. She could work with that. "OK."

37

MICHAEL pushed open the changing room door and emerged into the small reception-area-cum-café of his gym. His muscles ached, but in a good way. He'd really put himself through it today, trying to make up for all the sessions he'd missed of late. He'd been working out in Miranda's basement, but it wasn't quite the same. It was hard to stay on a treadmill when he knew she was upstairs, waiting to put him through his paces in other ways.

He'd hoped that the exercise would help clear out his brain, too, but that had been a bloody failure. He was as confused as ever. She was leaving soon, which meant that he should have asked the question "And what happens then?", but he hadn't, and neither had she. He'd ducked it like a coward, just like he'd ducked the more direct question of whether he'd go with her to Washington for her dad's birthday.

He knew he couldn't avoid the question – the big one, that is – forever, but he had no idea what the answer was. Miranda had never given him the impression that he meant nothing to her. This was something, what they had; he knew it in his bones. But was it something that could survive her being half a world away?

"Oh, hello." A voice interrupted his reverie and made

him realise he was standing in the middle of the reception area like an idiot. He turned towards the voice and found a woman wearing a sports bra, leggings, and a distinctly unimpressed look on her face.

"Priya?" he said to Cleo's former flatmate. "What on earth are you doing here?" He knew it wasn't to exercise. She'd once dropped him off here after he'd helped her move some furniture, and she'd shuddered at the very sight of the place.

She sighed dramatically. "A woman."

"Of course." He didn't even bother wondering what had happened to Ros. She'd lasted a lot longer than most.

"She's new to the area and wanted to know where she could work out." The way Priya said the last words, you'd think she meant "skin baby rabbits" or something. "This is the only gym I know in this part of town. Or anywhere, in fact. Why does it smell so odd?"

"This is the way gyms smell, Priya." He grinned. Priya wasn't born a princess, but she should have been. "So, you're hanging around hoping to run into her?"

"I was thinking of doing that, yes. But they keep trying to make me join!"

"Well, that is how they do things. I'm surprised they haven't kicked you out yet."

She waved her hand airily. "They can try. Anyway, now you're here, you can buy me a coffee."

"Oh, I can, can I?" But he was already moving towards the little coffee counter. Why not? Priya's company was always ... interesting.

He bought two coffees and started following her to

a table, but hesitated. "Do you mind if we sit away from the window?" It was probably unnecessary; nobody had followed him here, and the chances of a random stranger recognising him were slim to none, but precautions never hurt. He didn't want Priya to find herself in the press as "the other woman". Although knowing Priya, she'd probably find it hilarious.

"Good thinking, darling," she said, changing course. "I wouldn't want anyone I know to spot me in a gym."

"Perish the thought."

"So," Priya said when they were safely tucked away behind a pillar. "Cleo and Devon Grant, you and Miranda Janes. What is the world coming to?"

He laughed. "Aye, I know, right? It's so weird. I don't really know what to make of it all."

Priya sipped her coffee and made a face, which was fair enough. It was pretty terrible. "Enjoy it while it lasts, I say."

"Oh. Erm ..."

"Sorry, darling. God, this coffee is horrific, isn't it?" She pushed her cup aside. "That came out wrong. I didn't mean you were on the verge of getting dumped or anything. I just meant that whatever happens in the future, you're living the high life right now, so you might as well make the most of it." She shrugged. "I know it's not your scene, the whole glitz-and-glamour lifestyle. You are, in fact, the least likely person I know to enjoy it." A snort of laughter escaped him. She had that right. "But you might as well roll with it. Have fun. Go on adventures."

Adventures. Miranda had taken him on a couple of those already. And hadn't they always worked out? So maybe he should say yes to this trip. To be with her, away from the rest of the world, around the people who loved her, amid incredible nature ... were there really any downsides?

Except being sized up by her whole family at once, of course.

"Anyway." Priya was still talking, oblivious to his inner flip-flopping. "It's terribly unfair. Where is my Hollywood megastar, thank you very much?" She flipped her glossy dark hair over her shoulder.

"I'm very sorry. I'll have to ask Miranda if she knows a single celebrity who would be worthy of you."

"I'd settle for Seb Akao." She wiggled her eyebrows. "That boy is divine. And open to dating a civilian, according to that thing."

"What thing?" He took a gulp of his coffee. Horrific was probably overstating it. Besides, he'd paid for it, so he was drinking it no matter what it tasted like.

"The thing in *Buzz!*. I'm judging from your face that they did not reach out for comment." She rummaged in her pristine-looking gym bag and pulled out a magazine. "Here. If Cleo ever asks, of course I never buy this disgusting rag."

He looked down at the issue of *Buzz!* now in his hands. The cover star was Scarlett Smith, a former reality TV star he used to photograph who'd just "welcomed baby girl with partner Dan Theroux!" apparently. But in the corner was the headline "10 Times Celebrities

Dated Normal People", and there was a small picture of Miranda.

Ah, shit.

It wasn't as if this was some unexpected turn of events. Most outlets had taken the lazy route of copy-pasting the piece from the website Cleo worked for – where "our source", aka Cleo, had provided some basic background information and a couple of platitudes about it "being new but going well". He knew before he opened the magazine that *Buzz!* would have gone further, and he bet himself a bacon sandwich that he knew who'd written the article.

"OK," Priya said when he failed to say anything for several minutes. "I'm going to leave you to it. I think this smell is seeping into my hair."

He looked up at her as she stood, but he barely saw her. His mind was still on whatever he was about to find in this magazine.

She put her hand on his shoulder – very gingerly, as if terrified that she might come into contact with a stray droplet of sweat – and said, with uncharacteristic softness, "It's not worth worrying about. None of that crap matters. If you need to talk, call me, yeah?" And then she was gone.

He flicked open the magazine. Bacon sarnie it was, then. Arielle bloody Newton. Of course it was. They were practically warring factions at this point – Arielle, Baz and *Buzz!* against Cleo, Devon, Miranda and him. He steeled himself for the incoming bullshit.

The first thing that hit him was a picture of a house.

His mother's fucking house. Those bastards had gone to the trouble of taking a picture of his mam's house. Fuck's sake.

Miranda Janes's new boyfriend might be rubbing shoulders with the likes of Henry Deng and Devon Grant these days, but it's a far cry from his humble beginnings in a council house on the outskirts of Newcastle-upon-Tyne.

He wasn't sure whether to thank a lack of journalistic accuracy or the typical southern ignorance of northern geography, but either way he was grateful. His mam's house was generic-looking enough that it would be impossible to pin down her actual address from that picture and that description – it hadn't been a council house since the 80s, and it was on the outskirts of Newcastle in the way that Scotland was on the outskirts of England. His grandmother's house was much more distinctive, so he supposed it was a good thing they didn't seem to have found that. Or maybe they had, but it didn't fit the narrative they were writing for him. He let out a silent huff as he imagined Margaret's face if such a "lowbrow" publication had dared to publish pictures of her abode.

He returned his gaze to the magazine and continued to read the ... well, character assassination was probably being melodramatic. But bloody hell, did it feel like one right now. Most of the other articles had described him as simply "a photographer" – some had pointed out that he was behind Miranda's recent "hot new Instagram pics". But there was no way Arielle would have let him get away with that. It wasn't as if he'd ever tried to hide what he used to do, but Jesus, she'd gone out of her way to make it sound as grubby as she possibly could.

... more used to lurking around outside celebrities' houses than being invited in ...

There was undeniable truth in that. But fucking hell, that was a bit rich coming from Arielle. Where would she be without people like Baz – people like *him* – willing to sell their souls to her for thirty pieces of silver? The biggest scoop of Arielle's career had come because Baz had lurked around outside Devon and Cleo's holiday cottage for her.

He grabbed his fury over Arielle's hypocrisy with both hands and refused to let go as he shoved the magazine into his bag and left the gym in search of a bacon sandwich. Because if he didn't focus on that anger, then he knew the prickles of insecurity would turn into full-on knife blows. "Normal people", they'd said, and the rest of the article seemed to be an affectionate look at fancy celebrities with refreshingly regular partners. Maybe the part about him was supposed to be that too. But he couldn't help reading it differently. He couldn't help reading it as a list of all the ways in which he wasn't good enough for this life he now found himself living. He wasn't good enough to be described as an artist. He wasn't good enough for her.

He pulled out his phone and texted her.

MICHAEL: Are you at home? Can I come over?

She replied instantly to say that she was, and he hastened his steps towards the Tube, even though he'd had every intention of going home to check his post and see what had grown in his fridge since the last time he was there. He needed to see her. He needed to hold her and kiss her and let her touch eradicate these doubts that that stupid article had put in his head. When he was with her, none of it mattered. When he was with her, there was no room for doubt.

He reached into his bag, pulled out the magazine, and dropped it into the nearest bin.

38

"SUBLIME. This is really giving, my darling." Blade adjusted the hem of the leather skirt he'd squeezed her into. "Although you're supposed to look all sexy and sultry and miserable in an outfit like this. You've looked like a little ray of sunshine since you got that message. The new man, I presume?"

Miranda laughed, looking at herself in the full-length mirror. Her stylist always knew how to find just the right thing when she was in the mood for something different. "You got me. He's on his way over." And the thought had her wanting to hug herself like a delighted child. But then she'd wrinkle this gorgeous little silk top, so she refrained.

"Then we'll try these boots and I'll get out of your way." He winked at her. "It's nice to see you so happy."

"Thank you," she replied, giving him a huge smile. Blade had been working with her for years now. He'd seen her through so many new relationships, and he'd always helped her find the perfect eat-your-heart-out outfit at their inevitable end. Did he think it was going to be the same this time around?

Was it going to be the same this time around?

No, it wasn't. It was different. It had to be different.

She tried the boots and declared them fabulous just

as Michael walked in. She'd given him a key and a fob for the gate, of course. It was easier and safer than having him stand outside waiting for her to let him in. Not a sign that she was trying to move him in or anything.

"Hey, Michael," Blade said. "How's it going? You don't need something for tonight too, do you?"

"Huh? What? No." Michael gave Blade a brief, tight smile, but his mind was clearly elsewhere.

"Thanks for this, Blade," Miranda said, gesturing to the outfit. "You never miss. You can leave the blue thing, too. I'll find somewhere to wear it."

"Whatever you say, boss." Blade kissed the air either side of her cheeks and moved away to gather the discarded items of clothing, putting them carefully back into their garment bags. "I'll see myself out. See you later, Michael."

Michael muttered a vague farewell. Miranda shot Blade a grateful smile, then took Michael by the hand and led him into the kitchen.

"Tea? Coffee? Wine? Beer?" It was still a little early, maybe, but he looked like he could use a drink. Maybe she truly was becoming an honorary Brit, trying to solve a problem with beverages.

"Beer would be great," he said quietly, but as she turned to head for the fridge, he tugged on her hand and pulled her to him for a kiss. Which of course she didn't object to, but there was something about his demeanour that was troubling her. This was neither the easy affection or the searing desire that he usually kissed her with, but something ... sadder.

"What's going on?" she said, putting a hand to his cheek.

He closed his eyes for a second, then opened them again and shook his head. "Nothing."

"Well, that is clearly untrue. Let me get you that beer and you can tell me the truth." She fetched a bottle and handed it to him. "OK. Go."

He sighed. "I'm overreacting to an article about us." His brow furrowed, and she wanted to smooth away those lines until his face was clear again.

"Arielle's?" she asked. He nodded. "My publicist sent it to me earlier. It could have been worse, all things considered."

"I know. I've been bracing myself for worse since Paris. But ..." He let out another sigh, one that seemed to contain the weight of the world. "It just felt a bit shit, you know? Those pictures of you looking so glamorous, and then this reminder that I'm just some scummy guy who doesn't belong in your world."

"Hey, no," she said sternly. "I am not going to let you believe their bullshit." He looked taken aback, and she didn't blame him; she rarely cursed out loud, but she was brimming with far too much indignation to watch her mouth. "You don't have to be proud of the job you used to do, but you don't need to let it shame you now, either. It's in the past, and you always tried not to hurt people. They were the ones who used your stuff to sell their papers, so don't you dare let them convince you you're the bad guy here." She brushed a lock of hair back from his face. "And although I'm beyond pissed that they published a picture of your mom's house, where you come from is nothing to be ashamed of either. Both of you did what you did to survive, to help each other survive. She raised a good, kind man with no support from anyone. You've earned your place in any world you want to be in, Michael."

Anything else she might have said was lost as he crushed his lips to hers in a hard, demanding kiss. She kissed him back as deeply as she could, hoping that somehow her kiss could help banish his insecurities, tell him that he was, always had been, enough.

"Thank you," he said raggedly when he released her. "And I'm sorry. This must be so boring for you, me constantly freaking out about this shit."

"Nothing about you bores me."

He gave her half a smile, and she could tell that he didn't really believe her. Damn Arielle. Why did that woman always have to cause so much trouble?

"Anyway," he said, his hazel eyes sweeping over her body, "you look gorgeous. What's this in aid of?"

"Oh, this. A friend invited me to a gig tonight." She bit her lip. "I didn't think I'd be seeing you. Do you want me to cancel?"

"What, just because I've got myself in a shitty mood?" He kissed her fingers. "Of course not. Go. Have fun."

"Why don't you come with me? It'll be fun, and I know Brix will want to meet you. They're so nice."

Michael's eyebrows shot up. "Your friend is Brix Lyon? The gig you're going to is the one that sold out in about seven minutes flat?"

"Uh-huh." She nodded. "Brix is a friend of Tom, my ex. They went to art school together or something. We stayed in touch after Tom and I broke up. One thing about all these disastrous relationships – I did at least make some good friends out of them."

"Brix is amazing. I listen to that album at least once a week."

"So come."

He looked conflicted. "I don't know, Miranda. I don't want to be a downer. Plus, I promised Hugh I'd try to keep a low profile for a while."

"You did?" This was news to Miranda. "Why?"

Michael shifted uncomfortably. "Oh, he's just worried that all this stuff about us might be a distraction from my art or something."

Well, that was one she hadn't heard before. Of course, she knew that "There's no such thing as bad publicity" was total nonsense, but could dating her actually be bad for Michael's profile? She tried not to take it personally. Hugh's role was to help Michael, so she supposed that was what he thought he was doing. But she wasn't about to let Hugh's opinion stop her from trying to cheer up *her* man.

"It's hardly the Met Gala, sweetie. We'll just be at a concert, like thousands of other fans. And do you really think your bad mood is any match for a sold-out Brix Lyon show? I'll bet you a thousand dollars that you're smiling before the end of their first song." She turned on her most persuasive smile. "What do you say?"

He laughed affectionately, and she felt a surge of

satisfaction that she'd managed to lift his spirits. "Is there ever any point in saying no to you?"

"Very little," she said with a grin.

"OK, fine." He sighed in mock defeat. "Future me would punch me in the face if I missed the chance to see Brix Lyon live. But while you are dressed like an emo teenager's fantasy made flesh, I am going to have to wear whatever's cleanest out of whatever I've left here."

She hadn't thought of that. "Should I get Blade to come back? I can send him to find you something. Or Frank could take you home? Or–"

"Babe, chill." He put his hands on her arms and gave her the quickest of smiles. "The jeans I'm wearing will do, and I'm pretty sure I have at least one T-shirt around here somewhere. Unless ..." A look of worry crossed his face. "Unless you think I need something better? I don't want to embarrass you. Maybe I should just ..."

She kissed him lightly on the lips. "What you have will be perfect. Tonight will be perfect. You'll see."

39

THE wall of noise took its time to abate once Brix left the stage for the final time. Michael's voice was hoarse from all the cheering and singing. That gig had been incredible. He and Cleo used to go to gigs all the time, and since she'd been gone he hadn't ever felt like it. He was glad Miranda had persuaded him to come. He stole a glance at her – she was looking at him as if she were reading his thoughts, and there was a definite hint of smugness in her eyes. Fine. Let her be smug. She deserved it, because she'd been right. This had been a good idea.

He took her hand, not caring if someone might be taking a picture. "Thank you," he said into her ear.

"You're welcome," she said, squeezing his hand. "You owe me a thousand dollars."

"Michael, Miranda!" a voice boomed across the VIP area over the last gasps of applause. "Great to see you here!"

Brad Conway was approaching them, his arm slung around a woman with the most flawless skin Michael had ever seen.

"I've been reading up on him," Miranda murmured. "He's quite the mover and shaker in all kinds of circles, it seems." She turned her head towards Brad. "Brad, darling! How wonderful to see you. Did you enjoy the show?"

"Do you need to ask?" he replied, grinning widely. "Brix cannot put on a bad show. Although ask them about the open mic night at my first venue." He winked. "Now there's a story."

"Oh, so you know each other?" Miranda asked.

Brad waved a hand. "We go way back. I know all kinds of people. Say, Michael, I'm glad you're here. We never got a chance to talk again at the opening."

Ah, yes. He had promised Brad they would talk more, and then going down on Miranda in a cupboard had taken priority.

"So sorry, Brad," Miranda interjected smoothly. "That was my fault. I came down with such a headache. Anyway, where are my manners?" She turned to Brad's companion, who had legs about twelve miles long and an intensely serious face. "It's Jodi, right? I think we met before, maybe at Fashion Week?"

Jodi – presumably, because she didn't correct Miranda – looked them coolly up and down. "Which one?"

Miranda laughed, completely unfazed by the woman's unfriendliness. "You know, I don't remember! They run into each other, don't they? And of course it must be even worse for you. I think it was after you walked for Elie Saab in that unbelievable cape."

Jodi's face seemed to warm up by about one degree, maybe two. "Paris. Right. We were at the Vogue party."

"That's right! What a party that was ..."

And before anybody seemed to understand what was happening, Miranda had drawn Jodi aside into a separate, almost animated conversation, leaving Brad and Michael standing there a little awkwardly. Or at least Michael felt awkward. He had the feeling Brad never did.

"Wow," Brad said. "The famous Miranda Janes charm in full effect. It's quite something, isn't it? Jodi never warms up that quickly."

"That's Jodi being warm?"

"Oh yeah. We've been dating three weeks and I've never seen her be that friendly with anyone."

"Oh." He wasn't sure what to say to that. But Brad spared him and changed the subject.

"I saw your Instagram picture from the Tate Modern the other day. Did you catch the climate change exhibition? That photo series – whew."

"Yeah, I did. I was blown away."

Brad nodded enthusiastically. "Incredible, wasn't it? The sense of scale was extraordinary, and then once you stopped feeling stunned by that, the tiny details took over, and ... wow."

"I know, right? It was like every time you blinked, you opened your eyes again and noticed something new. Miranda practically had to drag me out of there ..."

And they were off, talking about the exhibition, about one of the other displays, about their favourite artists, about so many things that Michael hadn't talked about in so long. It was weird – for someone allegedly trying to become an artist, he'd almost forgotten about the art. His batshit personal life seemed to have taken over.

"So ..." Miranda's voice broke into their conversation, which had somehow got around to avant-garde jazz, although quite how was a mystery as neither of them liked it. "I think the staff would kind of like us to get out of here."

Michael looked around. There were only a handful of people left, and members of staff were indeed lurking at the edges of the room. He and Brad must have been talking for a lot longer than he'd realised.

"Babe," Jodi purred, sliding her hand over the sleeve of Brad's suit jacket. "Brix is throwing an after-party at their hotel. We're going, right?"

"Of course, angel." Brad turned to Michael and Miranda. "You guys will come too, yeah?"

Christ. Could he handle another celebrity party? Another night of talking to people he didn't know about lifestyles he didn't understand? And then there was the attention. Michael thought of Hugh's face as he beseeched him to keep a low profile.

"Why don't we go for just a little while?" Miranda said, giving him that smile he found so hard to resist. "You haven't met Brix yet, and I'd really like you to."

Damn it. He could never refuse this woman anything. All she was asking him to do was meet her friend. And he had been having a great time talking to Brad ...

"Sure. Let's go."

* * *

"So let me get this straight," Hugh said. "I recommended that you try to keep things low-key for a while, and you interpreted that as 'get pictured outside a celebrity party with your movie-star girlfriend plus a model'?"

"Erm, yeah." Michael grimaced. Hugh's flat suddenly felt suffocatingly small. "I mean, no. That's not how I interpreted it. I didn't mean for that to happen." He looked at the picture on Hugh's screen again. "I see how it looks, though."

Brad had got a phone call just before they arrived at the party, so he'd been a few seconds behind Michael, Miranda and Jodi in getting out of the car. Literally a few seconds. But that was all they needed. Suddenly Michael looked like some kind of scrattily dressed playboy, two women on his arm. Not that either had actually been on his arm, or walking all that close to him, not even Miranda. Perspective could be a bitch.

Hugh sighed, and Michael struggled against the urge to apologise. He didn't need to; he'd done nothing wrong. But Hugh was disappointed in him nonetheless. Oh, Hugh's manners would never let him say it, but Michael knew when he'd failed to live up to someone's expectations. He'd had enough practice.

Grow a fucking pair, Hedley. He took a breath. "Look, I know that picture is kind of ridiculous. But is this really such a big deal? All I did was go with the woman I'm seeing to meet a friend of hers. Am I not allowed to have a life?"

"Of course you're allowed." Hugh locked his phone screen, removing the offending picture from sight. "I'm not saying this is your fault. I'm just ... concerned, you know that. My mission is to get you taken seriously as an artist. That's not an easy task in this city. Between this and that article ... well, it doesn't help. Your background–"

Frustration tightened its grip on Michael's chest. "What about my background? Because I didn't go to private school with people called Tarquin and Penelope?"

"No," Hugh said firmly. "That's not what I mean. I'm not going to deny that there are some terrible snobs in the art world, but by and large that kind of thing shouldn't be much of an issue. It might even help. Reverse snobbery, authentic working-class experience, all that."

Michael snorted. That was easy for Mr Humberstone-Ridley to say.

Hugh ignored him. "I meant your career. It's been almost a decade since you were last in a fine art environment. You know you're taking a non-traditional route into this. Spending time on your craft and networking with the right people in the right places is going to help you, not being seen at raucous after-parties with models."

The "right" people. How many times had he heard that before, whenever his grandmother had taken it upon herself to give him career advice? The phrase made him want to throw stuff. He refrained. Hugh's ornaments were probably heirlooms.

"I was networking!" Michael didn't bother telling Hugh that the party had in fact been pretty chilled. That was clearly beside the point. "I was talking to Brad Conway for a lot of the night. The model is his girlfriend."

Hugh rolled his eyes. "Brad Conway is nothing but a starfucker who likes to throw his money around. His gallery probably won't last five minutes, and if it does it'll show nothing but selfies of influencers."

Michael opened his mouth, closed it again. Where was this coming from? He'd never heard Hugh speak like this, so full of something that he didn't want to call contempt. He'd always been reassured by the idea that Hugh wasn't a snob, that he wasn't secretly judging Michael, but maybe he'd been wrong all along. A prickle of unease crept up the back of his neck.

Michael had been pleasantly surprised by Brad last night. The first time they'd met, there had been something about him that seemed too slick, too over the top. He definitely was slick and over the top, but that was just his way. Behind it all seemed to be a decent guy with a genuine love of art. Or was that all for show? Maybe he was just pandering to Michael because of Miranda. Perhaps he really was, in Hugh's words, nothing but a starfucker.

Although the epithet quite literally applied to Michael too, so ...

"Listen, Michael." Hugh's voice, sounding much more like his usual measured but friendly tone, broke through Michael's thoughts. "I'm sorry. I shouldn't have acted like I was berating you for having a social life. But I think we need to make sure that you're seen in a few more helpful places, if you are serious about the gallery route."

"I am serious. I swear." He had wanted this for so long, and everyone was counting on him to do it. He couldn't let a few paparazzi pictures derail him. Hugh could help him fix this, right?

"Tomorrow night, then." Hugh nodded firmly. "There's a talk on war photography at Somerset House. We'll go, I'll introduce you to some people. Let's get you known for the right reasons."

40

MIRANDA smiled as Courtney's name flashed up on her phone screen. Miraculous – a rare moment where both of them were free and awake.

"Courtney, sweetheart, how are you?" Miranda said.

"Hey, M. Not as great as you, by the look of it. Taking the new man out on the town and all."

Miranda giggled. "Yes, our hand was forced. You know how it is."

"Oh yeah. How's he dealing with it?"

Miranda frowned. "Um, OK, I think?"

"You don't sound too sure," Courtney said.

"Well …" Miranda blew out a breath. "I think the whole media-circus thing in general, he's OK with. I mean, he knows how it goes, so he's pretty much rolling with it. But …"

"But what?"

"The *Buzz!* article really freaked him out. And he has this mentor, Hugh, who's supposed to be helping him break into the art scene, and I think Hugh's worried about the effect all this will have on his career."

"What? Having a higher profile is … bad?"

"Well, that's what I thought. But I don't know. I guess I don't have the right kind of fame, or something."

"Wait, did this guy say that?" Courtney sounded horrified.

"No, no, of course he didn't," Miranda replied. *But is that what he thinks?* She brushed the thought away. "That's just the vibe I'm picking up from what Michael says about what Hugh says. I might be reading too much into it."

"Probably," Courtney said reassuringly. "Fame opens doors, M, especially when there's talent to back it up. I'm sure they'll both see that before long."

"Yeah. I hope so."

There was silence for a second, before Courtney said, "So, I have to ask you something ..."

Her uncharacteristic hesitance put Miranda instantly on alert. She had a feeling she knew what was coming. "Sure, sweetie. Fire away."

"God, I hate myself. I know this is pathetic. I know I should be talking to Henry about this, and I know I don't even need to. But ... the other night, those photos. Who was she?"

Poor Courtney. She sounded so distressed. But surely she knew she had nothing to worry about? Henry adored her.

"Her name's Eleanor," Miranda said, calling up the information from the part of her brain that was so good at storing all of that. "They work together. She's something senior in HR. Henry said he brought her to the dinner to make up for loads of horrible meetings, and because she's from the same part of England as Michael so he thought they'd get along, which they did. She's sweet, very married, and there wasn't a single hint of anything non-platonic between them, Court, I swear."

She felt Courtney's relief as if they were in the same room. "Thank you. I just needed to hear that."

"Of course, sweetie. But haven't you spoken to him about it? Is everything OK between you?"

"It's fine. We're fine." Courtney's reply was the least convincing one Miranda had ever heard in her life.

"Honey, if something's up, just talk to him."

"Yeah." Courtney was silent for several seconds, then said brightly, "Anyway, enough about me and my neuroses. How are you? Are you coming back to the States anytime soon? I miss you."

Miranda missed her friends too, but the question hit her like an anvil to the stomach. "A few weeks. Rehearsals for *Ocean* start soon. I'll be in LA the whole time."

"Ooh, yay." Courtney sounded much more like her usual self now. "I can't wait to see you. But I bet you'll miss London, huh? And Michael ..."

Miranda couldn't even answer. They still hadn't had The Conversation. She wanted to believe that they were both taking it for granted that they'd stay together, but she knew it wasn't that simple. "Michael. Yeah. I ... we ..."

Courtney could apparently read silences. "What was it you said to me thirty seconds ago? 'Just talk to him'?"

"I know." But it was a lot easier to dish that advice out than it was to follow it.

What is wrong with you? You're Miranda freaking Janes,

and you can do anything. You didn't let Damia slip through your fingers. Don't let Michael either.

"Hey," his voice called out. Speak of the devil.

"Is that him?" Courtney said. "I'll let you go. Thanks, Miranda. I don't know what I'd do without you."

"It's OK, you don't have to go," Miranda protested.

"Nah, it's fine. My personal trainer will be here soon anyway. Acting has destroyed my core strength, according to Anders." Miranda could practically hear Courtney's eye-roll. "Besides, one of us is on the same continent as her man. Go take advantage."

Miranda laughed as the man in question appeared in her living room doorway, looking delicious in a fitted black T-shirt. "OK, if you say so. But call me anytime you need to, you hear?"

"I will." Courtney blew a kiss down the phone. "Bye."

"Bye."

"Who was that?" Michael said, sitting down beside her and dropping a kiss on the side of her neck.

"Courtney." Miranda tilted her head to let him do it again. "She's missing Henry, I think."

It was the perfect opportunity, to segue into talking about separation. But Michael was still dropping soft, fluttery kisses on her neck, and his arms looked so damn good in that shirt and … ah, screw it. Difficult conversations could wait.

* * *

"I was thinking," Miranda said as Michael moved purposefully around her kitchen making some kind of pasta thing that smelled delicious, "I had a nice time with Jodi and Brad the other night, didn't you? Jodi is hilarious in that kind of deadpan way you Brits are so good at, and Brad is just so easy to talk to."

Michael made a non-committal noise. "Do you have any paprika?"

She waved towards the collection of spices she'd bought when she first moved in. "There may be some over there. God knows how old it will be, though. We should see them again some time, don't you think? I know Brad said his gallery was full for now, but he'll still need artists in the future, right? And he's very well connected."

"Hmm. Maybe." He appeared to be concentrating very hard on his sauce. "This needs something ..."

That wasn't exactly an enthusiastic response. But she knew what he was like when he was focused on something. She decided to let him be and just watch him as he cooked. She loved the way his brow wrinkled as he tasted the sauce, seasoned it a little more, kept tweaking it until he was satisfied. She set the table and poured them drinks, and waited until Michael had set down a plate of pasta in front of her.

"So, should I call them? We could go out, tomorrow night, maybe?"

Michael shook his head. "I have to go to a thing with Hugh tomorrow night."

"Oh? What kind of thing?"

"Some talk at Somerset House. Hugh thinks I need to be seen at more 'serious' art stuff."

He rolled his eyes, and she could hear the air quotes in his voice, but something about his words stung anyway.

"As opposed to hanging out with me at my deeply unserious stuff?" she said lightly. Or she hoped it was light.

He seemed to take an age to finish swallowing the bite of pasta he'd just taken. "I didn't say that."

"Did Hugh?"

"Not in so many words," he mumbled, not meeting her eyes. He dropped his fork with a gentle clatter and lifted his head. "I'm sorry. You know that's not what I think. I don't even think it's what Hugh thinks. But I've had no luck on my own. I don't know the right people, and Hugh does. So I think I should play this his way for a while."

She arched an eyebrow. "Which is?"

"Which is keeping out of *Buzz!* magazine and in events with people who are in danger of disappearing up their own arses." He smiled at her, that small, uneven, uncertain smile that never failed to tug at some spot behind her ribcage. "You had to change your image to get what you want. Now so do I."

That was different, she wanted to argue. She had never changed who she was or what she did or who she hung around with. She'd made the most superficial changes on the most superficial of platforms, so that AJ could see her for who she really was and what she could do.

But maybe it wasn't that different. The world needed to see what Michael could do, and if he needed to avoid the limelight in order for that to happen, she could live with that. It wasn't as if she objected to more cosy nights in whenever he wasn't putting in the Serious Artist hours with Hugh. The number of those nights available was dwindling, after all ...

And now she was sad again, great. She must not let herself mope.

"Hey. What's up?" Michael was looking at her with concern.

"Nothing," she said, smiling. "We can give the red carpets a miss for while."

He reached for her hand and entwined his fingers with hers. "Thank you for understanding."

"Of course. You know I'll do anything I can to help you, right? I only want good things for you, Michael."

"I know." He kissed her fingers, then let go of her hand and picked up his fork. "Finish your pasta before it's stone cold. I bought you a doughnut for dessert. Actually, I bought us one doughnut to share. I know you said you'll have to go back into pre-rehearsal health mode."

"Oh my god, you're the best." How was she supposed to not fall in love with this guy? She'd been a fool to think it was possible. He always knew what she needed and did his best to give it to her. She wanted to be that for him. She just had to figure out how.

* * *

"That will be …" Miranda looked at the card in front of her. "Two thousand pounds, please."

Michael groaned. "Would you accept thirteen pounds, Old Kent Road and, erm, five kisses on that bit of the back of your neck?"

She giggled. The thought was very, very tempting. "No. I do not take sexual favours in lieu of rent, Mr Hedley."

"Then I guess you win. Although I'm not convinced you didn't cheat."

She gasped. "How dare you? I am just very good at this game. I always win."

"No," he said dryly. "You shock me."

She threw her winning Mayfair hotel at his chest. She loved this stage of a relationship, where you felt comfortable enough to take the piss out of each other, as they said over here. "My family won't play this game with me anymore. My dad is a terrible loser, and Jen says it brings out all my worst instincts."

"Well, pet, if your worst instincts are to become a ruthless capitalist monster, I can see where she's coming from." He leaned over the board and brushed a kiss across her lips, so she was fairly sure he was kidding.

"Speaking of my family …" She took a quick breath. "Did you think any more about coming to the falls?"

Apparently, tidying away the Monopoly board had suddenly become an urgent and interesting priority. "Hmm?"

"My dad's birthday. You said you'd think about it." Did that sound whiney? Maybe a little. "I don't mean to pressure you or anything. But we should book a flight if you want to come. Which you totally don't have to do."

But lord, she wanted him to want to. The idea of being out there, cut off from the whole world except the people she loved best, surrounded by nature, had taken hold of her and she couldn't let it go.

"I don't know, Miranda." He was separating all the bank notes and putting them in the box, making sure each one sat neatly in the correct compartment. "It's not that I don't want to spend the time with you, because of course I do. But it's a family thing. I'd feel like I was intruding. They want to be with you, not some random bloke they don't know from Adam."

"I told you before, they love people. It's not that strange for one of us to bring someone else along on a trip. Jen's best friend came with us to Disney World once because she was going through a divorce and Jen didn't want her to be alone. And you're not just some random guy. You're ..."

His eyes met hers. The question neither of them asked hung in the air between them. One of them should do it. Why wasn't she doing it? She'd never been afraid of this before.

But she chickened out. "They all know about you and want to meet you," she said instead.

Michael let out an uneasy little chuckle. "I've never had to meet a woman's parents before. Cleo's knew me – and hated me, pretty much – for most of my life. And it was never an issue with anyone else, not even close." He put the lid back on the box. "I'm kind of ...

not great with families in general, to be honest. I don't know how they're supposed to work, because mine just fucking ... didn't."

There it was, that pain in his eyes that she saw whenever he talked about his family. Miranda tried not to take hers for granted, but the simplicity of the love they all had for each other meant she didn't always remember that other people had more baggage.

She scooted closer to him and put her hand on his arm. "You have a wonderful family. You, your mom, and Cleo – that's a family. The way you've always loved each other and looked out for each other, that's real, and that's beautiful. The hard and unconventional parts don't make that count any less."

Michael slid one hand into her hair and pulled her close for a sweet, deep kiss that took her breath away. He leaned his forehead against hers, and she thought she maybe saw a tear in his eye. "I ... thank you." He swallowed. "When do you need an answer? About the trip?"

She thought about Aisling's last email on the subject. "Monday, probably, if we're to have any hope of getting a decent flight."

"OK," he said softly. He put his arm around her, and she leaned her head on his chest, listening to the beat of his heart. "I'll let you know by Monday."

41

HUGH was waiting for him at the east entrance. As Michael approached his mentor, his first thought was that it was so quiet. Jesus Christ, what had he become? This was what it was normally like when you went somewhere. You were outside, and then you went inside. Just like that. No avoiding the press or posing for them, delete as applicable. A few weeks with Miranda and he seemed to have forgotten how the actual world worked.

He was fervently glad that Hugh couldn't tell what he was thinking.

"Good, you made it. Let's get a drink," Hugh said tightly. Whoa. What was up with him? Was he still pissed off about the pap shots?

He stifled a sigh. This was going to be a fun night.

He followed Hugh inside, past the various small groups of people milling about. Was it his imagination, or were some of them giving him funny looks? *It'll be your imagination, you bellend. You're not that important.*

As soon as they entered the bar area, Hugh got to work.

"Rhys! Good to see you. Rhys, this is Michael. He's a new mentee. Michael, Rhys, an old mentee."

"Effie! It's been too long, darling. Sorry I didn't

make your opening, but I caught the show before it came down. Stunning, really."

"Ash, your programme for this season is so interesting. You have to tell me more about that concept."

And on and on and on it went. Michael smiled, shook hands, nodded, tried to think of interesting things to say, mostly failed. This event wasn't that different to the ones he'd been to with Miranda, when it came down to it, but despite the glitz and the glamour of those, they'd always been easier at her side. She had an extraordinary knack for starting conversations, for working out what people had in common, for putting people at ease. Hugh was great, of course, but it wasn't quite the same. When Hugh went into schmooze mode, Michael felt as though he ceased to exist.

When the talk finally, blessedly, started, he sank into his chair as if it were a life raft.

Christ alive, he wished he were somewhere else. Anywhere else. Half his brain was trying to pay attention to what the speaker was saying, because at least if he listened he'd hopefully have something to say to people afterwards, but the other half wouldn't stop wondering where it would rather be.

It wanted to be with Miranda, no point in denying that. For just a second, he let the whole of his brain picture being with her, somewhere that wasn't here. Somewhere peaceful, beautiful, quiet, somewhere far away from her world and his. Somewhere, he realised, that sounded very like the cabin she'd been talking about. Shit, did he actually want to go to Washington?

Had he come around to the idea of meeting her whole bloody family? That was something he hadn't expected.

He felt an elbow in his side. His lack of attention had not gone unnoticed by Hugh. Oops. Time to do some listening.

He was glad he did. The talk was fascinating. The photographer was a superb speaker – witty and passionate about his subject despite the sometimes harrowing details. Michael felt himself start to relax. By the time the crowd broke out into applause, he'd begun to think that maybe this night wasn't going to be so horrible after all.

"That was great, wasn't it?" said the woman next to him with a friendly smile.

Michael returned it. "Really great. Are you into photography?" Stupid question, given her attendance at a photography-related event, but he had to start somewhere.

"A little. I cover visual art for an arts website, so I know a small amount about a wide range of things, I suppose. I've been to this whole series of talks so far, and they've all been excellent."

"Oh, I didn't realise they were part of a series. I'll have to check out the others."

"You should." She extended her hand. "I'm Suzy."

He shook it. "Michael. I'm a photographer."

"I know." She looked a little sheepish. "Sorry. I'm a secret *Buzz!* fan."

He couldn't completely stop a small groan escaping. Before he could form a reply, Hugh interjected.

"Let's go to the bar. Excuse us, Suzy, is it?"

Michael offered her an awkward wave as Hugh hustled him away. Was it just him, or was that pretty rude? Hugh was never rude. Something was definitely up with him.

But Hugh just smiled. "Don't worry. We'll find you some people who won't know who you are."

"OK." But it hadn't been that terrible, had it? He'd been having a pleasant conversation, and he could have brought it back to a non-Miranda-related topic in a second or two, probably.

"Hugh!" cried a small man with very round glasses as they reached the bar. "I didn't know you were coming tonight."

"It was fairly last minute." Hugh caught the attention of the barman and ordered two glasses of red. "It's good to see you. How's the show going?"

"Good, I think. Had a very positive review in *ArtScratch*, which surprised me. I never thought they would write a kind word about any of us again after that whole debacle with Leona."

The debacle with Leona was apparently an amusing rather than a disastrous one, judging by the hearty laughter, but god knew what that meant.

"Michael, meet Oskar. He's exhibiting at Preston's at the moment. Very exciting multimedia work. You should check it out."

"I'll try." He offered the small man a smile. "Nice to meet you."

"Ooh, a northerner!" Oskar sounded delighted.

"Don't get many of you in these parts. What brings you to the Big Smoke?"

"I live here," he said, bemused. This was London, for crying out loud. Hardly anyone was actually from here. "I came for uni, never left. I'm a photographer. Hugh is mentoring me."

"Ah, I see. I did wonder if old Hugh had ditched Aidan for a younger model."

Michael laughed politely, but Hugh did not.

"Yes, Michael is a very promising talent," he said stiffly. "Excuse me for a second, please. I see someone I must say hello to."

Crap. Michael tried to breathe evenly as Hugh walked briskly away. This was fine. He was a grown man. He could have a conversation with another grown man. What would Miranda do? She'd ask a question, that's what she'd do, and she'd be genuinely interested in the answer.

"So, Oskar, tell me about your show. What's it about?"

It sounded fascinating. Michael didn't know a lot about multimedia work and admitted as much, and Oskar seemed only too happy to have an enthusiastic audience. *People love talking about the things they love. That's all you need to remember.* Miranda had told him that once, and she was right. She was always right.

Some other people drifted over, and Michael's heart plummeted. Ah, shit. One of them was Kimiko, the photographer from Brad's opening. The woman had been decidedly unimpressed by him. But maybe that had just been nerves on his part, or a bad day on hers.

"We've met," she said coolly as Oskar tried to introduce them.

Or maybe not. Still, it could be worse.

"I've seen you somewhere," one of the newcomers said. Michael had forgotten his name already. Jack, maybe? "Did you used to work at the Arts Council?"

"No, sorry. Not me."

"Perhaps you've seen him in the Sidebar of Shame," Kimiko said over the rim of her wine glass.

There was the worse. Oskar's eyes swivelled to him, as did the rest of the group's. "Really?"

He waited for Kimiko to explain, but apparently she was about to do no such thing.

"Er, yeah. Maybe." Fuck, what was the best way to say this? "I've been ... pictured with Miranda Janes a few times."

What the hell was wrong with him? Why didn't he just say he was seeing her? The rest of the sodding world knew that, so why was he tiptoeing around it?

"That's it!" the guy – was it James, not Jack? – said, snapping his fingers. "My flatmate is obsessed with those crappy celebrity magazines. Aren't you the guy who used to be a pap?"

The eyes on him widened. Hugh was going to lose his shit. In that very posh way he did, obviously.

He rubbed at the back of his neck. The room was suddenly way too hot. "Aye. I was." Maybe if he kept his answers brief, they'd change the subject.

There was contempt, there was disdain, and then there was whatever Kimiko was looking at him with.

"And now you're an artist. Interesting path." He had to admire it. The emphasis she put on the word "artist" was incredible. Managed to imply he was nothing of the sort while saying exactly the opposite.

"Would we have seen your work anywhere, Michael?" Jack-or-James asked. "Other than in the red tops, obviously!"

A hearty laugh went up. *Et tu, Oskar?* Michael felt his face flush.

"Probably not," he said, trying to keep his voice light.

"Not unless you follow Miranda Janes on Instagram," Kimiko put in.

Fuck's sake. Where the fuck was Hugh? Michael was dying here.

He forced a smile. "Well, hopefully with Hugh's help, I'll be able to find somewhere else soon." Guilt twinged in his stomach as he said the words. It felt a little too much like accepting Kimiko's premise, like agreeing that featuring on Miranda's Instagram was a huge joke. Those pictures were great and he knew it. He was proud of them, and he'd loved everything about taking them. But what good would it do him to admit that now, here, to these people?

"Can I get anyone a drink?" When in doubt, get a round in.

Nobody took him up on the offer, but Michael headed to the bar anyway. He knew he should have stayed and stuck out the conversation a little longer, but he just couldn't.

How was he ever supposed to fit into this world?

They'd all been making art their whole lives, while he'd spent his hanging out on pavements, wasting so many years. And all he had to show for it was an ever-dwindling stack of cash and a reputation for all the wrong things.

He ordered a shot of rum and downed it, letting it burn its way down his chest. Getting hammered at this kind of thing was undoubtedly a terrible idea and Hugh would definitely not be impressed, but what did it matter? He was fucking up anyway, like he fucked up everything.

I'm sorry, Cleo. I tried.

42

THE only thing as nice as a spa day with an old friend, Miranda decided, was a spa day with a new friend. Things in her life were about to get extremely un-relaxing, so when Jodi called and invited her to check out London's most fabulous new spa, Miranda had jumped at the chance.

Jodi had been right about the fabulousness of the spa, and Miranda had been right about Jodi. Behind the frosty exterior lay a sharp brain and an even sharper sense of humour.

"Thanks for coming with me today," Jodi said as they relaxed in a hammam filled with gentle, scented steam. "The rest of my friends get tired of indulging my spa obsession."

"Oh, anytime. Today has been just what I needed. We should hang out more."

"Definitely," Jodi said, closing her gorgeous dark eyes in contentment.

"In fact, I was thinking we should have dinner or something, the four of us. You, me, Michael and Brad." OK, so Michael hadn't been all that enthusiastic about the idea when she'd first floated it, but the two guys had gotten along great, hadn't they? They could keep it low-key. Miranda knew plenty of places where they could avoid being spotted.

"Sounds fab, babe. If I'm still around, of course."

"What do you mean?"

Jodi opened one eye. "I don't think Brad and I will last long, to be honest."

Miranda's face must be displaying her shock, because Jodi sat up straight and looked at her properly.

"Don't get me wrong," Jodi said. "Brad is a great guy, and we're having a load of fun. I know he looks like your typical fuck-em-and-chuck-em wide boy with more money than sense and style put together, but that's not it. He's clever, and kind, and so interesting, and very respectful. But the man lives life at a million miles an hour. He's like a ride at Alton Towers – fast and exciting and" – she winked – "will make you scream, but then it's over and it's someone else's turn." She shrugged. "It is what it is."

"Wow." Miranda pulled her eyebrows down from where they'd risen to in surprise. "I was not expecting to learn all that about him today."

Jodi lay back down and closed her eyes again. "The only thing that holds his attention for long is art. That's his thing. Did you know, he looked me up because he liked my *Vogue* spread? And not just because he thought I looked good, but because he loved the whole artistry of it. We spent most of our first date talking about what it was like to shoot. He's really interested in that kind of intersection of art and fashion, you know? That's why he was so interested in Michael."

"Then we should definitely get them together," Miranda said thoughtfully. Brad's gallery might not have openings right now, but that didn't mean there wouldn't be opportunities in the future. And even if nothing professional ever came of it, it'd be fun.

"Speaking of Michael ..." Jodi drawled. "What's the deal with you two? Is it serious, or is it more a me-and-Brad thing?"

It was one of those rare occasions where Miranda wasn't sure what to say. Her standard line to the press had been "very new, very happy", and to her closest friends ... well, that was a little more complicated, what with one of them being his ex-wife. Jodi was so straightforward that it was hard not to tell her the truth, but Miranda couldn't figure out how to do that, or what it even was. *Well, I'm desperately in love with him and not sure how to make him fall desperately in love with me? It's the best relationship I've ever been in yet somehow also the least defined? I've never had less of an idea of what the future holds?*

She was pretty sure she said all that in her head, but maybe Jodi heard some of it in the silence anyway, because she said, "I've seen the way he looks at you. You two seem good together. I'm sure you'll work it out."

Would they? Or were they running out of time?

* * *

A small cluster of photographers were waiting on the pavement as Miranda left the spa. Somebody must have seen her arrive. Either that, or someone at the spa had tipped them off, and she hoped not. The spa had been wonderful, but if they couldn't be discreet, they'd crossed themselves off the list for anyone with any kind of profile. Being snapped with post-spa red skin wasn't what anyone wanted.

Miranda gave them a brief smile and got into her waiting car. She'd always been more tolerant of the paparazzi than some people she knew – cough, Devon Grant – but since meeting Michael she was no longer sure what she thought of them. In some ways, she had more sympathy for what a miserable job it was, but the things he'd told her about the way some of them operated made her want to throw them all into the sea.

Frank pulled away from the kerb and headed for home. Home. In a few short weeks, that would be LA again. Temporarily, of course. London was her home now, she was sure of that. It wouldn't be the worst thing in the world, being back in California. She loved the weather, and her LA house, and so many of her friends were based there. She'd usually be looking forward to going back, but not this time.

She really needed to start getting things organised; she'd have so little time after Washington. But that would mean thinking regularly about the fact that she was leaving, and Miranda was assiduously avoiding doing so, for obvious reasons. She couldn't do it forever. She had to face the truth.

After she answered this phone call that was blessedly interrupting that train of thought.

"Aisling, darling. How was the night away?"

"It was unbelievable, Miranda. Thank you again. You really didn't have to."

"I had to get my favourite assistant an engagement present. I'm glad you enjoyed it."

"We did. Anyway, I'm calling about your flights for next weekend. The seats are going fast on that direct flight. There are only a few left. I'd be concerned about waiting until Monday to book."

"Damn." Miranda chewed her lip. She'd promised to give Michael time to consider it, but once again, time was in short supply. She couldn't bug him about it again. But also, she absolutely did not want to sit around in a connecting airport for hours.

She took a deep breath. "Book them." If he didn't want to come, well, she'd be down a few grand but there'd be one more seat between her and anyone who might be able to see her cry.

"For the two of you?" Miranda could already hear Aisling's fingers tapping over her keyboard.

"Yes. You still have all his details, right?"

"Yup. I'm on it as we speak."

"Thank you, sweetheart." Miranda hung up. She hoped Michael wouldn't be mad that she'd booked him a ticket without asking first. It was a practical matter, that was all. And she should think positive – he'd probably say yes anyway. Why wouldn't he?

* * *

To her surprise, when she arrived home, Michael was

already there, sitting on her sofa with a bottle of beer.

"Sorry," he said. "I hope you don't mind that I let myself in. I did try to text you but my phone died as it was sending." He waved over to where it was charging in a corner.

"Of course I don't." She sat down by his side. "What's wrong?" He looked as if he had the weight of several worlds on his shoulders.

He slumped back against the sofa cushions. "Last night was fucking horrible."

"Oh no. Why?"

"People recognised me. I barely got to have any conversations about anything real, because I was too busy being the butt of their jokes." He took an angry swig from his bottle.

She put her hand on his shoulder. "Sweetie, I'm sure it wasn't like–"

"It was exactly like that. Hugh was right. These people aren't going to take me seriously. They all know each other, and they all talk in the same way, and they acted like I was some kind of zoo exhibit."

His anger seemed to fade into bitterness, but her own was rising. How dare they treat him that way? She knew what that was like, to have your talent overlooked because of what people thought they knew about you, and she knew how much it burned.

"I don't know if I can do this," he said, and the quiet despair in his voice made her heart hurt. "If this is the way it's always going to be, if that's the way they're always going to see me ..."

"No, Michael. Don't talk like that. Don't think like that." She stood. "I'm going to get myself a drink, and then we'll figure this out. We'll find a way to make them see you as the artist you are." She stopped and put her hand on his shoulder. "I won't let you give up on yourself."

43

MICHAEL watched her go, trying to feel grateful for her support. But how could she help him fix this? She was part of the problem.

No. His brain scrambled to erase the thought. That wasn't fair. She wasn't the problem. These people and their snobbery were the problem. Michael's inability to deal with them was the problem. Michael and the stupid decisions he'd made were the problem.

Being with her wasn't one of those stupid decisions. Was it? He'd never thought so, but all day long he'd had to fight hard to keep the thought out of his brain – were they just completely wrong for each other? It wasn't her fault – she was wonderful, she really was, and he'd been letting himself fall for her because how could he not? But she was a bright, vibrant butterfly breathing rarefied air. And he was nobody, a miserable twat with absolutely nothing going for him. She'd be leaving for LA soon anyway, and she'd have better things to do than spend time on her phone listening to him drone on about how the shred of a career he had was circling the drain. How long could he hold her interest once they were apart?

She came back into the room holding a glass of wine and another beer for him. He took it and fiddled with the label as she sat back down.

"So," she said, determination in her voice, "what can we do? How can we fix this?"

He bit back a sigh. "I'm not sure this is something you can help me with."

"Why not? Two heads are better than one, babe. There's always a way forward."

Of course that was her attitude. He normally admired it. Today it just felt as though she didn't understand.

"I'm thinking I might do what Hugh advised. Take a step back from the fine art for a while. There'll be loads of opportunities for me to work on more commercial stuff, more fashion-related. I could be good at that, and I think I'd enjoy it." It made sense. Baby steps. He needed to ease back into the world of serious photography, not throw himself straight into something he couldn't handle. And, he realised, surprised, the thought didn't fill him with dread.

But Miranda was looking at him in horror. "But that isn't what you want, is it? That wasn't your dream. You wanted to be in the art world."

"But the art world doesn't want me!" The admission felt like a dagger in his gut. "Maybe I've just got to face that."

"Nonsense. You went to one event where a few people were awful. You can't let that stop you."

On some level he knew she was right. He was giving up too easily. Perhaps he'd just had the bad luck to run into a tiny minority of arseholes, and he just had to try, yet again, to find people he could actually connect with. But fuck, the thought of putting himself through weeks and months and years of nights like that one was enough to make him want to stick his head in a blender.

She continued, almost as if he wasn't there. "If the people from last night were terrible, then you need to find new people. I refuse to believe that they represent the entire art scene. I saw Jodi today, and she said that Brad really liked you. Let's have dinner with them. It'll be fun, and you can talk to Brad about this. Maybe he can help."

This again? Hadn't he told her he wasn't sure about that? "It's a nice idea, but I don't think hanging out with Brad Conway and his supermodel girlfriend is going to help this situation. It's doing exactly that that got me in trouble with Hugh!" He was letting his voice rise, which he knew he shouldn't, but all of his frustration was bubbling over and he didn't know how to control it.

"Maybe Hugh's wrong!" she cried, a stubborn set to her features. "Did you ever think about that? Maybe Hugh's doing just what you're accusing all those people of, judging Brad based on superficial things. Brad genuinely cares about art, and he was definitely interested in you. Why are you so against the idea of having dinner with the man, for heaven's sake?"

It was a reasonable question. He didn't have anything against Brad, as such. But he couldn't stop thinking about the way Hugh had described him – a starfucker. "Why are you so set on the idea? For all we know, Brad's only interested in me because of you anyway."

"Is that really what you think?" she asked, and he

didn't think he was imagining the flash of hurt that crossed her face.

He let out a sigh, feeling himself deflate. "I don't know. Maybe. No. I don't think so. I'm just not sure he can help me, or if you can help me, or if anyone can help me. I'm not like you, Miranda – I can't look at a problem and instantly see all the ways I could beat it. I just need ..."

"What?" She looked into his eyes, and he hated the fragment of pain he saw there, because he knew he'd put it there with the way he'd been carrying on. "What do you need? I only want to give that to you, Michael."

"I know," he said softly, closing his eyes. Space. That was what he needed. This conversation had got too heavy and heated. It had probably been a mistake to come here when he was in such a fucking mood. "I just need a minute." He kissed her on the cheek, grabbed his no longer dead phone and headed out to the garden. He sat down in the beautiful Mediterranean corner he'd shot Miranda in all those weeks ago, seeing nothing, wondering what the hell he was supposed to do.

44

THE urge to follow him outside, to wrap her arms around him and try to take away his pain, was almost uncontrollable. Miranda couldn't bear to see Michael like this, so despondent, so defeated. How could he let one bad night derail him like this?

Her mind was whirring with plans and ideas. This couldn't be the end for him. When he calmed down, he would see that. She'd set something up with Jodi and Brad, maybe here, away from the prying eyes of the press, so that Hugh couldn't object. A sour taste came to her mouth at the thought of Michael's mentor. She failed to see how Hugh was actually helping him. He seemed more concerned about her and her effect on Michael's reputation than he did the actual art. Was he another one of those people who thought he knew everything about women like her? Frivolous and foolish, no real help to anyone or anything serious? He'd see. They'd all see.

Wait, no. She needed to stop thinking like this. This wasn't about her. This was about Michael. This was his career, and maybe she needed to step back and let him do things his way.

But if his way was quitting ...

Her phone buzzed with an email, and she picked it up, grateful for the distraction. It was Aisling, confirming her flight details. No, confirming *their* flight details. To both of them.

Oh, hell.

Ten seconds later, he appeared in the doorway. "What's this? Why is Aisling sending me flight details?"

She stood up to face him. "Yes, about that–"

It seemed he wasn't in the mood to let her explain. "You said I had until Monday. You booked it without asking me?"

She grimaced. "Yes. But the seats were selling so fast. Aisling was concerned we'd miss out. I didn't want us to have to get a connecting flight."

He ran a hand through his hair. "But you didn't even ask if I'd decided yet. You knew I was still thinking about it. Would the flights really have sold out in the thirty seconds it would have taken you to ask?"

"I couldn't have asked. You said yourself your phone died."

He narrowed his eyes. "Did you even try?"

"No," she admitted, her shoulders sinking. "But I didn't want to put that pressure on you, making you think you had to decide right then."

"So you thought it was better to present me with a fait accompli? Did you think I'd just say yes to you, like I always fucking do?"

Whoa. Where was this coming from? Why was he talking to her like this, with such bitterness in his tone? She took a deep breath, trying to pretend each of his words wasn't hitting her like a shower of stones. "It wasn't like that. I didn't want you to feel backed into a corner because of something as stupid as flight availability. I figured I'd rather waste money on a seat that went unused than do that to you."

"Must be nice to have that option," he muttered, and anger flared in her chest.

She drew herself up to her full height. "Yes, actually, it is. I have a lot of money, and I can use it to solve problems. You never seemed to have an issue with that before."

Even from across the room, she saw his jaw clench tight. "And what the fuck is that supposed to mean?"

"I'm sorry," she said hastily. "That came out wrong. I didn't mean to imply you liked me for my money or anything like that. I know that isn't true. I just meant that it's easy for money to cause problems between people, and it never has for us before, and I don't want it to now. Is it ridiculous that some people dream their whole lives of travelling first class and never will, yet I can afford to drop thousands on a ticket that might not even get used? Of course it is. But it was an option for me in that moment, and I took it."

He lifted his head and looked her straight in the eye. "And there wasn't a single part of you that thought you'd be able to persuade me to use it over the next few days and I'd never know?"

If there was ever a good moment to issue a denial, it was now. He was mad at her, that much was clear, and she desperately wanted to make that stop. She should tell him that her decision was purely a pragmatic one.

But it would be a lie, and she was pretty sure he knew that.

She sighed and took a few steps closer to him. "Is that so wrong of me? To want you with me? To want one magical weekend with all the people I love?"

Oh no.

The moment the word left her lips, she wanted to reach for it and stuff it back into her reckless, impulsive mouth. She saw the look of stunned panic that crept into his eyes. This wasn't the way she'd wanted to tell him that, but it was too late now. It was done, and Miranda Janes didn't do or say things she wasn't willing to stand by.

So, she took another deep breath and threw all caution to the wind. "I love you, Michael. I wanted you to come meet my family because I'm in love with you, and I wanted them to love you too. I wanted to spend time with you getting away from it all, so I could show you how much you mean to me, how much the thought of leaving you is killing me." She'd never felt so vulnerable in her life, standing in the middle of her living room, while he stood feet away, saying nothing. The silence that followed her words seemed to last an eternity.

Eventually, he slumped into the armchair by the door. "Fuck, Miranda," he said in a voice laced with despair.

Well. That wasn't the reaction she'd hoped for. Her legs felt as though they might give out, so she walked back over to the sofa and sat down on it, trying to retain some shred of elegance but feeling as if there were a lead weight in her stomach.

They sat there, her on the couch, him in the chair,

saying nothing. Her eyes were fixed on him, but he seemed to want to look at anything but her.

Her insides twisted in on themselves. Why had she said anything? Had she thought he would fall into her arms, declare how much he loved her too, and sweep her straight to bed?

Yes. That was, if she was being honest, exactly what she thought he'd do. Or at least what she'd hoped for.

"You can't love me." Finally, he broke the silence, shattered it into a million pieces.

"Don't tell me what I can and can't do," she said, hoping for levity but not managing it.

"I'm all wrong for you, Miranda. We both know that. You need a man who can take on the world with you."

"But you can be that man, Michael. Why won't you believe that?"

The sadness in his smile almost cracked her heart in two. "You think you can make me a better man, someone worthy of being by your side. I don't know, maybe you could." He pushed himself to his feet and crossed the room to stand in front of her. He bent down and tipped her chin up so she was looking into his beautiful hazel eyes. "You could make the world bow to you, Miranda, should you demand it." He brushed a soft kiss over her lips, and her brain refused to acknowledge what her heart already knew – that it was a kiss goodbye. "But you deserve someone who's good enough already. That isn't me."

And then he turned around, and he left.

45

MICHAEL went home. He cleaned the flat, removing the dust that he'd allowed to settle over everything in the last couple of weeks. He emptied the fridge of all the now unidentifiable food items, and went to the shop to replace them. He slept for twelve solid hours. He batch-cooked a load of healthy meals. He processed an Etsy order, and uploaded a new shot of the river he'd taken the other week. He texted his mam and said he'd ring her soon. He went to the gym and pounded the treadmill so hard he almost collapsed.

In short, he got his life back in order. He returned everything to normal.

But nothing was normal, because he wasn't normal. He was a man walking around with a hole where his heart should be. Because no one with a heart could have caused the look of devastation on Miranda's face when he left her.

He told himself, a million times a day, that it was for the best. She might be hurting now, but it wouldn't take her long to come to her senses and get over him. She'd bounced back after failed relationships before; the whole world had watched her do it, over and over. He was just the latest in the line. By the time she was in LA with AJ Hollinger and Seb Akao and all those other glittering people who belonged in her world, he'd be nothing but a memory. He could picture her now, at some party high in the hills, sipping a glass of something expensive and laughing that crystal-clear laugh of hers. "*Can you believe it? I thought I was in love with him! Imagine that!*"

He held on to that image of her, sparkling, vibrant, untouchable, and pushed away every single other one that he had. Her cheek cradled in his hand. The secret smile she gave him across a crowded room. Her naked body beneath him. Any image that suggested she could have really been his, that they could have belonged together.

It was a fantasy, and he'd let himself get caught in it for too long. Time to get back to reality.

And his reality, right now, was that he had no job, no art career, and a mentor who was supremely pissed off at him. He had to fix all of those things. The last was probably – hopefully – the easiest. He pulled out his phone and sent Hugh a message.

* * *

Hugh had insisted on taking Michael for lunch, suggesting the restaurant they'd met in weeks ago. As he waited for Hugh to arrive, Michael couldn't help but notice how different it felt from the last time he'd been here. How different *he* felt. He'd been so nervous, felt so out of place. He still did, to a certain extent, but after weeks of Miranda's luxury lifestyle, he finally didn't feel as if the waiters were about to turf him out onto the street at any second. He wouldn't say he felt comfortable, as such, but it was ... OK.

"Michael, so sorry I'm late." Hugh sat down opposite him, and Michael's jaw almost dropped. He'd thought Hugh had looked a bit tired at Somerset House, but it was nothing compared to how he looked today. His clothes were impeccable, as always, but his stubble looked accidental rather than artfully cultivated, and the bags under his eyes could have been seen from space.

"No, no, don't worry about it." Michael couldn't hold back the question. "Hugh, is everything alright?"

He didn't expect Hugh's extreme British Gentleman mask to slip, but to Michael's surprise, he heaved a huge sigh. "I've been better, if I'm honest. I owe you an apology. I abandoned you the other night and I shouldn't have done. I was there to help you, and I let you down. I've been having some ... personal issues of late, and I have allowed them to take over. I probably wasn't in the right headspace to be trying to mentor someone, to be frank, and I'm deeply sorry."

Personal issues ... Michael remembered that Hugh had stalked off just after Oskar mentioned Aidan. Shit, were they having relationship trouble? It was none of his business, so he wouldn't ask, but he felt a surge of sympathy for Hugh.

"I, er, I hope things get resolved for you soon," he said, somewhat feebly, but it was the best he had.

Hugh acknowledged Michael's words with a nod. "How did it go, anyway? I did try to find you again later but I think you'd left."

The groan left Michael's mouth before he could catch it.

Hugh arched an eyebrow. "That good?"

"I had a decent chat with Oskar," he said, deciding to start with the not-disastrous part of the evening. "But then this woman, Kimiko, came over and told everyone who I was, and ..."

"Ah. Yes, I know Kimiko, and she can be ... prickly. She has had to work very, very hard to break into the art world, and I think it's made her, understandably, a little suspicious of people who she perceives have had an easier ride. It's a shame, because you probably have more in common than either of you might think."

Michael snorted. "Aye, well, I won't be rushing to tell her that anytime soon."

"Quite," Hugh said with a dry chuckle.

"Anyway, she dropped me in it, and then everyone seemed to think it was the most hilarious thing they'd ever heard." Michael shrugged. "And maybe they're right. Maybe you were right. I've been thinking about what you said. If there are opportunities out there for me right now, commercial ones, maybe that's the route I should be taking."

Hugh said nothing. He gestured for a waiter, ordered a bottle of wine, then looked thoughtfully at Michael. "I know that was my suggestion, but that may be jumping the gun. The networking might not be getting off to the smoothest start, but that's not the be all and end all. I haven't given you enough support – or any support, really – on the creative side yet. There's so much to do there, and I should have made more time for that."

Michael huffed a laugh. "My creative side. I don't even know where that's gone. Everything with Miranda just took over, the last few weeks."

"You can say that again."

"Well, that's not something we have to worry about anymore," he said flatly.

"Oh." Hugh looked disconcerted. "So you ..."

"We split up." If it had been his decision, and it was for the best, why did it hurt so much to say? It felt like someone was digging his intestines out with one of these expensive forks.

"I'm sorry to hear that, Michael."

"Are you?" he asked as the waiter poured their wine.

Hugh met his eyes. "Of course I am. I don't know either of you well enough to say this with any authority, but you did seem happy together, from what I saw. And you don't, if you don't mind my saying, seem all that happy today. So of course I'm sorry."

"Even though you didn't approve?" He didn't know why he was pursuing this line of discussion. It wasn't as though it mattered, not now.

"It wasn't like that. The publicity surrounding your relationship may have created some complications with regard to your profile, and that did cause me concern, but that was only ever about your career. It's not my place to interfere in your personal life." He took a long drink from his wine glass. "But it may have been that my own ... circumstances coloured some of my reaction. And that is unacceptable, and for that I apologise again."

Michael gave a half-hearted shrug. It was all irrelevant now. If he was supposed to feel something about Hugh's words, he was failing at that like he was failing at pretty much everything else.

"But you were right," he said at last. "Me and Miranda, it was a problem. You tried to warn me, and I didn't listen. And now ..."

"And now?"

"I think," Michael said, "that I just need to work. I need something to do, to focus on. I'm so grateful that you want to help me, Hugh, but the art stuff, it feels too out of reach right now."

Hugh looked at him sadly. "I mean, sure. I can help you out with some commercial contacts. If that's what you want."

"That's what I want."

He didn't know if that was true. He didn't know what he wanted anymore. He only knew that wanting things had led him here, to breaking Miranda's heart. So maybe it was safer not to.

46

IF she had to have her heart broken, Miranda supposed she was glad he'd done it before her trip back to Washington and not after. She'd been able to fall off the plane and straight into her sister's arms. She'd missed her family so much, and she'd never needed them more than she did right now.

She was here, with the people she loved, and that was always cause for celebration. And Miranda would be damned if she let anything, least of all her train-wreck love life, spoil her dad's birthday trip. So she let Tommy and Izzy's excitable affection soothe the edges of her battered soul. She let her parents' love enfold her and make her feel safe.

All things considered, she thought as she lounged on one of the cabin's comfortable couches on the second morning of the trip, she'd done pretty well. No one seemed to have noticed that she had fallen apart.

"Milkshakes! Milkshakes! Milkshakes!" Tommy and Izzy chorused as they danced into the room.

"Kids, please," Bryan said. "We are two miles from the nearest cabin and I think even they can hear you."

"Sorry, Daddy," Izzy said breezily. "Aunty Rand, are you coming into town to get milkshakes?"

"Aunty Rand is staying here with Mommy,"

Miranda's mother said, putting a gentle arm around her granddaughter's shoulders. "They're going to have some nice peaceful grown-up time."

Her mother's tone was cheerful, but the slight meaningful edge to it told Miranda that she hadn't been fooling her family for a second. After a flurry of shoe-finding activity and reminders about sunscreen and not letting Tommy jump around too much if he was going to drink a whole shake, quiet descended on the cabin.

"So," Jen said, handing her a mug of coffee and sitting down at the other end of the huge sofa. "How are you holding up?"

Miranda shrugged. "Pretty crappy." She didn't cry, thank heavens. She'd done nothing but for twenty-four hours after he left. There were no tears left in her body.

"I bet." Her sister gazed at her intently. "It was different this time, huh?"

That was the thing, wasn't it? It was. He'd been different. They'd been different. Miranda had been heartbroken before, plenty of times. But not a single one of those times had carved something out of her like this one seemed to have done. Had it all been in her head, whatever special thing she thought had existed between them? It must have been, because how else could he just walk away like that?

"Yeah," Miranda said. "I really thought it was."

"So what happened?"

"I don't know. We had a fight, and then ... I don't know. He told me he wasn't good enough for me, and he left." She would never, as long as she lived, forget the look of pain and regret on his face. He'd been smashing her heart into a million pieces, and yet she still somehow ended up feeling sorry for him.

"Walk me through it, babe."

So Miranda told Jen everything, how things seemed to have been OK, how she'd been sure he'd been on the verge of agreeing to come this weekend, how she'd tried to help with his career, and how it all seemed to fall apart in one stupid conversation.

By the end of it, Jen's mouth was hanging open. "Let me get this straight. You booked him a flight to come meet your whole family at once after you'd been together, like, three weeks, and then when he freaked out about that, you decided that the best thing to do was tell him you loved him?"

"Well, when you put it like that ..." Miranda exhaled heavily. "It wasn't like that, though. I honestly didn't mean to pressure him about this weekend, and then the love thing just ... slipped out."

"Oh, Randa," Jen said, and the pitying look that accompanied her words sent a surge of irritation through Miranda. "I told you not to terrify him."

She tried to supress it, tried so hard. Her sister was wonderful, and Miranda absolutely did not need to yell at her when she was only trying to be supportive. But the irritation mixed with Miranda's sadness and frustration, and the temperature of all those feelings rose until they bubbled over and she couldn't stop herself.

"And what would you know, Jen? Who are you to be

dishing out relationship advice? You've never had to go through this. You don't know what it's like, over there with your perfect man and your perfect little family."

She could feel her mouth running, the words pouring out like a river whose dam had broken. She could see the stricken look on her sister's face, and she hated that she'd put it there, but she still couldn't stop.

"Everything comes so easy for you, Jen. You have everything you ever wanted, and maybe it's everything I've ever wanted too, but I don't even know, because I have to work so fucking hard for everything, and it still slips away from me every goddamn time. You could never understand that."

The second the words left Miranda's lips, she wanted to grab them back. God, what was she doing? This wasn't her. Shame joined the tempest of emotions in her stomach, and hot tears sprang to her eyes.

"I'm sorry. I'm so sorry," Miranda mumbled as she fled the room.

* * *

Miranda leaned on the railing of the cabin's deck, blowing out her breath in an effort to pull herself together. The trees around her, the sound of the falls in the distance, the birdsong – the majesty of nature should have been soothing, but barely any of it pierced her humiliating self-pity. This weekend was supposed to have been so different. There should have been nothing but joy, love, laughter.

She let herself picture, for one weak, beautiful moment, what could have been. He could have been here, taking in their glorious surroundings, basking in the happiness of her family's love, because she knew without a shadow of a doubt that they would have loved him.

But instead he'd chosen to burn it all down, to throw away what they had like it was nothing, like she was nothing, and here she was, crying over yet another man who didn't love her enough, and lashing out at the people who did.

She heard the cabin door open and the creak of wood as her sister stepped out onto the deck.

"I'm sorry, Jen. I didn't mean that."

"Yes you did," Jen said evenly, coming to her side. "But you're wrong." She leaned on the railing, right next to Miranda, their arms touching. "You think everything comes easy for me? Maybe you're right. But did you ever think that it's because I only ever take the easy option? That my whole life, I've wasted opportunities because I was too scared to try?"

Miranda stared open-mouthed at her sister. This was what Jen thought of herself? How could that be?

"Yeah, you work really fucking hard for everything, and you know what? That's incredible. I could never do what you do, go after what I want as fearlessly as you do. You amaze me, and every day I tell Izzy that she can achieve anything her heart desires, just like her Aunty Rand."

Something inside Miranda thawed and unbent. "You do?"

"Of course I do. You have no idea how many times I've wished I were more like you." Jen took Miranda's hand and squeezed it. "But, Rand, people aren't goals you can achieve. They're messy and unpredictable and all kinds of screwed up, and you have to let them be."

Miranda let her sister's words settle in her mind. "You think I pushed him too hard."

Jen smiled. "I'm saying that maybe it was a possibility."

"You're right." Miranda's shoulders slumped with the admission, the realisation. "God, you're totally right. I didn't tell him how I was feeling, I didn't ask him how he was feeling, I just decided I could plough through his defences. I was so determined to make him mine that I never just ... asked him if he wanted to be."

"Well, don't you think that maybe you should do that?" Jen said, tilting her head.

An ache formed in the pit of Miranda's stomach. "Don't I already have the answer? He left me, Jen. I told him I loved him, and he bailed."

"Because he was scared! And because he didn't think he was good enough for you."

"Or maybe he just doesn't love me." Saying it out loud, god, it hurt. That ache in her stomach intensified until she didn't know how she could bear it. But somewhere beneath it, buried deep in the pain, was a flicker of anger, and she held on to it like a life raft as she let the words continue to fall out. "Because I always thought he knew me, Jen. From the very beginning, he always saw me, the way no one else did. So he knows that I'm pushy and that I go after the things I want. But he should have also known that I was only ever trying to help him, because I love him. That I don't care about him being "worthy" of me. That I don't want a better man, I want him, only him, the way he is. How could he love me, if he couldn't see all of that? If he couldn't believe it when I told him all of that to his face?"

"Oh, Miranda." Jen pulled her into a hug, and Miranda leaned against her sister and let her tears fall again. "It sounds like you've both gotten yourselves all mixed up. Why don't you talk to him about it?"

"And how do I do that, when he's the one who left? You just told me I was pushing him too hard."

Jen stroked her hair. "You give him a bit of time, a bit of space. Then you call him, and you tell him how you feel."

It sounded so simple when she said it like that. So sensible. So very Jen. And Miranda knew that normally she'd agree. But could she really bring herself to lay her heart on the line like that again, when there was every chance he would only smash it into even smaller pieces? Why should it be up to her to put herself through that?

Her pride was all she had left, and it had gotten her through a hundred heartbreaks. She had never been the one to go crawling back when it was over, and she wasn't starting now.

"Rand? What are you thinking?" Jen said.

Miranda pushed herself out of her sister's arms. "I'm thinking that you might be right, but maybe so is he, in a way. Maybe I do deserve a better man. One who doesn't give up so damn easily. I fight for the things I want because that's who I am, and maybe he couldn't handle that. But I also know that some things are worth fighting for, no matter what. I should be one of those things to him, and apparently I'm not."

"But maybe you are and he doesn't know how. I still think you should just talk to him."

"I won't beg him to love me, Jen. I do have some pride, you know."

Jen smiled, a little sadly. "Never doubted that for a minute."

Miranda felt a tiny hint of resolve creeping in. It wasn't her usual kind, the steely type that gave her energy and sent her off on her next mission to conquer the world. This was sadder, smaller, a weary kind of resigned determination that she would not give in to the pain this love had left her with.

She had a life most people could only imagine. She was about to shoot the role of her dreams. Whatever she was going through now was nothing but the latest in a long line of romantic setbacks. She'd thought she'd finally found someone who saw her for who she truly was and could love her for it, but she'd been wrong, and she'd get over it. She always did.

47

IT had taken Michael ten days to realise that he'd been a complete fucking idiot.

Well, he'd known he was a complete fucking idiot right from the start, but it had taken a few days for him to fully comprehend that the scale of his idiocy was such that he'd thrown away maybe the greatest thing that had ever happened to him for no sodding reason. Then it had taken a few more days for him to admit that what he actually needed to do was call Miranda and explain that he'd been an insecure, frightened arsehole, apologise, and beg her to give him another chance. Then he'd remembered that she was in the States with her family and that he should wait until she was back in the country before he rang her.

So that had all taken ten days, and now Michael was standing in his living room, phone in hand, still trying to figure out exactly what he should say. He only knew it was the opposite of all the shit he'd spouted on that awful, awful day when he'd left.

Why had he done that? What was wrong with him? Miranda Janes had told him she was in love with him, and he had decided to tell her that she couldn't be. Who the fuck was he to decide that? If she'd decided that she could love him, he should have just thanked whichever gods had made that happen and told her he loved her too.

Because he did. He knew that now. He'd known it all along. He'd started falling in love with her the moment he met her, and it was only his fear that had stopped him from admitting it.

And apparently was still stopping him admitting it now.

"Your phone is right there, you dickhead," he told himself out loud, remembering when, eighteen months ago, he'd said those exact words to Cleo – without the dickhead part, of course. He hadn't quite understood, then, why she didn't do it. Bloody hell, he got it now, though.

What if he was too late? She'd been away with her family, people who loved her and were bound to have reminded her that she could have any guy in the world and didn't need to wait around for some English wanker to pull his head out of his arse. What if a weekend of space and time and clear air was all she needed to realise that she didn't have to put up with this kind of shit?

Well, maybe he was too late. If he was, that would be his own fault, and he would have to live with that. But he owed her an apology. He'd completely overreacted to the flights, and although he still didn't think that Brad Conway was the man to help him launch a career, Miranda had just been trying to help. He'd thrown all that back in her face.

Before he could talk himself out of it again, he scrolled to her number and pressed it.

It rang for at least six hundred years, then went to voicemail.

Well, shit. In all his worrying about what to say, he'd never considered that she might not even answer. Never mind. He'd try again later. Give it a couple of hours.

He needed something to do – something that would absorb him but not take him away from his phone, just in case she called back. He'd sort all his camera kit out, that's what he'd do.

Man, he had a lot of shit. It took him half an hour just to round it all up, pull all the long-neglected stuff from the back of the cupboard, delve into every pocket of every camera bag and retrieve it all. He laid it all out on the spare room floor, determined to check and catalogue and organise every last filter and lens cap, the kind of thing that sounded desperately boring but actually he kind of loved doing.

She didn't call back.

When three hours had passed, he tried again. Still no answer.

On his third attempt, he only heard three rings before his call was sent to voicemail, and Michael felt his stomach plummet to the floor.

So. She knew he was calling, and she didn't want to talk to him.

Maybe she's busy, in a meeting or something. You don't know that she's ignoring you.

He didn't believe himself.

He gave it one more hour, during which he took pictures of all the stuff he was never going to use again, ready for eBay. Then he blew out a huge breath. He hadn't wanted to do it like this, but it seemed he didn't have a choice.

MICHAEL: I'm sorry. Can we talk?

And then he waited. What else could he do?

48

"SO, I've spoken to Rose, and she'll have everything in the house ready for you. Your flights are booked, as is the car to pick you up from the airport. Frank will be there by Tuesday. Nora sent through some release forms for you to sign ..."

Miranda tuned out as Aisling continued to run through the list of preparations for LA. It was rude of her, but she knew she didn't really need to listen too hard, even though there was tons to do and very little time to do it in. Under normal circumstances, she probably would have stayed in the States after her dad's birthday instead of flying back. But she'd wanted more time ...

A gentle huff escaped her. Aisling glanced at her but kept talking, probably entirely aware her boss wasn't paying attention. But Aisling would be on top of everything; she always was. Miranda was really going to miss her. She'd have an assistant assigned to her for the movie, but they were never Aisling.

Her eyes roamed around the garden. It was a beautiful day, so they'd decided to sit outside while they worked. Or while Aisling worked and Miranda sat there remembering the day of the photo shoot out here. Which was better than if they were inside, when the kitchen would remind her of every meal he made her, when the sofa would remind her of every time they'd cuddled up on it, where every single inch of every single room reminded her of Michael.

She looked down at her phone, as she was currently doing roughly seven thousand times a day. Every time, she had to stop herself from returning one of his messages or calls. And every time, she wondered whether she should. He'd apologised – wasn't that what she wanted? And he wanted to talk. That was a good thing, right? Why would he want to talk unless he wanted another chance?

Trouble was, Miranda was no longer sure that was what she wanted. She missed him so much it hurt. But that wasn't the only thing that did.

His rejection of her still hurt. She didn't know if talking to him could soothe that away, not yet. And his lack of belief in himself, in them, in her, still hurt, and that was the bigger issue. That wasn't something that could be fixed in the short time they'd been apart.

Maybe she was being foolish. The best course of action was probably to talk about it, figure out what they both wanted. Perhaps she was throwing away her chance at happiness by refusing to speak to him.

But she was tired, so tired, of following the path of most resistance. She'd finally learned that – how had Jen put it? – that people were messy and unpredictable and screwed up and sometimes you just had to let them be. Let her include herself in that for once.

"Sweetheart," Miranda said, probably interrupting her assistant mid-sentence. "Can we finish this tomorrow? I think I'll go do some packing."

"Of course," Aisling said, her carefully neutral face betraying only the slightest flicker of concern. Or was it pity? "I have pretty much everything under control, and I can email you with the things you need to decide or do. Do you want me to help you pack?"

"No." Miranda forced a smile. "I can take care of it." She needed to go through everything she owned and make sure anything that he'd ever touched stayed here in London. If she was escaping to another continent, she was going to do it as completely as she could. Let the memories stay locked up here until she was strong enough to face them.

She'd gotten as far as dumping the contents of three drawers onto her bed when her phone rang.

"Hey, Courtney," she said, answering the video call.

"Hey, babe. How are you doing?" Courtney's voice was full to the brim with sympathy.

"Still feeling kind of flat," Miranda said honestly. It felt good, if you could call it that, to share this with her friend. Of course, Jen had been amazing, but it was different talking to someone else for whom the course of true love hadn't always run smooth. And obviously, she couldn't talk to Cleo about any of this. She knew Cleo cared about her, and she knew she'd be worried, but Michael needed her more right now, and Miranda wasn't about to put her in the middle.

"It'll get better, honey. You still don't want to talk to him?"

Miranda sighed. "I do and I don't, you know? Part of me so wants to believe that I could just answer the phone, and he'll say he loves me and that will be that, but ..."

"Is that really so unlikely?"

"No. I guess it's not. I don't think that's what I'm scared of, that he won't say that. I just don't know if it's enough."

"What would be enough?" Courtney asked, a thoughtful look on her face.

"I honestly don't know. I feel like I don't know anything anymore. What to do, what to think, how to handle this. I love him, and I'm pretty sure he loves me, if he'd only have the balls to admit it. But when he walked away, it hurt me. And I guess ..." Miranda's chest tightened. "I hate to say it, but I guess I'm kinda pissed at him."

Courtney was looking at her as if she'd lost her mind. "Why do you hate to say it? Babe, the man dumped you because you bought him a plane ticket. You're allowed to be pissed at him."

With her free hand, Miranda started sifting half-heartedly through the clothes on her bed. "I just ..."

Courtney held up a hand. "Miranda, sweetheart, I know that you are very good at pushing away negativity, and it is one of the things everyone loves about you. But you don't have to do it 24/7, you know. Sometimes things suck. Sometimes people suck. And right now, Michael sucks. The boy done fucked up, and the only thing he can think of to do is text you? Let him stew."

Despite herself, Miranda found a tiny giggle escaping. "OK, fine. Maybe he does kinda suck a little bit.

But I know I played my part in this. I've already done all that soul-searching."

Courtney rolled her eyes. "Maybe you were ever so slightly the pushy Miranda we all know and love. But he should have talked to you properly about it, instead of running away like a little baby."

Miranda stared right into her phone's camera. "Hmm. Talking about your feelings properly. Now there's an idea."

Brown eyes stared right back. "We aren't talking about me."

"Honey, I never said we were." But Miranda kept up the direct look. She didn't want to talk about herself anymore. Time to do what she did best – help someone fix a problem. OK, so maybe that was what had got her into this mess, but she felt pretty confident that there was only one right answer in whatever Courtney and Henry's situation was.

Courtney cracked. "Fine." She sighed. "Something's up with him and I don't know what, but I can't just keep asking how he is and hoping he'll tell me. And then lying when he asks me if I'm OK, because I'm not. I need to tell him that I know that something's going on and that he needs to talk to me about it."

"Yes. Yes you do." Miranda smiled gently at her friend. She hoped those two could work it out. They had the kind of love she used to dream about.

"Ugh," Courtney said. "Love. Why do we do it to ourselves?"

Miranda let out a huff of laughter. Damned if she knew.

49

MICHAEL felt the sweet, sweet relief of the moment his front door came into view. Was there anything better than that feeling? He'd been on his feet all day, taking pictures of a women's football team, a job that Hugh had helped set up for him that had been a lot more fun than he'd expected. It felt good to be working again. But it had been a long day, and now he was looking forward to a beer, the chicken tikka masala that was in the freezer, and an evening of doing precisely nothing.

So when he walked into his flat and found his best friend sitting at his kitchen table eating a packet of crisps, he nearly jumped out of his skin.

"Cleo? What are you doing here?"

She rose to meet him as he crossed the kitchen in two strides and pulled her into a massive hug.

"Sorry for just being here. Maybe it's the jet lag, but for some reason it didn't occur to me that you might not be in when I got here. I still have my key, and I figured I'd just come in and wait. I've been here ages, and I was going to text you but I fell asleep. Oh, it's good to see you. I've missed you so much."

"I've missed you too." He kissed the top of her lovely, familiar head. "But you didn't answer. What are you doing here? Why are you in London?"

"Courtney finally decided she needed to come and see Henry about whatever's going on there, so I hitched a lift. She got me an interview with Declan Hainey so I'd have a work reason. But mostly I'm here to see you, you idiot."

"OK ..." He still wasn't certain his question had been answered, but he was really bloody hungry. He went over to the freezer. "Have you eaten? Do you want some curry? And why are you here in my flat without telling me? And why am I an idiot?"

Cleo sat back down and picked up her crisps. "Of course I want curry. And if you don't know why you're an idiot, then you're even more of an idiot than I thought you were."

"Miranda."

"Bingo."

He sighed. He couldn't exactly tell her it was none of her business, after everything he'd done to get her and Devon back together, could he? He pulled two portions of chicken tikka masala out of the freezer and found some microwave rice in the cupboard. He debated making proper rice and decided he couldn't be arsed. He'd probably need to save his energy for defending himself.

"So you flew all the way here to have a go at me?"

"Obviously," she said, unperturbed. "But I can wait until you've fed me."

She wasn't quite true to her word. He'd barely taken his first bite before she said, "Tell me what happened, then."

He blinked in surprise. "She hasn't told you?"

"She told me you broke up. Nothing more." Cleo took a swig of her beer. "I get the sense she didn't want to put me in the middle. Which she needn't have worried about, because you didn't even bother telling me at all."

He winced. "Sorry, Clee. I guess I was just trying to figure it all out in my own head before I spoke to you."

"And have you?"

"I mean, I figured out that I'm an idiot. But we both already knew that."

"True." She waved her fork in the air. "Spill."

He told her the whole sorry tale. Jesus, now he was saying it all out loud, it was even more obvious that he'd handled everything about as well as the government had handled Brexit. From the look on Cleo's face, she apparently agreed.

"So you broke up over ... a plane ticket?"

"I mean, the same way you and Devon broke up over a photo," he said pointedly, because even though he knew she was right and he was so grateful she was here, he wasn't about to let her get off too easily.

"Point taken," she said. "And what did you say to me when that happened?"

"I told you to pick up your phone and talk about it. And I did! I swear. I called her as soon as I'd pulled my head out of my arse. But she won't talk to me."

"You phoned more than once, right?" Cleo glared at him accusingly.

"Of course I did. I tried a few times a day for a few days, then once a day for a few days after that, plus texts."

She raised an eyebrow. “And that’s it?”

“What do you mean, “it”? I don’t want her to take out a restraining order against me, for crying out loud.” Michael picked up their empty plates and stacked them neatly by the sink, because even when he felt like there was a gaping hole in his chest he still couldn’t bring himself to make a mess of the kitchen. “Or send Frank round. He’s fucking terrifying when he wants to be.” He sat back down with a thud.

“Have you left her a voicemail? Written her a letter? Been round to see her? Sent her flowers? Hired a fucking plane to skywrite ‘I’m sorry I’m such a dick’ over her house?” Cleo seemed pissed off with him, but he was fucked if he knew why.

“What? Have you lost your mind?”

“Have you?” She threw her hands up in the air. “Miranda Janes – *the* Miranda Janes, a sexy, talented, intelligent, world-famous actress who happens to be the nicest woman on the entire bloody planet – falls in love with you, and you balls it up and think that pressing a button on your phone a dozen times is all you need to do? Jesus Christ, Michael, I know you don’t like stepping out of your comfort zone, but give your head a wobble.”

“It’s not about comfort zones, Cleo,” he said, although even as the words left his mouth they had that tiny prickle of untruth about them. “I don’t want to hassle her if she wants me to leave her alone. I wouldn’t blame her if she did. If she wanted to work things out, why wouldn’t she just pick up the phone?”

"Because she's pissed off with you, obviously!" She was pretty much yelling at him now. He hoped his neighbours weren't in. "She's hurt and angry, and maybe she's tired of doing all the bloody running! Maybe she wants to see if you can actually get off your arse and go after what you want for once."

Cleo's words hit him like a punch to the gut. "Is that what you think of me?" he asked quietly.

She seemed to deflate a little. She reached over the table and covered his hand with hers. "Mate, you know you're one of my favourite people on earth. I love you and always will. But ..." She exhaled heavily. "But you've never exactly been the putting-yourself-out-there type, have you? You stayed in a job you hated rather than follow the dream you came to London for. And yeah, you're making progress now, but how long did it take you to start really trying, even after you promised me you would? And would anything have ever happened with Miranda if she hadn't made it happen?"

Michael said nothing as the weight of Cleo's accusations settled on his chest. They weren't even accusations, were they? She was just making him face facts. If any good things had ever happened for him, they weren't down to anything he'd done. His ticket out of the paparazzi had been down to Devon. Meeting Hugh had been because of Miranda. Even Cleo – he'd never pursued her. They'd just sort of happened. As for Miranda, she'd wanted him, and she'd gone after what she wanted. And she'd tried to encourage him to do the same.

"You can be that man, Michael. Why won't you believe that?"

"You're right. Is that what you want to hear, Clee?" He stood up and started pacing the kitchen, which felt far, far too small all of a sudden. "That I'm a coward? That I've spent my entire life fucking up because I'm too scared to try? Because if I try, then I'll fail, and then maybe somebody who matters will confirm all the worst things I've always believed about myself?"

"Oh, Michael." She was on her feet and next to him in a second, wrapping her arms around him. "Of course that's not what I want. I didn't say any of that to hurt you." She stepped back and looked him in the eye. "But it's so frustrating, seeing you like this. I hoped that when we got you out of that life, things would change, you know? That you'd see in yourself what I see, what your mam sees ... what Miranda sees. This wonderful, kind, caring, so, so talented man who can achieve anything he wants. Who deserves to be happy. Why are so you convinced that you don't?"

"Because all I've ever done is make people's lives shit!" The swirl of bilious self-loathing he normally tried to keep trapped down inside was finding its way out. He paced the kitchen again, putting some distance between him and Cleo. "The people whose pictures I took, my mam, you ... and now Miranda. What have I got to offer anyone?"

"Oh, for fuck's sake," Cleo snapped, and he practically did a cartoon double take. She'd never spoken to him like that, not even right at the end of their marriage when all they ever did was fight. "Have you heard yourself? Enough with this self-pitying crap. It's bollocks, Michael, and you know it. Your mam adores you. You light up her life, and yeah, it was hard for her being abandoned by your dad and her mam, but how the hell was that your fault? You were a literal baby, Michael. She chose you and doesn't regret that for a second, so who are you to decide her life's been shit because of it?"

She took a breath. Apparently she wasn't done. But her face softened.

"You didn't make my life shit either. Far from it, you absolute tool. You were my first love, and I'll treasure that forever. You loved me when no one else did, and I don't know where I'd be today without you. Marrying you wasn't the wisest decision I could have made, granted, but we were kids, and we were being manipulated. All that stuff with Margaret, I never blamed you for any of it. My life was better – is better – because of you, so I'm not having you saying it wasn't, OK?"

"Yes, sir," he mumbled.

"And last of all, you definitely didn't make Miranda's life shit." She gave him a gentle smile. "We never talked much about you, but she seemed really happy. She might be feeling sad and hurt and angry right now, but that doesn't mean you can't fix it."

A flicker of hope tried to spring to life somewhere inside him, but it sputtered out as quickly as it started. "I don't even know if she wants me to." He flung himself back down into his chair, and Cleo grabbed his hand again.

"Look at it this way. She hasn't answered, but neither has she blocked your number, told you to fuck off, or been seen out wearing some fabulous dress and a 'Michael who?' smile. I don't think she's purposely testing you, because she doesn't play games like that, but she's also not the type to leave a door open if she wants it shut."

"Not a no is all you need ..." he said under his breath.

Cleo heard him anyway. The woman had ears like a bat. "Excuse me? Do we need to have a refresher chat about enthusiastic consent?"

"Not like that, you arse. It's something she said to me once." He sighed. "Maybe you're right."

She grinned at him. "I'm always right."

* * *

Cleo was fast asleep in Michael's spare room. She'd made a polite offer to go to a hotel or the farmhouse that Devon had bought from the guy he used to rent it from, but they both knew that there was never any question of either of those things happening. She'd always have a home here, just like he'd always have one with her.

And Michael was lying awake, thinking over everything she'd said, everything Miranda had said, everything anyone had ever said to him or about him his whole life. And for the first time ever, the voices of the three women who knew him and loved him best started sounding a little bit louder than all the rest.

Nearly all of them. One still chimed in his head, the cut-glass accent reopening the thousands of tiny scratches on his skin. Her last insult – *you're a disgrace to this family* – rang in his ears as if it were yesterday. Did he really want those words to be the last ones he'd ever hear from her?

He wasn't even aware that he'd made the decision, but he was somehow on his feet and heading for the living room, where a cream envelope had lain in a drawer for weeks. He took it from its hiding place and sat down on the couch, just holding the envelope, staring at the shaky handwriting on the front without seeing it.

"Stop being such a fanny and read the bloody thing," he said into the silence of the room. Softly, because he didn't want Cleo to wake up and ask him why he was talking to himself.

He opened the envelope.

Dear Michael,

As I try to write this letter, I find myself at something of a loss. Perhaps it is an impossible task, to find words to excuse or explain a lifetime of poor behaviour.

Instead, I offer you this: I am sorry.

I owe you more than this, I realise, but I also recognise that you may want or need nothing from me ever again. That is my fault, and my burden to live with.

Perhaps you will not believe it, but I regret my harsh words to you, and especially those I said to you when we last saw each other. You are not a disgrace, Michael, and you never were. You have looked after your mother when that should have been my responsibility, and you have had the strength to no longer tolerate me and my many unkindnesses. You understand what family truly means, and God knows you did not learn that from me.

If it were my place to be proud of you, please know that I would be.

With regards and regret,

Margaret.

Well.

He read the letter again, and again, then he read it a couple more times for good measure, trying to let the words sink in. He should have already known from Cleo's letter that it would be like this, an unreserved, unflinching apology, but it seemed as though the core of him hadn't truly believed that. There'd been some part of him braced for more cruelty, for a barb only he could see, for something that would, as always, make him feel like a disappointment.

There was none of that. Just genuine regret. An emotion he hadn't known his grandmother was capable of.

And she was proud of him, and she recognised that her pride might mean nothing to him. Michael tried to sift through his feelings to figure out what it did mean. It didn't give him a warm feeling, not in the slightest. And it didn't make his insecurities fall away, or erase any of the years of disparagement from his brain. But it wasn't nothing, either.

She was wrong about him, and she was able to admit that after all this time. Maybe his teachers had been wrong about him. Maybe Kimiko and all those art wankers were wrong about him. Maybe he was wrong about himself.

Or maybe he wasn't. He was the one who'd made his choices. He was the one who'd screwed up, so many times. He was the one who'd let other people make him believe that those screw-ups were all he was.

He was the problem.

But for the first time, the thought didn't fill him with despair and self-recrimination. Because if he was his own problem, maybe he could also be his own solution.

Maybe he could finally believe that Miranda was right. He could be the man she believed he was, the man who deserved to be loved by her. But he needed to prove that, and he needed to prove it not to her, but to himself.

So when the sun rose and Michael, still sitting in the same spot on his couch, picked up his phone, it wasn't to call her again, or to call an Uber to take him to her house, or to order flowers, or to book a sky-writing plane. It was to send two messages.

> To Brad Conway: Hi, do you have time for a drink tonight, or sometime soon? I'd like to ask your advice on something.

> To Miranda: I'm going to leave you alone for a while. There's something I need to do. But I am not giving up.

50

"AND then he says, 'You didn't tell me about the freaking alligators!'"

Everyone laughed as AJ finished his story. Well, everyone except Miranda, who'd apparently zoned out at whatever moment the alligators had come into it so did not get the joke. Still, she'd been at AJ's little cast get-together at his home for a whole two hours, so she supposed only zoning out once wasn't too bad. She was improving. The Michael fog she'd been trapped in was lifting. She still didn't know what his text meant, but she also wasn't attempting to find out. There was a time she would have. She would have called Cleo and wheedled the information out. Or even just called Michael and asked him straight out what was going on.

She hadn't done that this time. He was doing something, she'd let him do it. She couldn't promise to still be waiting for him when he was done, but for once Miranda was just going with the flow. It kinda sucked. But she knew it was what she needed to do.

A glass appeared in front of her face. "Marg for your thoughts?"

She looked up into the grinning face of Seb Akao. "Seb, you're an angel. But you don't want my thoughts. They're very boring."

He flopped down onto the couch next to her. "I don't think you've ever been boring, Miranda." He flashed that devastatingly handsome smile at her again, but now she saw the shadow in his eyes that marred the full Hollywood effect.

"Hey," she said. "Everything OK?"

"That obvious, huh?" He took a gulp of his own margarita.

She shrugged. "You're a very good actor, but I have a nose for this stuff."

"Girl trouble, you know?"

Oh yeah. She knew. "Want to talk about it? I'm a really good listener. And good at helping other people with their relationship problems, I'm told. Not so much my own."

He sighed. "I just broke up with my girlfriend."

She put her hand on his arm. "I'm sorry to hear that. I didn't realise you were seeing someone."

"We hadn't been together long. But I thought it was going well. She's a nice girl. Not in this business, but maybe that's the problem. She freaked out when she saw those photos of you and me leaving Gracias Madre last Saturday."

"Ah." Miranda's heart went out to him. This was an occupational hazard of theirs, and one they were all used to. But when you dated people who weren't, it was tough. There'd been six of them there that night, but the paparazzi had focused on her and Seb, obviously.

He ran a hand through his glossy black hair. "Yeah. It totally got to her, and I tried to be sympathetic and reassuring and everything, but there's only so much you can do, right? I mean, we're gonna get photographed together again, and then there's all the stuff in the actual movie. You've gotta have trust, to do this."

"Absolutely. I mean, on the one hand, it takes some getting used to, this life, so maybe she just needs a little time and you guys can work it out. But on the other hand, if the trust isn't there, it's rough."

"Yeah." Seb looked thoughtful. "Your guy is cool with it, though?"

A little huff of laughter escaped her lips. "My guy. Not sure we can call him that anymore."

"No?" He cocked his head to one side.

"No. I mean, to answer your question, he was always cool about stuff like that. He used to be a paparazzo, so he knew the score better than anyone. But ... yeah. It's ... complicated, I guess." She didn't even know if that was true. They weren't together – wasn't it that simple? But something inside wasn't ready to let go completely. Not yet.

"Well," he said, turning his deep, dark eyes on her, "if it ever gets uncomplicated ..." He gave her a devilish smile that, admittedly, did have her sipping her margarita to wet her suddenly dry mouth. "Or you want to make it more complicated, let me know." He winked at her, but it was somehow friendly and not sleazy, despite his words.

She laughed, and he joined her, thank goodness. She'd been hit on with much less finesse and grace, and she knew in an instant that although the offer may have been genuine, the rejection of it wouldn't cause problems.

"In another life, I'd be tempted," she said. He was a spectacularly beautiful man, and there was a little frisson of something there, enough to give them great chemistry as Faran and Damia, anyway. But she knew from experience that that tension wasn't always worth exploring. And definitely not while she was so completely in love with another man.

Or getting over another man. Whichever it was. Ugh, she'd better not start thinking about that again or she'd never stop.

Seb shrugged good-naturedly. "I guess I did only break up with my girlfriend last night." He smirked. "Maybe she's right about me after all."

She gave him a mock-scolding look, just as her phone rang. "Excuse me, Seb. My assistant back home."

She answered the call as she headed for the pool terrace. "Aisling, darling. Everything OK?"

"Yes, yes, nothing to worry about," Aisling said. "I just didn't want to email you this without a heads-up. Are you OK to talk for a second?"

Miranda was curious. "Fire away."

"I've had an email from Michael."

Even though she'd been talking about him not five minutes ago, his name still caused a little stutter in her chest. "What about?" she said evenly.

"They're release forms. He wants to use some photographs of you."

The stutter turned into a fully fledged pounding. "That's fine," she said quickly.

"You don't what to know which ones? What for?"

They were very sensible questions, and ones Miranda knew she should ask. But she was letting things be. That's what she'd decided to do, wasn't it? If he'd wanted to ask her himself, he could have. He'd gone to Aisling, so maybe this was supposed to be some kind of surprise. Maybe this thing he needed to do was some kind of grand gesture that she wouldn't want to spoil. She held on to that idea, ridiculous as it was, because the alternative was that he was now using her image to further his career in some way and that was the only reason he hadn't cut things off completely.

"Can you sign them digitally for me?" she asked Aisling.

"Erm, yes, but ..."

"Then do it. Run it past Kate, but tell her I don't have a problem with whatever he wants to do." Her publicist would spot anything dubious, but Miranda trusted Michael. He was many things, but she didn't believe he'd do anything to damage her career or reputation. Cleo and Devon would murder him if he did, for one thing. And for another, he was a good man. She still believed that.

And whatever he was planning, she'd find out soon enough.

51

"MATE, will you calm the fuck down?" Brad said as Michael paced the floor. "I mean, I know this is literally the biggest night of both your career and your love life, but I only had this floor put down three months ago and you're going to wear tracks in it at this rate."

Michael absolutely could not calm the fuck down. Brad was right – this was the biggest night of his life. There were so many ways he could fall flat on his arse, very publicly. But there was only one thing that really mattered. Would she be here?

"She'll be here," Cleo said, as if she'd read his mind. "She's no fool. She'll know why we've brought her to London. She would have objected by now if she was going to." She grinned. "And Devon's under strict orders to bring her here by hook or by crook."

"Ha." Despite himself, he managed a smile. "Then, for his sake as much as mine, I hope she doesn't say no. I'd hate to be caught between you with your mind set on one thing and her set on the opposite."

She winked at him. "He knows which side his bread is buttered."

Michael's legs wanted to walk around again, to get rid of some of this nervous energy, but he managed to stop himself. "It's OK, isn't it? I mean, it all looks OK?"

"It looks fabulous, Michael. I can't believe you pulled this together so quickly."

Michael nodded at Brad. "Thank this guy. Which I can't do enough, by the way."

Brad waved a hand. "Are you kidding? How could I say no? I'd been thinking about turning this into a temporary exhibition space anyway, and doing it in three weeks was kind of fun."

Michael looked around the space. It wasn't a slick one by any description – if you peered closely enough, it looked like what it was, a former storeroom that had had a wall hastily knocked down and been given a coat of paint. In one way, he'd been happy with that. After all, the memory of this room would be seared forever into his brain. But he also wanted to make tonight spectacular, so he'd filled every available space with plants and flowers to hide its sparseness.

"Besides," Brad continued, "I'm terrible at relationships. Being part of your grand gesture might be the only romantic thing I'll ever do in my life." He laughed. "The guests will be here any minute. You ready?"

"As I'll ever be."

Brad walked off towards the entrance, and Michael adjusted the cuffs of the suit Brad had insisted he buy. He'd sent him in the direction of his tailor, saying, "Go big or go home, dude." And this was all about going big.

"Relax." Cleo put her hand on his arm. "It's going to be fine. I'm so proud of you."

He gave her a hug, hoping it conveyed some of how

grateful he was that she was here. "I'm pretty proud of me too."

The only question was, was it enough?

"I'm opening the doors," Brad yelled.

The first guest to arrive was Hugh, and Michael was delighted to see that not only did he look like himself again, but Aidan was with him. Next was Suzy, the critic he'd met at that terrible night at Somerset House. Oskar and a few more of Hugh's artist friends showed up. He'd even invited Kimiko, and the guy whose name, it turned out, was neither Jack nor James but Stuart, although he wasn't sure if they'd deign to appear.

Jodi's arrival caused quite a stir, and Michael smiled to himself. *You ain't seen nothing yet.*

The event was going to be a success. Yet none of it would matter if ...

Cleo touched his elbow. "They're on their way."

He closed his eyes and let the hope he'd been trying to keep at bay surround his pounding heart. She was coming.

52

WHEN Cleo, Devon and Courtney had shown up at her door and told her they were taking her on an adventure, Miranda was suspicious.

When they'd boarded Courtney and Henry's jet and she'd been told it would be a long flight, she'd started to hope.

When they'd touched down in London, she'd been pretty sure.

When Devon had knocked on her hotel room door and refused to tell her why she wasn't staying in her own house or where Cleo had disappeared to, she knew.

And now they were pulling up outside the Conway Gallery, Miranda's heart was beating so fast that she was starting to fear for her health. She sat frozen on the back seat of the car. She knew she needed to get out, but she couldn't.

Whatever he'd needed time to do, while he allegedly wasn't giving up, it seemed he'd done it. Now it was time to see what it was. And if it was enough.

"Miranda?" Devon's voice was soft. "You OK?"

"I ..." She licked her lips and tried again. "What did he do? This is ... a good thing, right? Right? I mean ... what if ... I ..."

"Whoa. Never thought I'd have to say this to the most together woman in the world, but chill. I'm gonna have to break my vow of silence, because this is too unlike you." He gave her the smile that made audiences all over the world melt into their seats. "He did a good thing, Miranda. I promise. You want to go in there and see."

The knot of unidentifiable emotions in her stomach unfurled, ever so slightly.

OK, Miranda, you can do this. It's time to find out what's going on.

What was she so nervous about? She wouldn't have come all the way here if there wasn't still a chance for them, would she? But what if the time apart had been too much? What if he hadn't even brought her here to get her back? What if this was all some elaborate plan by their friends without his knowledge and she'd flown five thousand miles just for her heart to break all over again?

"Miranda." Devon's deep voice broke into her endless questions. His famous blue eyes were twinkling. "Get on out there."

She took a deep breath. "OK. I'm going. Aren't you coming?"

"I'm going to sneak in the back, if that's OK with you."

She laughed. "Some things never change." She reached for the door handle. "Here I go ..."

She stepped out of the car, smoothing her dress as she stood. She'd gone for a dramatic backless red dress, almost exactly the same shade as the simple one she'd worn that night in Paris. She wondered if he'd notice. Of course he would. He noticed everything.

Rope barriers formed a path to the gallery's front steps, and paparazzi crowded either side of them. She flashed them a smile that she knew would betray nothing of the nerves tangling around inside her. Why were there so many of them, though? Judging by the ropes and the huge security guards policing them, this was planned for. Which meant this was potentially a pretty high-profile event for such a small gallery. What in the world was going on?

A burly man in a suit opened the door for her, and she stepped inside to find Brad Conway waiting for her.

"Miranda, delighted to see you again," he said, kissing her on both cheeks.

"And you, Brad." She was delighted, but she was also puzzled. The last time she'd suggested Brad might be helpful, it hadn't gone well. Clearly something had changed.

"Now our guest of honour has arrived, I guess we can get this party started. Can I get you a drink?"

"No, thank you." She just wanted to find out why she was here.

"Then allow me." Brad offered his arm, and Miranda took it as he led her through the bar area, which was full of people she knew and people she didn't, all dressed up to the nines and sipping champagne – Cleo and Devon, Courtney and Henry, Hugh and a man she assumed was his fiancé, Jodi, Brix, and ... she didn't have time to take in any of the other faces, because Brad was whisking her towards a room off to the side.

"Welcome to the Conway Gallery's first special exhibition, 'Seen' by Michael Hedley," Brad said, his voice tinged with something that sounded like pride.

Tears sprang to Miranda's eyes. Whatever else, Michael had his work on display. That was worth celebrating.

"Go ahead." Brad withdrew his arm from hers and gestured towards the room. She took a step forward. There was something about the space that looked unfinished, but the eye was drawn from that by the stunning floral displays between ... pictures.

Large photos hung from the ceiling on invisible wires, and Miranda couldn't help but gasp as her eyes fell on the first one. Henry Deng, sitting behind his desk, his expression serious, his suit as sharp as his cheekbones. He radiated power, wealth and status. And then beside it, Henry again, but wearing a T-shirt, his hair slightly rumpled as he ran a hand through it. A little half-smile was on his face, and he looked for all the world like a male model who'd just got out of bed. She was looking at the Henry that Courtney had fallen in love with, and the effect was dazzling.

She could have looked at those two pictures of her friend for hours, but she forced herself to move on. All the other pictures were in similar pairs, and Miranda felt more and more stunned with each one she took in. Brix, singing into a microphone, eyes closed, next to Brix swamped by a huge hoodie, grinning goofily. Jodi

Alper striking an angular pose in a chain mail halter, juxtaposed with a shot of her wearing no makeup but looking no less beautiful, her head thrown back in a laugh.

Declan Hainey, a UK country singer who'd collaborated on Courtney's new album, was pictured hunched seriously over his guitar, then thrusting his fist in the air while wearing a Leicester City soccer jersey. Scarlett Smith, from that reality show, wearing a ton of makeup and a tight minidress, followed by her in an oversized white shirt, her hair piled messily on top of her head, cuddling her newborn to her chest, looking exhausted but happy. Becky Nolan, Miranda's neighbour, smiling prettily in a flowered dress, then in jeans and a T-shirt, hands on hips and staring defiantly at the camera, her wedding ring notably absent.

Miranda was speechless. Some of these people were her friends, and in their pictures she felt like she was seeing them the way she always had but the rest of the world rarely did. In the pictures of the people she didn't know so well, she felt like she'd gotten to know them better in just seconds. Pride welled up in her heart and threatened to overflow. She'd always known that this was what he was capable of. Did this mean he finally realised it too?

She let her gaze turn to the photos in the middle, the ones she'd known were there the minute she walked in but hadn't let herself see while she took everything else in.

There it was – the BAFTAs picture. It had been her

favourite picture of herself for years, until he'd started taking more and every single one had been a revelation. But seeing it now, larger than life in the centre of this room, she was taken back there. Her heart had been in tatters, and she'd been determined not to show it. She hadn't shown it, and the rest of the photographers had captured her red-carpet-ready smile. But Michael ... he'd captured the moment before that, and the photo was nothing but resolve that the world wouldn't see her broken. And next to it, she was laughing. It was in Paris, the morning after everything changed. Her joy spilled out of the picture and into the room. She'd been so happy. He'd made her that happy. And it looked like he saw that, the way he saw everything.

She stood looking at the two versions of herself, two of the best versions, and a tear slipped from her eye. She couldn't believe he'd done all this. How had he even done all this?

"Do you know," the most familiar voice said into her ear, "what an arse-on it was to get the rights back to that shot?"

"Michael," she said, and if she thought the pictures had taken her breath away, it was nothing compared to the sight of him. His jaw was clean-shaven, his hair looked freshly cut, short and sharp at the sides and longer on top, and he was wearing a navy blue suit that looked like it had been made for him. Hell, maybe it had been. But more than that – there was something in the way he held himself, the way his hazel eyes were smiling. This was a man at ease with the world and his place in it.

What the hell had happened to him?

She wanted to ask, she had so many questions, but nothing seemed to want to come out of her mouth. He didn't appear to mind. He turned to face her and took her hands in his.

"Thank you for coming. I hoped you would, and everyone said you would, but I didn't know if I'd pushed you too far away. It was a risk I had to take, though."

No, still no words. She nodded gently, because it was clear he had more to say.

"I've missed you all this time, Miranda, so much. I stopped calling because I knew that if you answered, I would beg you to take me back, and maybe you would have done. And I wouldn't have been ready. I needed to figure out for myself if I could be who you said I was, the man to take on the world with you. I wasn't him then, no matter how much we both wanted it to be true."

She swallowed down the lump in her throat enough to say, "And do you think you are now?" Because she understood now that it was his answer, not hers, that mattered the most.

"Yes," he said with a quiet firmness she didn't even recognise. "I'm not perfect, and I can't promise never to freak out about anything ever again." He stepped closer, holding her hands tighter, and her eyes were full of tears now, because nothing had ever meant as much as this moment. "But the last few weeks ... I figured out what I wanted and I went after it. And it felt good. It was fucking terrifying, but I felt alive in a way I've only ever felt ..." His eyes met hers. "When I'm with you."

"Michael–"

"Wait, I'm not done." His new confident stance dropped, just a little, just enough for his head to dip and the front curl of his hair to do that thing she loved, and he gave her the sweet smile that she'd seen every night when she closed her eyes, no matter how much she'd tried not to. "I love you, Miranda. I loved you when I walked away, but I was too much of a coward to admit it. I think I've loved you since the moment we first kissed. And I'm so, so sorry that I hurt you."

Miranda's heart was floating somewhere among the clouds. She brought her hand to his face, and he closed his eyes and leaned in to her touch. "I'm sorry too, Michael. I was trying so hard to get what I wanted that I forgot to let things just be what they'd be." Her voice dropped to a whisper. "But I love you too."

She tasted salt on her lips as they found his in the sweetest, most perfect kiss.

And then she heard a huge "Whoop!" from behind them.

53

MICHAEL broke away from Miranda's lips with a laugh. He knew at least one of those voices that was ruining his romantic moment. He turned to see Cleo, Devon, Courtney and Henry in the entrance to the room, smiles on their faces. Cleo and Courtney, of course, were the whoopers.

"Couldn't give us even a minute, could you?" he said, beckoning Cleo over with his head.

She threw her arms around them. "I'm sorry. I got overexcited."

"It's alright. You've earned it, I reckon. Thank you, all of you. I couldn't have done any of this without you."

"Sure you could." Devon clapped Michael on the shoulder and kissed Miranda on the cheek. "Maybe not as quickly, though."

"How did you even do all this?" Miranda asked. He took her hand and wound his fingers around hers. "This kind of thing doesn't come cheap or easily, I imagine."

"With a little help from my friends," he replied, marvelling at how naturally the words slipped from his lips. "OK, a lot of help from my friends, and yours, and Courtney's, and ... you get the picture."

"Really?" Miranda looked at him in surprise.

"Yeah. I've discovered that when people want to help

you out of love and kindness, you don't actually have to be a dick about it."

A beautiful smile spread over her face. "Who knew?"

Indeed, who knew. Well, he knew it now. He thought of all the ways people had helped him – Brad had let him use the gallery for free, although he was sure it didn't hurt that an event featuring some of the most famous people in the world was a huge publicity opportunity. Courtney had hooked him up with Declan. Aisling had helped him get in touch with Becky and Brix and conspired with Miranda's LA assistant to find the only gap in her schedule and keep it free. Devon had insisted on paying for the drinks. Henry had refused to take anything but a modest carbon offsetting donation for the use of the jet. All of them had been all too happy to help him, and it gave him a warm glow to think that they'd done it because they wanted Miranda to be happy. He would repay them all by spending every minute of his life making sure that she was.

Their friends slipped away to join the rest of the guests in looking at the pictures, and Michael felt a burst of pride at the quiet exclamations and murmurs of appreciation he heard around him.

He slipped his arm around Miranda's waist, where it belonged. "You have no idea how desperate I am to get you out of here, but ..."

She tipped her head inquisitively at him.

"But we're not going anywhere just yet."

"We're not?"

"Nope. I spent a significant chunk of my life savings

on this suit, so I need to show it off. We're going to stay here, drinking the finest champagne Devon Grant's money can buy and mingling with all these good people. We're going to tell them all about my work, and how you're killing it in LA, and it's going to be great."

She looked at him, her mouth hanging open. "Who the hell are you?"

"New and improved Michael Hedley, pet. Get used to it."

She laughed. "As long as you don't improve so much that you stop calling me 'pet'."

He nuzzled her cheek, inhaling the scent of her that he'd missed so bloody much. "Never. I swear."

She pressed a soft kiss to his lips, and it took every ounce of self-control Michael had not to let it turn into something much less public-friendly. She grinned at him. "Then let's mingle."

* * *

By the time they got back to the hotel, Michael was exhausted and energised all at the same time. The evening had gone brilliantly, better than he'd even dreamed. Everyone had loved the pictures, especially Becky Nolan, who said she was going to hang her second one in the hallway so that every time Aaron came to pick up their son he'd have to see her "in all my fuck-you glory". Even Kimiko had grudgingly complimented his work, although he still didn't think he'd ever actually impress her. But it was major progress that he no longer gave a crap.

In the lift, Miranda went for the button of the floor she'd been on earlier, but he covered her hand with his and pressed a different one. She raised an eyebrow.

"One last surprise," he said.

"Oh!" She let out a gasp as he led her into a familiar room. She turned to him, eyes shining. "Where it all began. You really did the most, huh?"

"That was the idea." He looked around the site of their first shoot together. The rich colours and textures seemed even more vibrant tonight, but maybe that was because she was radiating a happiness that brightened everything around her.

There was so much still to talk about. But as the air around them seemed to heat and thicken, he realised there was only one thing he wanted to say right now. Slowly, as if he were moving through melted gold, he reached for her and drew her body against his. "I love you."

"I love you too."

If the words tasted perfect on his tongue, it was nothing compared to the way she did as he finally kissed her the way he'd dreamed of for all these weeks. He stroked her smooth bare back as her body melded into his, and the only thing less believable than the fact she was in his arms again was the fact that he'd ever thought she didn't belong there.

He'd learned his lesson, he vowed, as he took her by the hand and led her to the bed he'd photographed her on all those weeks ago. There'd be no letting her go ever again.

54

PERFECTION. Everything about this night was perfection. Especially ending up here, in this room where they'd started. She'd wanted him even then, and now he was hers. Maybe forever, but for once Miranda wasn't letting her brain get ahead of itself. They had all the time in the world.

There were much more immediate matters to focus on. Like the way Michael had moved behind her and brushed her hair over one shoulder, exposing the back of her neck to him. He leaned in, not quite touching her but close enough that she felt his breath on her skin like a kiss.

"I have missed you," he said in a soft, low voice that seemed to promise her everything she'd been craving for the last few weeks. He slid the straps of her dress off her shoulders, and it fell to the floor, leaving her wearing nothing but her paper-thin thong – a dress like that didn't allow for anything more substantial. Her entire body was crying out for his touch, but he only ran his hands over her arms. "So much."

"I missed you too," she whispered, turning to face him.

Instead of kissing her, he traced a finger over her collarbone. "Is that right? I wonder if you thought about me as often as I thought about you, at night, alone in the dark." His other hand delicately skimmed her hip bone.

"I tried not to." She shivered. His body was still at least an inch away from hers, and it was too damn far. She shifted closer, but he moved away, keeping that frustrating, tantalising distance between them.

"I tried, too." His voice had dropped until it was as barely-there as his touch. "Every time I thought of you, this mouth" – the very tip of his tongue flicked over her bottom lip – "this body" – her neck – "I tried to push it away, because otherwise I would have begged you to come back to me. When I let myself remember everything, the way you felt and the way you moved ..." He spread his hand over her ass. "It was so ... fucking ..." He pulled her sharply against him. "Hard."

Oh, *Jesus*. Hard wasn't even the word. And then his lips were on hers in a searing kiss that took the breath out of her lungs and into his until she was drowning in him. She felt her nipples harden against that flawless jacket, knew she was impossibly wet for him. She wanted to beg him to get inside her, they'd wasted so much time and she needed to feel him, but she knew it would do her no good. He wasn't a man to be rushed.

Cupping her ass cheeks with both hands, he picked her up and deposited her on the very edge of the bed. "Spread your legs for me." He gave her a little smirk. "Please."

"Well, since you asked nicely." She parted her thighs, and he dropped to his knees at her feet.

"Christ, I've dreamed of being here," he murmured, and then he buried his face in her, licking and lapping as if he had been starving for her. Miranda collapsed back on the bed. Everything inside her turned liquid, molten under his relentless tongue. She gasped as he pulled her closer to his face and pleasure hit her like lightning. It was good, so good, but she needed more.

"I want you," she choked out through heavy breaths. She needed him inside her. She'd waited so long ...

"Do you, now?" He stood, still fully dressed. God, he looked beautiful. She wanted to buy him as many of those suits as he'd let her, just so she could look at him in them. Then watch him take them off. He unfastened his watch and placed it on the nightstand, then reached into the inside pocket of his jacket, took out a condom and set it down beside the watch.

She raised an eyebrow at his preparedness. "You were pretty sure your plan would work, huh?" Not that she was ungrateful. Far from it.

"I had faith." He stepped back to her end of the bed and leaned down. "And hope. And when all I had left was hope, that was still more than enough." He buried his hand in her hair and kissed her, exploring the corners of her mouth as she tasted herself on his lips. She reached up to push his jacket from his shoulders, but he pulled back. "You want this off?"

"Yes please," she murmured.

"Your wish is my command." He kissed her again,

until she was gasping with desire, then picked her up and moved her to the top of the bed, laying her back against the pillows. “Give me a second.”

He stepped away and carefully shrugged off the jacket, then turned to drape it over the back of a chair. Over his shoulder, he said, almost nonchalantly, “Keep yourself busy. But don’t touch between your legs.”

Oh, good god. What was he trying to do to her? The gruff edge to his voice was the sexiest thing she’d ever heard. “Ordering me around now, are you?” She tried for an arch tone, but she knew her words came out as more of a moan, and her hands had already floated to her stomach.

“Yes. I can stop, if you want.”

“Please don’t.” She skated her hands upwards until they found her nipples, already tight and hard beneath her fingers.

“Good girl,” he said, undoing the top button of his shirt. He took his sweet time over the rest, unfastening them one by agonising one as she ran her hands over her body, the graze of skin on skin almost more than she could take. She writhed under her own touch, and his eyes never left her.

He watched her as he finally removed his shirt, letting her see the lean, toned torso she loved so much. He watched her as he unbuckled his belt and unzipped his pants in leisurely, unhurried movements. The only sign of his need for her was in the intensity of his gaze. Until his pants fell from his hips and her mouth went dry. Even through his boxers she could see how hard he was for her, even though she hadn't so much as laid a finger on him. She stroked the top of her thigh with one hand and her breast with the other, wondering how long she could last before she begged him to make love to her.

The answer was, it turned out, about two seconds after he was naked in front of her.

"Please, Michael," she gasped. "I need you."

"Sure," he said easily, but the glitter in his eyes told her he wasn't done teasing her yet. He grabbed the condom and rolled it on, then crawled over her and kissed her. He groaned into her mouth as she let her kiss tell him how much she wanted him, if he couldn't already tell from the slickness between her legs.

He kneeled between her thighs, seemingly content to just stay there, the bastard, his dick nudging at her but never giving her what she was so desperate for. Instead, he licked his thumb and brought it to her clit. Sparks flew to every cell of her body as he stroked her until she was almost sobbing with need.

"Please ..." she gasped. This was torture, exquisite, white-hot torture. With his free hand, he guided his cock to her entrance and slipped inside her, just an inch and then, with a groan, he stayed there, letting her feel him. She writhed, trying to take in more of him, but he let out a low chuckle and shifted back, increasing the pressure on her clit, and she felt a wall of pressure building inside her as her legs started to shake. This was too much, she couldn't take it, she had to ...

"God please Michael please fuck me please." The

words tumbled out of her in an incoherent rush as she reached out for him, and in one swift thrust he sank all the way into her and captured her lips with his, and that perfect, perfect sensation of him finally being deep inside her was all it took. Digging her fingernails into his shoulders, she cried out into his mouth as a wave crashed over her, making her whole body tremble.

"Oh, Jesus, Miranda," he murmured. He kissed her sweetly, then pulled back as she tried to catch her breath. "Do you need a minute?"

She shook her head. "Hell no. Stay right there."

"Happy to." He kept his movements slow and gentle until she felt like she'd returned to this plane of existence. "God, I've missed you. Missed this."

"Mm-hmm," she mumbled, because as she lifted her hips to meet him and pulled him closer, tension was building in her core again. Fireflies danced across her skin as they moved together, faster, harder, making up for every second they'd lost.

Her orgasm ripped through her as Michael hissed, "Holy shit" and she felt him shudder to his own climax. He collapsed against her, then immediately propped himself up again so he wouldn't squash her, and that gorgeous act of consideration made her thundering heart squeeze.

She looked into his beautiful hazel eyes. "I love you, Michael Hedley."

He kissed her tenderly. "I love you too. I promise I'll never lose sight of that again."

She smiled. "You'd better not."

* * *

It was three a.m., but neither of them could sleep, so they lay curled up together on the couch, drinking the wine they'd ordered from room service.

"Tonight was incredible, Michael," she said, toying with the tie on his fluffy white hotel robe. "The show, I mean. I can't believe all the thought you put into it, and how much work it must have been to pull it off. I know that a lot of it was about you proving something to me and yourself, but Michael ... the pictures. They were phenomenal."

His cheeks turned adorably pink. "Thank you. I really loved taking them. In fact, it made me realise something – this is what I want to do. That kind of picture. That's who I am."

At the contentment in his voice, she felt her lips curve into a smile, but she said nothing, letting him continue.

"I've been chasing the fine art thing because, well, I guess because it was my dream, and because I promised Cleo I would. But the kid with that dream, he's long gone. I spent my twenties doing something I despised in many ways, sure, but it's also true that I was good at it. Taking those faces that people think they already know and finding something new in them – that's always been what I loved. Seeing everyone's reactions tonight just solidified that this is what I'm supposed to do. And that's not the kind of thing you can easily sell in galleries, because until you're a huge name shooting other huge names, it's not what collectors are after. Unless they're massive creeps, I suppose. So I need to explore other avenues for that, and I'm going to."

"Yeah?" she said softly. She couldn't see his expression very well from this angle, but she didn't need to. She knew that that wrinkle in his brow wouldn't be there.

"Yeah. It's time to stop worrying about what I should be doing or what people think I should be doing. It's time to chase the dreams that are truly mine, in the now. You taught me that."

She pushed herself up to sit and look at him properly. She was right. He looked calm, certain. At peace. She could have burst with pride and happiness for him. "You taught me something too," she said. "You taught me that I don't have to be hustling for what I want every second. You made me learn that sometimes what you need is to have a little patience and let things be." She laid her hand against his cheek, her heart feeling so full of love that she thought she might cry. "It hurt me to let you go, but it was what you needed. It was what we both needed."

"I'm sorry." He put his hand over hers and leaned in to her touch. "I'll never let you go again."

"Damn right you won't."

She winked, and he laughed. He picked up his wine glass and held it up to her. "A toast," he said.

"To what?" She raised her own glass.

He kissed her softly on the lips, then touched his glass to hers. "To taking on the world."

Epilogue

"MIRANDA! Miranda! Seb! Over here! This way!"

Michael watched as Miranda and Seb walked the red carpet, turning their most charming smiles towards the assembled crowd of photographers. For a brief second, he almost wished he were there in the scrum, capturing her with his camera, because tonight she was dazzling. She was always dazzling, but right now she was radiating such joy that it seemed to refract out of each sparkling crystal of her dress.

It was the London premiere of *An Ocean of Fallen Stars*. Michael hadn't been able to fly out to the world premiere in LA; he'd been busy shooting Declan Hainey's next album cover. But he was more than happy to be here tonight, in the city they both loved, watching her shine.

And bloody hell, was she shining. She was an ocean of stars all on her own. And now the whole world was seeing it. There had been Oscar buzz around the film from the moment it was announced, and it had only grown more intense as time went on. From the second the reviews started to hit, it was clear that everyone involved had turned in the performance of their lives, especially Miranda. Critics who would always have been snobby about her romcoms in the past were falling over themselves to praise her range. The whole world was bowing to her, and she couldn't have deserved it more.

"Mr Hedley, Ms Hedley, would you like to come and take your seats?" one of the army of clipboard-wielding event assistants asked.

He turned to his mother, whose expression hadn't got any less excited than it had been when she first arrived in London yesterday. "Ready?" he said, holding out his arm.

"Oh, yes, I suppose we should go inside. But look at her, Michael. Isn't she beautiful?"

"She is." He was already looking. He always was.

He turned to follow the assistant, then cast one last glance over his shoulder at the woman he loved.

She met his gaze, and in her beautiful blue-green eyes he saw everything he'd always seen – her strength, her power, her kindness, and more love than some people saw in a lifetime. He pulled out his phone and quickly snapped a picture of the secret smile meant for him and only him. Then, his beaming-faced mam on his arm, he followed the assistant into the cool darkness of the cinema.

Want to know how Cleo and Devon found their happy ever after? Snap up *The Scoop*!

And look out for Courtney and Henry's story – coming 2024!

Acknowledgements

FIRST and foremost, the hugest thank you to everyone who has read, reviewed, helped promote, or just generally been brilliant about *The Scoop*. Becoming a romance author has been a dream come true, and I couldn't have done it without, you know, people who wanted to read my book. I know a lot of you have been waiting for Michael and Miranda's story, and I hope you love them just as much as I do.

Sarah G, Jill, Sarah C, Fiona, Helen C, Helen W – there aren't nearly enough words in the universe to express my gratitude for your support and feedback, especially when I was having all my various wobbles! And a grateful shout out to Vikki, for your super speedy and incredibly sharp-eyed read!

My subject-matter experts, Cheryl Murphy Lowrance, Ben Hines, Simone Rudolphi, and Jon Bradley – I'm so grateful for all your insights, and I apologise to Simone, Jon and fine art photographers everywhere for taking liberties with the dynamics of the art scene! Special thanks to Ben for never tiring of helping me replace "he [DID SOMETHING WITH THE THING]" with actual terminology.

David, David, Adam, Aidan, Pauline, Ed, Suzanne, Christie, Susan, and everyone else in my writing group who I've probably mortally offended by leaving them out – so much of this novel got written in our Sunday sessions, and your support has been invaluable.

Thanks to Judith for pointing out how many times I described something as "perfect", Elizabeth for being patient with my endless "Can you just change that colour a bit, but not like a lot?" requests, Eleanor for making the inside of the book look beautiful, and Holly for drawing stars to my very vague yet awkward specification!

My family – thank you for being so supportive even though I won't let you read my books.

My husband – My love for you is deeper than an ocean of stars. I don't know how I'd write about love without you.

About the author

KW Thomas lives in the north east of England with her husband and two children. By day (and sometimes by night), she is a freelance fiction editor, and any spare time she has after she's through with work, housework, life admin, refereeing her children's arguments, and, erm, faffing about on the internet, she spends reading, and now writing, romance novels, because the world always needs more love.

Printed in Great Britain
by Amazon

28118346R00220